THE TOTALLY TRUE STORY OF GRACIE BYRNE

SHANNON TAKAOKA

CANDLEWICK PRESS

This is a work of fiction. Names, characters, places, and incidents are either products of the author's imagination or, if real, are used fictitiously.

First edition 2023

Library of Congress Catalog Card Number 2022923378
ISBN 978-1-5362-2878-6

23 24 25 26 27 28 APS 10 9 8 7 6 5 4 3 2 1

Printed in Humen, Dongguan, China

This book was typeset in Stempel Garamond.

Candlewick Press
99 Dover Street
Somerville, Massachusetts 02144

www.candlewick.com

For anyone who has ever
felt anxious, awkward, or unsure.
You're not alone.
And you are enough.

DO YOU EVER WISH YOU COULD WRITE YOUR OWN STORY?

I don't mean like an autobiography or a memoir—something you write when you're old, when you're looking back. I mean, what if you could write your life story *before* it happens, the way you *want* it to happen? Wouldn't that be awesome? You could be whoever you wanted . . . the Chosen One, secret royalty, or even just a little famous or kind of cool.

I guess what I'm saying is, some creative control would be nice. Because despite all that stuff that teachers like to say about "charting your own course" and being the "captain of your destiny" and whatnot, most of the time I feel like my story is actually being written by someone else—someone who does *not* get me. At all. The voice is all wrong, for one. I think it needs to be bolder, more confident, and always ready with a snappy comeback at exactly the right moment. And the plot? It *sucks*. Nothing good is ever happening. It's like my entire life has writer's block.

Revisions are urgently needed. Because if I don't take over this narrative soon, *The Story of Gracie Byrne* is going to flop—spectacularly—before I even make it out of high school.

SEPTEMBER 5, 1987

I CLICK MY PEN ONE, TWO, THREE, FOUR, FIVE TIMES. IT'S MY ritual before I write. *Click, click. Click, click, click.* I run my hand over the blank page of my college-ruled spiral-bound notebook. All that white space. So many possibilities. It makes me feel like I'm on the edge of a diving board, about to launch myself off. *Just go. Don't think. Just write.*

> *Everyone is curious about the new girl. She's from LA—here only temporarily while her father works on location for a film project. He brought her along to get her out of the Hollywood bubble, where there were too many parties and too much blow . . .*

Hmmm. Maybe the blow is a bit much.

The ice in my sweating glass of tea cracks and shifts. I take a sip, set the glass down on the coffee table, and position myself on the sofa so that I'm directly in the path of the box fan. I close my eyes and try to imagine an ocean breeze, but what I'm getting is more of a musty smell. Dust + Western-Pennsylvania-in-late-summer humidity = must. I click my pen and try again:

> *The whispers around school are that the new girl, along with her entire family, is in the Federal Witness Protection Program.*

Now *there's* an idea. I wonder what starting over with a new identity would be like. If I had to pick a Witness Protection name for myself, I would choose something more sophisticated and unusual. Like Dallas. Or Brooke. In real life, I guess I could go by Grace, which is at least somewhat grown-up, instead of Gracie, which is what everyone in my family calls me. Now's my chance, since I won't know a single soul when I walk into Morewood High on Tuesday, and not one single soul will know me. I'll be a blank page. Almost like I'm in Witness Protection. Except not.

> *The new girl spoke multiple languages: English, of course, but also Spanish, Mandarin, and even French, from the years she and her family spent living in Burgundy, where they own a vineyard.*

I roll my eyes at myself. Why would anyone move to Pittsburgh if they owned a vineyard in the South of France? I scribble over the Burgundy vineyard and glance at Hank, asleep on the scratched-up hardwood floor, his front paws moving in some kind of doggie dream. Even at rest, he's chasing something.

I flip the page . . .

> *The new girl is pissed. Pissed to be starting over at the worst possible moment: right in the middle of high school. Pissed at her mom, who doesn't understand why it's not so easy for her to just "make friends." Pissed at her brother, Jack, who, of course, excels so much at making friends that he has a surplus. Pissed at her dad, who left them three years ago for his new life with his new wife, which, as of two weeks ago, also includes a brand-spanking-new baby daughter. Pissed at the universe, for . . . everything.*
>
> *Actually, she's worse than pissed. "Pissed" makes her sound kind of tough, like a badass, like a girl who could hold her own in a fight or who plays drums in a punk band. Like a girl people are curious about. But she doesn't feel like a badass. She feels lost. Lonely. Terrified at the prospect of facing a sea of new faces on Tuesday and not being able to do anything but freeze.*

Nope! I cross out the entire passage with a giant X. Too much realism.

Hank's explosive bark blasts me back into the present. The one where I'm not a cool / possibly troubled California party girl, the mysterious / possibly dangerous daughter of a mafia hit man, or . . . *European*. I'm just me. Sweaty, cranky, and still stressing over what I'm going to wear to school next week. Except for the shoes. I found a pair of shiny black oxfords on sale a few days ago, and I *think* they look sort of cool.

At the window with his paws up on the sill, Hank's ears are perked and his fur is standing on end all across his back. I follow his stare to the moving truck that just pulled up across the street. It must be the new neighbors, the ones Mom won't stop talking about in her chipper, hopeful voice. She heard there are three kids, the oldest in high school, like me, and twins around the same age as Jack. "See?" she'd said. "Now you won't be the only new one at Morewood."

Hank continues to bark, bark, bark, and I tell him to shush, but instead of taking my advice, he emits a frustrated sound that's half cry, half yelp before skidding across the floor and hurling all eighty pounds of his canine self at the flimsy screen door, knocking the entire thing off its hinges. He jumps back for a second, startled by the clatter of the screen as it falls onto the porch, barks once at it, and then he's out the door.

Shit.

Shit. Shit. Shit. Shit.

No time to find shoes—Hank's still not used to this house, let alone this neighborhood, and we're on a busy street. When he's in a protective frenzy, he doesn't pay attention to cars or anything else. I bolt after him, jamming my bare toe on the corner of the fallen screen as I go.

Holy. Mother. Of. God. A wave of pain takes my breath away.

At the edges of my consciousness, which is currently 99 percent focused on my throbbing toe, there is barking and barking and more barking. *Forget your toe, Gracie. Get the dog, before he's roadkill.*

I force myself to look up, and spot Hank on the sidewalk in front of our house, not on the street at least, tangled up with a guy and a girl, both about my age, and a small dog that looks kind of like Toto. The other dog is even more aggressive than Hank—baring its teeth, its wiry hair puffed out all over its body like a porcupine—but in this particular case, I can't say I blame it. Hank is bigger by about seventy pounds. And he started it.

I run-hop up to them, repeating, "Sorry, sorry, sorry," while simultaneously doing this ridiculous dance with Hank where I lunge at him to try to catch him by the collar and he leaps back, just out of reach. The girl is also trying to reel in the terrier, now a full-on ball of blind rage as it tries to bite Hank, who, in response, yelps as if he has actually been bitten and runs into the street.

"*HAAANK!*" I yell as he darts directly in front of an oncoming Camaro.

It blares its horn and screeches to a stop. Hank pauses—perhaps his dog-life is momentarily flashing before his eyes—and then takes off again. The driver rolls down his window to shout at the three of us, "Control your goddamn dogs!" Nice.

I can't *see* where Hank went, but I *hear* him, barking somewhere behind the moving truck that is parked across the street. Seconds later, I hear a crash.

"Hey," a gravelly voice, close to me, speaks. For the first time, I get a good look at the guy on the sidewalk. He's wearing a Ramones T-shirt and is ridiculously hot, with brown-green eyes and the kind of hair that could be categorized as tousled, in the best possible way.

My face heats up in an immediate blush, because of course it does. "Hey," I reply, trying to sound like I'm not a sweaty, red-faced mess.

He points to my toe. "You're, uh, bleeding."

I glance down at my bare feet and *oh my God*. Total carnage.

"I don't . . . feel so good," says the girl, now clutching the terrier in her arms as it continues to thrash and bark. She's straight from central casting as Hot Guy's companion—ridiculously pretty, like a teenage Michelle Pfeiffer with smoky eyeliner and glossy, bright pink lips. Her face, however, is paler than pale, with some green undertones. "I think I need to sit down."

"She has a thing about blood," the guy tells me. "And, like, maybe you should get a Band-Aid or something . . . ?"

As if things couldn't get any worse, right then my mom pulls the car into the driveway with Katherine in the passenger seat. I want to cry. Hank is somewhere across the street, on a nervous, freaked-out rampage, possibly about to get us sued.

Meanwhile I'm bleeding out in front of two complete strangers, one of whom is close to fainting on the sidewalk.

Mom gets out of the car and takes in the scene: me, Hot Guy, teenage Michelle Pfeiffer, one angry terrier, and a severely bleeding toe.

"Gracie, what's going on?" She glances toward the house across the street. "Is that Hank barking?"

"He knocked down the screen door and took off," I answer.

Nurse that she is, Mom begins to triage. Taking one look at Michelle Pfeiffer's greenish pallor, she says, "Oh honey, we need to find you a spot to sit down." To her hot boyfriend (he must be her boyfriend, right?), she says, "Here, you hold the dog, okay? Let's get your friend up on the porch." And then she looks at me. "Your toe is bleeding."

"I KNOW!" I didn't mean it to come out like that, but yeah, *I know*.

Mom leads the girl by the arm to one of the wicker chairs with the floral cushions on the front porch. "Put your head down, like this." She demonstrates. "I'll get you some water in a minute. I need to help my mother out of the car first."

But Katherine has already unbuckled herself from the passenger seat and is standing in the driveway. I'm nearest, so I hop over to catch her by the hand. We can't leave her alone this close to the street. She'll walk right out without even looking.

Mom, still on the porch, takes a deep breath. "Gracie, can you get her to come in? I'll find you a hand towel and some bandages, and then we can deal with Hank."

She pushes the fallen screen door to the side and disappears into the house. Michelle Pfeiffer keeps her head down, as Mom directed, and Hot Guy sits awkwardly next to her with the terrier, who is now trembling all over in his lap, which is an improvement over fury, I guess.

"C'mon Katherine," I say to my grandma. (It's no use calling her Grandma—she doesn't remember she's a grandma, and she definitely doesn't remember she's *my* grandma. She doesn't remember almost anybody she's related to, including Mom. Alzheimer's sucks.) "Let's get you inside." I gently pull her in the direction of the porch. *Please,* I telepath to her. *Just be quiet and cooperative. Just this once.*

No such luck. She gives me the worst stink eye, yanks her hand out of my grasp, and yells at full volume, "WHAT DO YOU THINK YOU'RE DOING? WHO THE HELL DO YOU THINK YOU ARE?"

The mail carrier dropping a package at the house next door stops in his tracks and looks our way. Michelle Pfeiffer lifts her head up. Hot Guy's eyes go wide.

Attention is focused on me from every direction, and not in a *Whoa, who's that girl?* kind of way. It's more like: *What the fuck is up with that girl?* I can feel the heat wafting off me as I break out all over in a fresh layer of sweat. After what seems like a lifetime, but in reality is probably about ten seconds, Mom emerges from the house with a glass of ice water and a hand towel. She gives the water to the girl and then hurries over to me and Katherine, passing me the towel. "Katherine, it's all right," she says. "Gracie isn't going to hurt you. How about you come up to the porch and I'll get you some lemonade?"

"Who's Gracie?" Katherine asks. But she seems to have already forgotten that a moment ago she didn't want to budge from the driveway. "Lemonade would be nice."

I follow them up the walkway that leads to the porch, sit on the bottom step, and wrap the towel around my foot, being careful to pull it tight around the bleeding toe. "Put some pressure on it," my mom says.

"I know." I raise my head and look toward the street, hoping that Hank might appear without us having to chase him down.

Instead, another guy around my age is standing at the end of our walk. His sandy-brown hair—somewhere between wavy and curly—is damp and his face is flushed. He looks like someone who has been carrying boxes into a house on a very hot day. *Cool.* Maybe the whole neighborhood can come by to see what's going on with my grandmother and my toe.

"Hi," he says, with the biggest sort-of-askew grin I've ever seen. Seriously. His mouth seems almost too big for his face.

"Well, hello," my mom responds in this *the more the merrier* voice that instantly irritates me.

He walks closer, to the foot of the porch stairs, and I look up. He's tall, kind of lean and wiry, and wears white tube socks with green stripes around the top. Basketball player? Shorts. T-shirt. Running shoes. Maybe a long-distance runner. Definitely a jock of some kind.

"Hi. I'm Tom Broder, from across the street." He gestures

with his thumb behind him. "We're just moving in, and I think we have your dog? He's in our backyard. I was going to try and bring him here, but he doesn't seem to want to leave, which is fine for now, there's a fence and a gate, but you might want to come get him when you . . ." His voice trails off and he glances around at all of us, registering Michelle Pfeiffer's ashen face, the towel around my foot, drops of my blood splattered all over the walk. "Oh, wow. Maybe he's not your dog? Did he *bite* you?"

"No, no," says my mom. "You definitely have our dog. Hank. He's . . ."

An asshole, I think.

". . . got a lot of energy," Mom says, before turning to Michelle Pfeiffer, who probably has come to the same conclusion about Hank that I have. "Are you feeling better, hon?" She pauses. "I'm sorry, what's your name?" *Ugh, I guess we're doing this? Right now? Shouldn't my mom go get Hank? Like, NOW?*

"Lisa," she says. "I am feeling better, thanks."

"And you are?" Mom asks Hot Guy.

Oh my God.

"Luke," he says.

I immediately store that one in my memory bank, though.

"And this is my daughter, Gracie." My mom gestures to me.

I lift my hand in a half-hearted wave. There goes my plan to start going by the more mature *Grace*. Like Grace Kelly. Or Grace Jones.

"I hope Hank didn't break anything over there," Mom adds, turning back to Tom-Broder-from-across-the-street.

"Ahhhh . . . you know, not much." Tom has a terrible poker face. "He followed our dog into the house and they both got a little rowdy."

"Oh, no," says my mom.

"And it turns out one of the movers does not like dogs. He dropped one end of a wardrobe. But I think it's salvageable."

Yikes.

"Anything else?" my mom asks.

Tom looks uncomfortable, like he doesn't want to lie but also doesn't want be the bearer of any more bad news. "Just . . . a vase. But it was one my brothers broke and glued back together months ago. So no loss there."

Mom sighs. "We'll replace it. I'm sorry."

"HEY!" Katherine, who has up until now been quietly rummaging through her purse, is now looking directly at Tom. "Who do you think YOU ARE?" (I don't know why, but this is one of her favorite phrases. At least this time she didn't add a curse. She swears a lot more now than she used to, although I can't say I blame her. I'd swear a lot too if I couldn't remember anything.)

"Uh . . . I'm Tom?" He's obviously confused. "We're moving in across the street . . ."

"This is my mom, Katherine," says Mom, who is now back to introductions.

"She has memory problems," I add, by way of explanation.

Katherine looks offended. "Who has problems?" One thing

that hasn't been affected by Alzheimer's: Katherine's hearing. She goes back to searching the contents of her purse, giving Mom the opportunity to return to her embarrassingly obvious effort to jump-start my social life.

After five minutes of chitchat—five minutes that feel like five lifetimes—Mom has ascertained that Tom is an incoming junior at Morewood, like me; that Luke also goes to Morewood and is a senior; and that Lisa graduated in June and has just started at the University of Pittsburgh, where coincidentally, Tom's dad will be working as a therapist in student health services. Tom's mom, a professor, will be teaching calculus at Carnegie Mellon, and his younger brothers will be going to the same school as Jack. Oh, and Lisa plans to study nursing.

At the end of her lightning round of questions, Mom promises to go across the street to pick up Hank as soon as she "takes a look at Gracie's toe." And then, *finally*, everyone disperses. Tom jogs back across the street, waving to us all as he goes, and Luke, Lisa, and Lisa's terrier, Coco (another detail gleaned by my mom), continue on their walk.

I breathe a sigh of relief as soon as the porch is clear, and watch them go. Luke's lean, muscular arm is casually draped across Lisa's shoulders. (Is that a tattoo peeking out of his Ramones tee?) She leans into him and he whispers something in her ear, making her laugh. Then he slips his hand into the back pocket of her jean shorts.

Why, I wonder, *isn't my life like that?* Hot pink lips. Shorts that make my ass look amazing. A boyfriend with cool clothes, great hair, and perfect cheekbones. His mouth whispering in *my* ear. His fingers stroking *my* back.

Instead, I have a feral dog, sweaty armpits, and an injury that, if it happened in a movie, would be 100 percent comedic.

"I don't think she's going to make it as a nurse," my mom says as they disappear around the corner. "Not with that reaction to blood. Now, let me see your toe."

I unwrap the towel. It's still bleeding, although not as badly as before.

"How'd Katherine's appointment go?" I ask as she inspects the cut.

She shrugs. "Oh, you know, fine. Her cholesterol is not great, so they're giving her new meds for that, and I got a referral for a senior day care just a few blocks away."

My "summer job" has been keeping an eye on Katherine while Mom is at work. Keeping an eye on her is why we moved here in the first place. My grandfather used to be the one to do that, but he died suddenly this spring of a heart attack. And two weeks after the funeral, Katherine nearly set the house on fire when she left a pie baking in the oven overnight. She couldn't be alone anymore, so Mom decided to sell our old place and move in here. My grandparents' house is bigger, in a good school district, and it's where Katherine is most comfortable. Plus Mom doesn't have to worry about a mortgage. It just makes sense. But that doesn't mean that I have to like the fact that I have to completely turn my life upside down right in the middle of high school.

Mom sighs. She's been sighing a *lot* lately.

"I think I'm going to have to take you to urgent care. This is going to need a few stitches."

"What are we going to do with Katherine?"

"Jack can watch her." She looks back toward the house. "Where is he, anyway?"

"At the park," I answer. Even though we've only lived here with Katherine since the beginning of the summer, my little brother is already like the kid mayor of the neighborhood. He's been running around with a pack of kids for weeks now, walking to the pool at the Y, disappearing for hours into the park.

As if our conversation had summoned him, he appears on the front walk, kickball in hand, face flushed and dirty, hair sticking up at all angles.

"What the hell happened to the door?"

When he reaches us at the porch stairs, he looks at my toe. "*Oh, man*, that's disgusting! What did you *do*?"

"Language," Mom says. "Gracie cut her toe." Even she is done explaining the chain of events at this point. "Jack. I need you to go across the street to the new neighbors' and get Hank. And then I need you to stay with Katherine while I take Gracie to get this checked out. You can put *I Love Lucy* on the VCR."

I Love Lucy is Katherine's favorite. It usually keeps her occupied for a little while.

"*Hank* is at the new neighbors'?"

"Long story," I say.

He shrugs, but says, "Sure." Even if Hank weren't corralled

in their backyard, Jack would find some other reason to go over, introduce himself, and probably get invited to dinner before the moving truck was even empty.

"That dog is a real son of a bitch," says Katherine, as if she'd been joining in the conversation all along. Alzheimer's is weird like this. Most of the time, Katherine seems lost in some other place—only vaguely aware of what's going on at any given moment. And then she'll say something perfectly lucid. Like a radio station that's all static picking up a brief signal.

"He is, Katherine. He really is," my mom says. "C'mon, let's get you inside."

Katherine and Jack are not watching *I Love Lucy* when we get home. He's watching a rerun of *Magnum, P.I.*, and she's snoring softly in her armchair, fast asleep. Which means she's probably going to be up half the night, pacing the upstairs hallway, keeping everyone else awake, asking the same questions over and over and over again. It's called sundowning—when Alzheimer's patients get restless after the sun goes down and are unable to fall asleep.

Mom sets a pizza box down on the coffee table. "Sorry. I know we had pizza two nights ago." Jack is already grabbing a slice, so I don't think he minds.

I lean on the crutches that I'm supposed to use for the next few days to keep the weight off my toe and propel myself toward the sofa so I can pick up the notebook and pen that I left there what now seems like ages ago, when Hank knocked down the front screen door. The door that has gifted me with six stitches. As a result, I have to either wear sandals or an old pair of sneakers with the toe box cut out for my first day of school. And accessorize with the crutches.

I turn and start hauling myself up the stairs.

"Don't you want some pizza, Gracie?" my mom asks.

"No. I'm not hungry."

Hank is sprawled out on my bed when I enter my room, and although I briefly consider kicking him off in punishment for his bad behavior, I let him stay. In his weird way, when he dashed outside to tangle with Coco, he was just protecting me. As if *I* am the most important person in the world. The Chosen One. Secret royalty. I do have to push him over though, so I have some space.

Hank looks like a cross between some kind of shepherd and a Great Dane, but we're not sure what he is. Mom let us pick out a puppy from the pound when Dad decided to move to Maryland with Kirsten (*not* Kristen, as she likes to remind everyone), and the people at the pound told us he'd be about forty pounds. Which was . . . not even close.

I settle myself against my bed pillows and close my eyes. It's still hot and I can hear the cicadas buzzing loudly outside. I wish I could call Hannah. It's definitely one of those nights when I miss my best friend so much it hurts. I imagine myself back in my old room, in my old bed. I actually wouldn't even need to call. I could just run—or, okay, hop—over to her house. We could lie on her game room floor, eat an entire package of

Chips Ahoy, watch MTV, and laugh till I no longer wanted to die of humiliation when thinking about the rest of the day. But now she's miles away, and the *only* phone in this giant, creaky old house is in the alcove under the stairs on the first floor. I don't feel like going back downstairs just so my mom can eavesdrop. Plus it's really too late to call, so I guess it's just going to be me, myself, and my humiliating thoughts.

I open my eyes, pick up my notebook, and glance at the shoebox on the floor next to my desk, which contains the (possibly?) cool shoes I will *not* be wearing on Tuesday. I click my pen and scribble a single line, practically tearing through the page:

> *It was the first day of school and the new girl already had a nickname: Big Toe.*

No, no, no. I scratch it out, already feeling the story slipping from my grasp.

"WHERE DID THEY TAKE THE LETTERS?"

Katherine is standing in the doorway of Grandpa's study, purse over her arm. She's restless and agitated today, and this is her third or fourth lap around the downstairs. She keeps circling through what my grandparents used to call the sitting room, the kitchen, the dining room, into the study, where I am, and then through the entryway and back to the sitting room again, and every time she comes around, she asks me the same question: "Where did they take the letters?"

I sigh. This last official day of summer is going to be a long one. Mom's working a holiday shift and it's raining, so we can't even get out for a walk.

Katherine asks questions about "them" a lot. "*Where did they go?*" "*Have they come back from church yet?*" "*Where did they take the letters?*" I have no idea who "they" are, or where these mystery letters might be, but I know by now that it's better to just play along.

"Oh, they took the letters to the post office," I answer as I haul several volumes of the *Oxford English Dictionary* to the heavy oak desk by the window. In addition to the dictionary—which is twelve volumes long and takes up an entire shelf—the study is overflowing with all kinds of books: novels, essay collections, poetry, *The Complete Works of William Shakespeare.* There's even a special *Shakespeare Lexicon and Quotation Dictionary* to go along with the *Complete Works.* And several thesauruses. Like our new neighbor Tom's mom, my grandfather was a professor. But instead of math, he taught English lit.

Katherine frowns at me. "What letters? I don't know what you're talking about."

"Never mind," I say as I start flipping through the dictionary. I sometimes find interesting words that might spark a story idea. Like . . . *pareidolia*: a psychological phenomenon in which the mind perceives a specific image or pattern where one does not actually exist.

Once, there was a man who was convinced he saw Jesus's face in a piece of toast . . .

Petrichor is another good one. It means the pleasant, earthy smell after rain. Or, *chartreuse*: a light yellow or green resembling the color of a type of French liqueur.

"I better get going." Quicker than I would've thought

possible, Katherine makes her way to the front door and starts twisting the deadbolt, Hank right behind her.

Yeah, that's not going to be good.

I hop over to them and grab Hank by his collar, feeling his muscles tense as he readies himself to run. Katherine is still trying to work the lock. "Can you open this?" she asks me, frustrated. I spot my brother sprawled on the sofa, watching TV.

"Jack. Could use a little help here!"

The best approach in moments like this is to distract her, and Jack is much better at sweet-talking Katherine than I am. It helps that even at twelve, he's still adorable, with his freckles and dimpled smile. Although Katherine doesn't remember they're related, I can tell she's charmed by him. He knows it too.

"I'm watching something."

"*Jack.*"

"*Ohhhh*, all right." He slides off the sofa. "Hey, Katherine," he says when he meets us at the door. "I was just about to scoop some ice cream. Want me to bring some out to the porch for you?"

Katherine's face brightens. "Oh, thank you, I'd love that!" She pats Jack on the cheek. "Aren't you a sweet boy."

"You wait here with Gracie, and I'll bring out your ice cream in a minute."

"Who's Gracie?"

"This is Gracie. She's my sister," he says. "She'll wait with you here. I'll be right back."

He pulls Hank farther inside with him.

"Close him in the study," I say. "I don't want him getting out."

I open the front door and steer Katherine to the wicker chairs on the porch.

She holds her purse tight on her lap as she sits. "Where did they put the letters?" she asks me. Again.

"They took them to the post office," I answer. Again.

"Oh."

She's quiet for a minute, watching the rain come down. I study her profile, trying to find something in her expression that reminds me of the grandma I used to know when I was little.

Although my grandfather taught English lit, Katherine was the one who told me stories. At least that's what I remember most about her from Before. Before she forgot I existed. Before my parents' divorce. Before this house was also *my* house.

Back then, Katherine was always ready with a story. Like the one about a girl who could walk on water, and who crossed the Atlantic Ocean on foot as a pod of dolphins swam alongside her, feeding her fish and keeping her company. And the one about an old woman who found a bag that turned pennies into pieces of gold. And my favorite: the one about a boy and girl who fell in love because they both made the exact same wish, on the exact same day, at the exact same time.

I always wanted her stories to be true. I wanted the stories I read in my childhood books to be true too. Maybe there was even a part of me that actually believed they were, until I got old enough to realize that special powers and magic wishes and wardrobes that served as portals to other universes weren't really possible.

Well, *except* in stories. Because stories are their own self-contained universes.

I guess that's why I love to write them. When you write your own stories, you get to create whatever reality you want. A brother and sister can run away to live in the Metropolitan Museum of Art. A girl can rescue her father from another dimension. Poor, obscure, plain little Jane can inherit a fortune *and* marry her soulmate, Mr. Rochester, who is very conveniently available by the end of the book. There's a kind of power in making it all up. And sometimes—okay, truthfully most of time—making it all up is just so much *better* than what happens in real life. Saturday's fiasco with my toe being a good example.

My attention is pulled away from Katherine by movement across the street, as the new family's Volvo turns into their drive and stops under the carport. The mom climbs out of the driver's side, Tom gets out of the passenger side, and two younger boys—the twins, I assume—burst from the back. They all start unloading groceries and carrying them into the house while a sweet-looking golden retriever comes out to greet them, wagging its tail. It doesn't bark or try to run out into the street. Their dog seems kind of perfect. With their station wagon and helpful grocery carrying, they *all* seem kind of perfect, as if they've been cast in a commercial for milk or

Kraft cheese. On cue, Hank starts barking like a maniac in the study. I know without looking that he's up on the window seat, hopefully not tearing down the drapes. And now they see me and Katherine, sitting on the porch. Tom waves, his mom waves, so I have no choice but to wave back.

"How's your foot?" he yells across the street.

"It's fine, thank you!" I'm not about to go into the details.

"Whew!" he says. "Glad you're okay! It was like a crime scene over there!"

Ha, yes. Yes, it was, Tom.

"Hank seems like he wants to come out and play again," he adds, laughing.

"Where did they put the letters?" Katherine asks.

Hank continues to bark, because he's the most embarrassing dog in the world and won't ever be cast in a commercial for anything.

"Sorry . . ." I say. But my voice is drowned out by Katherine's: "I SAID, WHERE did they put the letters?"

Oh my God! WHERE is Jack?

"I don't know, Katherine," I tell her.

I.

Don't.

Know.

Tom disappears into his house with a grocery bag right as Jack *finally* appears with two bowls of ice cream. One for Katherine, and one for himself. Nothing for me.

Katherine's face lights up again when she sees him. "There

he is!" she exclaims, clapping her hands. "Are you Anna's son?"

Anna is Katherine's sister, and Anna's son, Pat, is in his forties, but Katherine must still have a vague memory of him as a little boy. This is a thing with Alzheimer's patients. They forget the most recent stuff first—what happened last week, last month, last year, three seconds ago—but the more far away past is sometimes still there, almost as if it just happened. Lately, Katherine talks about Anna a lot.

"No," Jack says, "I'm Maggie's son."

Katherine shakes her head. "I don't know any Maggie."

Jack and I exchange a look. We're never really sure how to handle these moments. As the silence stretches, the rain slows to a stop, and steam starts to rise from the asphalt on the road in front. There's an earthy scent in the air. Petrichor.

Jack jumps up from the chair he was sitting on. "I'm gonna see what's going on across the street."

"Jack. Give them a little breathing room. They just moved in."

"It's fine!" he says. "Mrs. Broder told me to come over anytime."

I watch him run across the street, a little envious of how comfortable he is about just knocking on someone's door and inviting himself in.

Katherine yawns. She was up pacing most of last night.

"You look like you could use a nap," I tell her.

"A nap sounds good."

She follows me up the stairs without complaint, a sure sign

that she is tired, but does ask about the crutches I'm using at least twice. Both times, I tell her that I hurt my toe, which is an explanation that I've already given to her about a million times today.

"Is Anna coming?" Katherine asks, as I help her take off her shoes and get into bed.

"Maybe later," I say.

"You'll stay with me until then?"

I smooth her wiry salt-and-pepper hair from her forehead. "Sure, I'll stay."

I take a seat at the vanity table across from Katherine's bed and examine myself in the mirror. My shoulder-length hair is slightly frizzy from the humidity. I also spot a zit on my chin that's just about to fully erupt. Should go nicely with my outfit tomorrow, which I already know is going to look all wrong with the dorky sandals I'll need to wear because of my big, bandaged toe.

I sigh and study the wood inlay on the top of the vanity, tracing the pattern with my fingertips.

Back when I was little, Katherine used to let me sit here and play dress-up with her things. Curious if all the jewelry I used to layer on is still here, I open the center drawer. Inside, there's a black velvet insert with spaces to organize everything: little divots for earrings and necklaces, slots where you can slide in a ring. The jewelry is still surprisingly well-organized—maybe Mom helps her keep it that way—though there are also a few random items that Katherine must have picked up from around the house: a Star Wars action figure, a teaspoon, neon-blue nail polish that I've been looking for.

I select and clip on a pair of chandelier earrings made of gold filigree with a line of tiny oblong pearls dangling from the bottom. They're beautiful. I hold my hair up, turning side to side to watch them sway, and wonder where Katherine wore these. I've never seen her in them before. The Katherine of my childhood wore basic pearls with a skirt, jacket, and low-heeled pumps when she was dressed up, so it's hard for me to picture her wearing something so glamorous.

The room is alive with laughter and music and clinking glasses. As I walk through the crowd, my gold chandelier earrings sway.

I'm about to try on a ring with an onyx stone when an old-fashioned brass key catches my eye. I pick it up and immediately wonder if it's the one that opens the bottom right vanity drawer—the drawer that, for as long as I can remember, has *always* been locked. When we were younger, Jack and I were convinced that there must be something really valuable in there, like a stash of rare coins. One Thanksgiving, when I was in my Nancy Drew phase, I even had the idea to try and pick the lock with a bobby pin when everyone else was downstairs watching football. (It didn't work.)

I study the key in my hand. It's likely just a random one that Katherine picked up somewhere else in the house, but in honor of eleven-year-old mystery-obsessed me, I have to try it on the drawer.

Katherine is snoring behind me. I hesitate for a few seconds, feeling slightly conflicted about unlocking a drawer that is not mine, but curiosity gets the better of me. I lean down and push the key into the lock. It sticks a little, but once I wiggle and turn it, the internal mechanism pops open with a click.

I grin, half surprised that it worked and half amused at what terrible detectives we were. *The Mystery of the Locked Drawer*—solved!

As quietly as possible, I slide the drawer open. It's surprisingly heavy . . . Maybe there *are* a bunch of rare coins in here! I imagine Mom's face when I tell her . . .

Mom: Fifty thousand dollars? These are worth fifty thousand dollars!

Me: That's what the appraiser said . . .

Mom: Oh, Gracie, this is amazing. I'm so glad you found the key to that drawer!

But quickly I realize that what I'm looking at is mainly just a bunch of junk. Old perfume bottles, several decks of rubber-banded playing cards, folded-up gift wrap, and a heap of tangled scarves.

Silently laughing at myself for expecting something more exciting than recycled wrapping paper, I tug at a black chiffon scarf. It catches on something underneath. A hat box. *Hmmm* . . . maybe I don't have to give up on those rare coins just yet? I lift the box out of the drawer and open the lid. No coins. There's no cool vintage hat inside either, just a bunch of old photos.

Katherine shifts in her sleep behind me, reminding me that I should probably get going. I start to return the box to the drawer but change my mind. I bet Mom would like to see the photos, and maybe Katherine would, too, even if she doesn't recognize them as hers. And, truth be told, I'm a little intrigued about them myself.

I pull off the chandelier earrings and put them back in their spot in the jewelry drawer. Then I pick up my blue nail polish and Jack's Star Wars figure, and carry them, along with the hat box, out of the room, being careful not to step on the spot where the hardwood creaks or to put too much weight on my bad toe. I'll come back for the crutches when Katherine wakes.

The house is so quiet, I can hear the cuckoo clock marking the hour on the mantel downstairs. It's midnight, but I'm too amped up to sleep. I've overthought my outfit, optimistically applied Clearasil to the pimple on my chin, and have imagined multiple scenarios about how my first day at Morewood High might unfold, none of them inspiring confidence. I rearrange my pillows. And then I stare up at the ceiling, studying a crack visible in the moonlight. Katherine's hat box is under my bed, where I stashed it earlier, so I decide to take a look inside to distract myself.

Sitting cross-legged on my mattress, I open the box and start shuffling through a stack of the photos. They look like stills from a black-and-white movie, and Katherine is *so* young in them. There's a faded one of her and her three siblings as children, standing in front of a house. A number of pictures are of her with her sister Anna in their late teens or early twenties, including one on a street in New York City, where they are wearing fitted dress coats and hats, a blurred taxicab passing by in the background. I run my finger over the photograph. Katherine was beautiful back then, with big dark eyes, long lashes, bold lipstick, and her hair styled in soft waves.

There are also photos of her with a handsome guy in an army uniform, who does *not* look like my grandfather. For one thing, he's smiling. I don't recall my grandfather smiling for any photograph, ever. He's even serious in their wedding portrait. Also, this guy has thick, dark hair. My grandfather didn't have much hair at all, and what little he did have was light.

On the backs of the photos of the army guy, there's a date written: 1942. In the first one, he's leaning against a cement wall and Katherine is perched behind him, her chin on his shoulder and arms wrapped around his chest. In another, they're sitting at a round table littered with glasses and bottles. It looks like they're in a crowded restaurant, or maybe a banquet hall. He's wearing his uniform again, but she's wearing a satiny dress with a deep V-neck and flutter sleeves. It's a candid shot, so neither is looking at the camera. Instead, their faces are turned toward each other and they're laughing, like they've been sharing some secret inside joke.

I'm about to take another pile of photos out of the box when my hand grazes something at the very bottom.

It's a book.

I lift it out. It looks old. The velvet cover, a deep maroon, is faded and patchy, and the pages are edged with gold leaf. It even smells old, like the copy of *A Tale of Two Cities* I checked out this summer from Carnegie Library. But there's no title on the front or on the spine. Is it a journal? I begin to open it—maybe there's something inside about Katherine's mystery man!—but for the second time today, I hesitate. It feels wrong to read someone else's journal. When I imagine anyone reading one of my notebooks, I'm overwhelmed by mortification.

But Katherine probably doesn't even remember she has a journal, so . . . I open the book, expecting to see her handwriting, but the pages are all blank and pristine. *Boo.* I guess I'm not going to uncover any juicy family secrets or stories about Katherine's younger, wilder days.

I run my hand over the journal's first blank page. It definitely feels more "writerly" than my ninety-nine-cent spiral-bound, especially with the black ribbon bookmark attached to the spine. Maybe if I use this journal instead, my stories will be more . . . sophisticated.

I pick up the pen from my nightstand, click it five times, and begin to write:

> *The room is alive with laughter and music and clinking glasses as I walk through the crowd. A champagne cork pops. My satin dress, chartreuse, clings in all the right places. My gold chandelier earrings sway. I know, without looking, that all eyes are on me.*

I slide into a seat at a table with a view of the bar and watch a waiter pick up a flute of champagne. He carries it in my direction on a small, circular tray, and sets it in front of me. Sparkling bubbles rise from the bottom of the glass. I shake my head. "I didn't order this."

"From the gentleman at the table in the corner," he says, before he retreats.

I turn to look, but the table in the corner is empty. Never one to waste champagne, I lift the glass. As I take a sip, a shadow stretches across the candlelit tablecloth.

"Mind if I join you?"

Ha! I think to myself. *Don't I wish.*

I snap the journal shut, put it back in the box, and return to staring up at the ceiling in the dark, far too anxious and wired than anyone should be at close to one a.m. If I don't get some sleep soon, I'll be adding puffy raccoon eyes to my bangin' back-to-school look.

L'ESPRIT D'ESCALIER

IT FEELS LIKE I'VE ONLY BEEN ASLEEP FOR FIVE MINUTES WHEN I hear my mom calling from downstairs. "Gracieeeee! You are going to be late if you don't get a move on!" I open my eyes and slam down the button of the alarm clock that's apparently been blaring for—*oh, shit*—twenty minutes now? I sit up and pull back the covers, and as I do, something shines on my nightstand, catching the light streaming in from the open window.

Katherine's gold chandelier earrings—the ones I tried on yesterday at her vanity—rest next to . . . is that . . . a champagne cork? That's weird. I definitely remember putting the earrings back in her drawer, and I *know* they weren't there when I (finally) fell asleep last night. So how did they, and a champagne cork, get into my room?

I look around and glance at the closed bedroom door. Katherine must have left this stuff here, on my nightstand, in the middle of the night. But how'd she pull that off without waking me? She's not exactly stealthy.

I pick the earrings up, just to make sure they are solid and not a figment of my imagination. They are light and delicate, slightly cool to the touch, but definitely real. And what's the deal with the champagne cork? Was she *drinking*? A bottle of champagne? Maybe Mom was and Katherine lifted the cork from the kitchen counter or something. Katherine stashes a lot of weird stuff in various places. Yesterday I found a half-eaten donut in her purse, and also the TV remote. But why would my mom be drinking champagne after midnight on a weeknight? Unless she's becoming a secret alcoholic? People with a problem drink alone, after everyone goes to bed, right? But how many of them drink champagne?

The volume of Mom's voice has increased to "using my full name" level: "GRACIE KATHERINE BYRNE, ARE YOU AWAKE UP THERE? WE NEED TO LEAVE NO LATER THAN SEVEN THIRTY!" Well, she sounds like her normal self at any rate. Not drunk. So that's good. We have to leave early so Mom can drop Jack and me at our schools before the appointment that she and Katherine have to visit the senior day care in our neighborhood. The original plan was for me to drive myself to school in Grandpa's old Cadillac Seville, but now I'm not supposed to drive until Friday because of my stupid toe.

"I'm up!"

I set the earrings back on my nightstand, grab the loose black Bermuda dress shorts and white boatneck T-shirt I picked out to wear, and head to the bathroom to shower.

On the way to school, I'm already second-guessing my outfit. If this were a normal year, I would have run it by Hannah over the weekend. I'd also be meeting her out front before the bell rang, so we could compare schedules and make plans to reconvene at one of our lockers before lunch. We'd been joined at the hip since kindergarten. Lunch plans were a given. Now nothing is a given, and not knowing what to expect is really freaking me out.

"Oh, look, there's Tom from across the street." My mom points him out waiting for the bus at the corner. "Maybe we should give him a lift?"

"Where did they put the letters?" Katherine asks from the back seat.

No. No, no, no.

I'm already picturing the awkwardness. "Mom, there's no room." We'd have to wedge him in the back of the Tempo, next to my grandmother and Jack and my crutches. And then Katherine would start badgering him with nonsensical questions and then . . . would we have to walk into school together? Would I have to make small talk with him when I can barely keep a lid on my first-day panic as it is? *Just no.*

"There's room!" says Jack, who, like my mom, has always been a the-more-the-merrier type.

I glance in the side mirror and see the bus behind us.

"The bus is *right there*," I emphasize. "He's fine."

I'm half expecting my mom to ignore me and pull over anyway, but she keeps going. She's quiet for a few seconds, but I can tell she's thinking about saying something that will annoy me. She can't help herself.

"We could have squeezed him in. I don't know why you're so weird about everything, Gracie."

"I'm not being weird, Mom. *You're* being weird."

"For wanting to give our new neighbor a lift to school?"

"Yes! I mean . . . no."

"What is it, then?"

I just hate when she feels like she has to be social *for* me. "Never *mind*."

I sigh. She sighs. Our personalities are just very, *very* different. I know she was popular in high school. And had a popular boyfriend: my dad. They were high school sweethearts.

"I love you . . ." she says.

"I love you too," I answer.

"Today is going to be fine."

Is it, though? My stomach has more than butterflies. It feels like I've swallowed an entire hive of bees.

I'm almost late for first period, on account of the crutches, and the fact that my trigonometry classroom is the farthest possible distance from the front lobby, where I picked up my schedule from a box marked A–D. When I find room 256, I freeze in the doorway, deer-in-the-headlights style, as a sea of unfamiliar faces turns my way. It feels like all eyes are on me. I'm assuming it's because of the crutches and my huge bandaged toe sticking out of my sandal. And maybe the pimple that, as of this morning, has erupted like Mount Vesuvius on my chin.

My eyes scan the room, the faces of my new classmates blurring together like an impressionist painting.

Breathe, Gracie, breathe. I breathe.

A seat. I need to find a seat. I was hoping to secure a space near the back, where I could switch to being the observer, rather than the observee. But all the incognito spots are taken, so the only choice easy to navigate to with the crutches is the front row, where I will be face-to-face with our teacher, who is currently scrawling her name on the chalkboard: Mrs. Drazkowski.

In an attempt to distract myself from the fact that I still feel like that deer, frozen in front of the high beams of a semitruck on a dark, wooded road at night, I open the trigonometry textbook on my desk and start leafing through it as if it's a magazine in a dentist's office. Like a total dork. *Yes, everyone, I just loooove to read about trig. Fascinating!* There is chatter all around me now—an "I love your shoes!" here, a "How come you weren't at Becky's on Saturday?" over there—most of it blending into an indistinguishable buzz until Mrs. Drazkowski begins to speak. "Good morning, folks. Welcome to Trigonometry . . ."

For the rest of my morning classes, I decide I will do my best to haul ass and arrive early, so I can navigate to a seat near the back of the room.

When the bell rings for Lunch A, I find my locker and dump in all the books that I've collected so far: *Trigonometry*, a United States history textbook, a paperback copy of *The Craft of Essay Writing* for English, and *Chemistry Today*, which is huge and slightly intimidating. The hallway is filled with the sounds of hundreds of other books thumping into lockers, the metal clang of slamming doors, laughter, yelling—until it all blends into that buzz again. That buzz where multiple overlapping conversations become insect-like white noise in my head. Even though I'm in the middle of it, I feel outside of it. Like I'm in the eye of a hurricane. And here, in the hurricane's eye, all I can think about is the question that's been gnawing at the edges of my consciousness ever since I walked in this morning: What to do about lunch? I imagine walking up to a crowded table and asking if I can join. The confused faces betraying what everyone is thinking: *Who the hell is this?* Or worse: walking up to someone sitting alone.

Unfortunately, this leaves me with only one other, equally unappealing option: sit by myself. I decide that lunch is as good a time as any to acquaint myself with the library.

Art is my first class following lunch, and for that, I am relieved. I loved the art studio at my old school, and Morewood's studio is similar: The long drafting tables marked by smudges from charcoals and gouges from X-Acto blades. The stained sink, dotted with drops of dried paint. The chemical but not unpleasant smell of all the supplies. More importantly, art class permits me to "introvert" as much as I want. I rarely have to worry about being called on unexpectedly or taking part in class discussions.

I plant my crutches and swing myself toward a table near the back of the studio, sit, and watch the rest of the class file in. There are a few people I recognize from my earlier periods. Then, a few moments after the bell rings . . . *help.* Calvin-Klein-underwear-model cheekbones, tousled hair: Hot Guy—Luke—from my front porch two days ago. He's wearing high-top black Chuck Taylors, jeans ripped at the knees, a white tee, and this funky, fedora-like hat that would probably look ridiculous on anyone else. As he makes his way to the back of the classroom, I wish I could slide right under the drafting table and hide. Instead, I keep my head down and study the homage to Black Sabbath that's been etched onto the surface in front of me.

"Mind if I join you?"

Help. Help. Help.

I look up into his velvety-forest-moss eyes and immediately blush. Because of course I do.

"Sure," I say, trying to sound as nonchalant as possible.

"Heeeyyy," he says. "Aren't you the girl with the Cujo dog and the bloody toe? From Shady Avenue?"

I briefly consider some version of *I have* no *idea what you're talking about,* but instead just nod. Even if I could lie convincingly, the crutches and the bandages sticking out of my sandal are a dead giveaway.

"I thought it was you," he says, sitting down. He nods at my crutches. "Tell me you didn't lose that toe." The sly smile suggests he's messing with me.

"No," I answer. "I just had to get stitches."

"Ouch. Sorry. What's your name again?" He doesn't remember. Not that I was expecting him to.

"Grace," I say, and try to sound like I believe it.

"Nice to meet you again, Grace."

"Thanks." I only realize after that *thanks* makes absolutely no sense. How about *Nice to meet you again too,* or at the very least, *Likewise*?

Mercifully, our art teacher, Ms. Slater, saves me from further conversation, at least for the moment, by getting down to business.

"Welcome to Intermediate Fine Arts. Despite what you may think, this class is not an easy A, and I expect you all to arrive on time." She looks at Luke, and then down at her class list. "You are?"

"Carr," he says. "Luke Carr." Like a double agent. Licensed to kill.

"Great. Luke, you can help me pass around the paper and charcoals. Let's all get warmed up with some still-life sketches."

She pulls a sheet off a pile of objects lined up on a table near the front of the room. The pile includes an old clock, a broken ballerina figurine, a brass key, a miniature ship in a bottle, a sand dollar, and a couple of other things that I can't get a good look at from where I'm sitting.

"Come on up and take one or a few of these items back to your spot and draw."

When I stand, I accidentally knock my crutches over. They clatter when they hit the floor, and yet again, all eyes are on me. *Carr, Luke Carr* leans down and picks them up.

"Thanks," I say, standing awkwardly with my weight on one foot.

"No problem," he answers. I swing myself toward the table in the front and pick up the key, which is heavy and old-fashioned looking—a larger version of the one that unlocks Katherine's vanity drawer—and an empty mason jar. Ms. Slater offers to help me carry everything back to my spot.

Back at the drafting table, I put the key inside the jar and begin sketching, but Luke's presence is already upsetting the serenity I was expecting from my art class experience. How am I supposed to work while also obsessing about my side profile? My primary concern is not my still life; it's whether my Mount Vesuvius chin pimple is super obvious or not.

I sneak a quick glance to my right. Luke, dark locks of hair falling over his forehead, is sketching a garden gnome—the last item left after he was done passing out the charcoals. A copy of *The Catcher in the Rye* sits atop his stack of schoolbooks.

Everyone is pretty quiet for the rest of the period. Until my stomach growls so loudly that a goth kid sitting in front of me turns around, staring through an enormous amount of eyeliner, as if he could *see* where the sound is coming from.

"I think it was her," says Luke. He tilts his head my way as I wonder why I'm always such a disaster. Note to self: bring a sandwich tomorrow if I intend to spend my lunch period in the library. When the bell rings, Luke offers to take my items back up to the front desk. As he passes behind me, he leans over and whispers—*whispers!*—in my left ear.

"Thanks for swiping that key I wanted . . . Grace."

I feel like my entire head is on fire.

For the rest of the afternoon, I imagine that I said something—*anything*—witty in response to that whisper, instead of losing my ability to perform even basic speech functions. I could have replied in a flirty voice: "*Oh, didn't you know that I'm a professional thief?*" or "*A hundred bucks and it's yours . . .*" But of course I am the type of person who only thinks of something interesting to say hours or even days after an opportunity strikes to say it.

There's a word for that. For missing your chance to say something clever in the moment. It's a French word. Well, a phrase, actually: *l'esprit d'escalier.* The literal translation is "wit of the staircase," referring to a remark coming to mind on the stairs as one leaves a social gathering. It has since been used to describe the predicament of landing on the perfect reply too late, which is basically the story of my life.

When I get home from school, the earrings and champagne cork that Katherine left on my nightstand are gone. What is it with her sneaking around in my room? I sigh. She's worse than Jack.

A STORM BLOWS IN ON FRIDAY MORNING, COMPLETE WITH lightning, thunder, and pelting rain that blurs my view of the car ahead of me, even with the windshield wipers going at full blast. The good news is that I've been cleared to drive. I've also been cleared to ditch the crutches. And now that I have almost a full first week of school under my belt, the angry hive of bees that had taken up residence in the pit of my stomach has been replaced by something a little milder, but still unpleasant. A colony of anxious ants, perhaps. Or maybe misanthropic mosquitoes.

As I turn onto Wilkins, I spot a figure running down the sidewalk chasing the 7:55 bus, which has already left the stop. Tall and lanky, I'm pretty sure the runner is my neighbor Tom. And although he seems fast, there's no way he's going to catch that bus. A bright flash of lightning is followed almost immediately by a deafening clap of thunder. When I was little, Katherine used to tell me that thunder was "just the angels bowling in heaven." If so, that last one was definitely a strike. I come to a quick decision. I don't want to have Tom's unlucky demise-by-lightning-bolt on my conscience, so I pull over to the curb a little bit ahead of him and beep the horn of the Seville. Tom—T-shirt sticking, no umbrella—slows to a stop and looks in as I roll down the window. "Oh, hey!" he says, catching his breath. "It's you!"

Probably doesn't remember my name.

"Gracie, right?" he adds.

"Actually, it's Gra—" The next flash lights up the sky and the angels bowl another strike.

Tom flinches and steps closer to the car. "What?"

"Never mind! Do you want a lift?"

"Nah, I'd rather stay out here. Enjoy the weather." He grins. "I mean, YES. That would be awesome." He opens the door and gets in.

Now that I realize I'm going to have to have a conversation, the colony of ants is on the move again, crawling all around my insides.

Tom chuckles. "You know, for a minute I thought it was a senior citizen stopping to offer me a ride. Not because you look elderly or anything. I just didn't expect you to roll up in a giant Cadillac."

"It was my grandfather's," I explain.

He nods with this big, dopey grin on his face. "Ah, makes sense."

He nods again and then says, "So do you ever ask yourself, 'Well, how did I get here?'"

What is he talking about?

"Ummm . . . how did I get *where*?"

"You know . . . the large automobile. From 'Once in a Lifetime.' Talking Heads? I love that song. Any relation?"

"Any relation?" I'm so confused.

"David *Byrne* . . . Talking Heads lead singer. Gracie *Byrne* . . . is it spelled the same?"

"Oh. Yes . . . to the spelling. But no." I shake my head. "No relation."

"I didn't really think so," he says. "But wouldn't it be so cool if you were related to David Byrne?"

The rumor around school is that the new girl is David Byrne's niece.

"I guess . . ."

There's a pause. The windshield wipers swish back and forth in front of us.

"So how's your first week of school been going?" he asks. "I was wondering if we'd have any classes together, but I guess we don't. What elective are you taking? Are you Lunch A?"

Am I supposed to answer all of these questions in order, or . . . ?

"Art." I say, as I make a left onto Fifth Avenue. "And I think all the juniors are Lunch A."

"Huh. I haven't seen you."

I'm surprised he even noticed I wasn't there. Instead of explaining that I have spent lunch period in the library for the past three days, like a loser, I just say, "It's a big cafeteria." Which is true. Big, noisy, and crowded. My worst nightmare.

Another pause.

Tom again: "My mom said you're new to the neighborhood too."

"Yes," I say. "Well, sort of. My grandmother has lived here for a long time. We moved in with her earlier this summer. After my grandfather died."

I don't know why I'm telling him about my grandfather.

"Oh, no, I'm sorry," he says. "And your grandmother, Katherine. She has Alzheimer's?"

"Yes," I say.

"I'm sorry," he says again. "That's tough."

"Yes."

"So . . . do you do a sport?" he asks.

"No."

He narrows his eyes like he's trying to size me up. "Drama club."

Definitely not, I think. But I say: "You ask a lot of questions."

"Do I?"

"Yep."

He shakes his head. "Sorry. I didn't mean to monopolize the questions. Go ahead, ask me anything. My life is an open book."

"Uh . . . I don't have any at the moment?"

Tom makes an exaggerated *ooouch!* face. "C'mon, you've got to have one? You're making me feel like the least interesting person that ever lived."

I can feel my cheeks heating and want to say: *No, I'm the one who feels like the least interesting person that ever lived*, but instead I blurt out the first thing that comes to mind. "Okay," I say. "How do you like Pittsburgh so far?"

"Hmmm," says Tom, making a face like he's taking my super-boring question seriously. "I don't know yet. We haven't lived here long enough."

"Where did you move *from*?"

"Chicago. How about you?"

See, Gracie? I tell myself. *It's just small talk. You don't need to overthink it.* The stomach ants are starting to chill out a bit.

"Two hours east. Altoona," I answer.

"So not too far," he says.

Far enough to feel like I'm completely starting over. I wonder if he's as bummed about having to move as I am.

"Do you miss Chicago? Your old school?" I ask.

"Yes and yes," he says. "I loved my school, but mom got offered a tenure-track position at Carnegie Mellon, so here we are."

"I've never been to Chicago."

"Actually, it's kind of like here in some ways," he says. "Everybody is really into sports and foods involving a lot of meat—it's just bigger and busier."

"And there's a lake," I say. *Duh.*

"There's a lake." He nods. "But everyone keeps telling me about the three rivers."

"Ah, yes," I say. "After the Steelers, and the Pirates, and the Penguins, Pittsburgh is proud of its rivers, I guess."

"What are they again?" Tom asks.

"The Ohio, the Allegheny, and the Monongahela."

"The Monongahela is my favorite," he says. "For sure."

"Why?"

He shrugs. "I just like saying it. *Monongahela, Monongahela, Monongahela.* Try it three times fast. It's like a tongue twister."

"I . . . I'm driving."

"Oh, right, I forgot about the no-tongue-twisters-while-driving rule." He shakes his head.

I can't decide whether I find him annoying or amusing. Maybe a little of both.

As I turn into the school parking lot, I splash through a huge puddle and accidentally spray dirty water all over two girls walking from their car. They shriek. One of them is wearing white jeans. *Shit.*

Tom makes a sound like he's sucking in his breath. "Oh. That's unfortunate."

"Well, obviously." I think I recognize the girl in the white jeans from my PE class.

"That's Christina Merlotti, from my lunch table," he says, in a way that sounds . . . ominous.

"And?"

"I don't know her well, but she seems a little intimidating? But maybe it's just a front, you know? Like, she could be a total softie on the inside."

I pull the car into a parking spot and turn off the engine. We walk to the main entrance together. Christina is standing just inside the doorway and doesn't look anything like a secret softie.

"What the *fuck*, new girl?"

"Sorry," I say. "It was an accident."

"I was distracting her with tongue twisters," adds Tom.

She makes a disgusted face. "*What?*"

The bell rings.

"I have to get to class," she adds, walking away. "But you *will* be getting my dry cleaning bill!"

She dry cleans her jeans?

Tom's face is a little pink. "I just realized the tongue twister thing could have been interpreted . . . differently than I had intended."

Ohhhh. Now my face is pink. It's contagious.

"It's okay," I say.

"Maybe I'll see you at lunch?" says Tom.

"Maybe." But if Tom is sitting at Christina Merlotti's table, I have no intention of going anywhere near it. We part ways at the hall that separates the East and West Wings, Tom breaking in to a jog as he calls over his shoulder, laughing, "Thanks for the lift, Gracie! You WILL be getting my dry cleaning bill!"

That does make me laugh. A little.

* * *

In English, Mr. Rossi is walking up and down the aisles, lecturing about the essay we were assigned to read last night, "Once More to the Lake," by E. B. White. He's talking about layers of meaning when my mind starts to wander. I doodle on my notebook: *Monongahela*, *Monongahela*, *Monongahela* and draw a little river monster next to the words.

Three minutes later, my body registers before my brain that Mr. Rossi is standing right next to me. I nearly jump out of my seat.

"What are your thoughts, Ms. . . . ? I'm sorry, I'm still learning all your names."

I look up from my notebook. Mr. Rossi stares at me expectantly, an encouraging expression on his face. And without turning my head, I can feel the other twenty-eight pairs of eyes in this room, all on me, their owners grateful they weren't the ones who got caught completely zoning out during our very first class discussion.

"Byrne," I say.

Did you know that I'm David Byrne's niece?

"Ms. Byrne." He smiles and waits.

"I . . . uh . . . Can you . . . repeat the question?"

He sighs. "So. At the end of the essay, White talks about feeling the chill of death as he watches his young son get ready for his swim in the lake. Any insight about what his meaning is there?"

"I'm . . . not sure," I say, my face hot. I can feel the sweat beads gathering on my upper lip, my armpits getting moist. *Moist.* Such a gross word.

"Did you read the essay, Ms. Byrne?"

"Yes." I nod, trying to gather my thoughts. *There was a thunderstorm . . . and then people went swimming in the rain . . .* and there was a really good word that I highlighted . . . *languid* . . . or was it *languidly*? My mind has gone completely blank.

Mr. Rossi sighs again. "Never mind, Ms. Byrne. Next time, read the essay." I hear a snort somewhere to my left but don't dare move my head to see who it is. He continues down the aisle and another girl raises her hand. "Ms. . . . ?"

"Dunn," she says. "Paige Dunn."

"Ms. Dunn." He smiles. "Any thoughts about what White meant at the end of the essay?"

Paige seems like one of those people who are *always* ready. "The chill he feels represents his awareness of his own mortality. Watching his son gives him a sense of the passage of time."

"Yes, yes, exactly." Mr. Rossi nods in agreement, clearly impressed.

The most annoying thing about the whole situation is that I did know this. I did actually read the essay. It was all there in my head. But my head had left the building.

He then turns back to the rest of the class. "This is what I mean by looking for layers. We want to not just explore the surface of a piece of writing. We need to dig deeper . . . What was the author consciously intending? What about unconsciously? There's always more that we can think about and analyze." He claps his hands. "Okay, people, I'm going to pass out a list of reading options for your literary analysis essays. The first will be due in three weeks." He picks up a stack of copies from his desk and deposits a handful with each of the kids in the front row so that they can take one and pass them back.

"She's such a kiss-ass," I hear someone whisper to my left. She's dressed all in black—black racerback tank top, black stretchy tube skirt, black fishnet stockings, heavy black Doc Martens boots.

I'm still trying to recover from the exchange with Mr. Rossi, so all I can manage is a weak smile.

"Don't feel bad. I've been there," she says. "Getting called on when you aren't expecting it. Always embarrassing. That's why I've perfected the art of the strategic hand raise."

"What's that?" I ask.

"Volunteer for the first question posed to the class. Provided, of course, you can answer it. Then you're in the clear to zone out for the rest of the hour because teachers like to mix it up and not call on the same person twice."

"You didn't volunteer today," I say.

She laughs. "Yeah, well, you got to do the honors this time, whether you wanted to or not. I'm Mina."

"Gracie," I say, realizing too late that I've squandered another chance at Grace.

"I think we also have French together, eighth period."

"With *Madame* Linney?"

Mina laughs and rolls her eyes. "Yes indeed. She so desperately wants to be French." She studies her handout. "What book are you going to choose?"

"I don't know." My mind returns to the dog-eared copy of *The Catcher in the Rye* that Luke Carr had with him in art class. "Maybe *The Catcher in the Rye*?"

The bell rings and everyone gets up to gather their things. Mina slings her black backpack over her shoulder.

"We should try to read the same one," she says. "Then we can, like, I don't know, help each other out with our reports?"

I don't know why she thinks I'm going to be helpful after my huge fumble with E. B. White, but I say, "Sure."

"Only if you want to . . ." she adds.

I immediately start worrying that I didn't seem enthusiastic enough about her idea, so I add, "Yes. Definitely. I'd like to."

"Cool," she says. "Want to talk about it at lunch?"

"Okay," I say. "Today?"

"Yeah," she says. "Unless you have other plans."

I think: *No, Mina, I do not have other plans, other than eating a sad sandwich in the library.*

I say, "Nothing I can't blow off."

I pick up my backpack and follow Mina into the midday hallway chaos, but this time I do not step out of the way. I join the rest of the salmon, swimming in unison, upstream.

As I drive home from school, I replay the highs and lows of my day. High: I ate lunch with Mina and her friend Daniel, at a spot on the edge of the cafeteria, near the windows. Just the three of us, which was much better than a jam-packed table in the middle of the storm. I spotted Tom at one of those. He was talking with a cute girl who's in my French class and gesturing wildly about something while several other people at the table laughed. Obviously, Tom has had no trouble making friends. He is clearly a center-of-the-room, comfortable-in-the-chaos kind of guy. And I'm a hang-on-the-edges-with-a-few-trusted-companions kind of girl. Maybe we both have found our people.

Low: It turns out that Christina Merlotti *is* in my PE class. Which was fine when she didn't take notice of me at all, but now I feel like I have a big old target on my back on account of this morning with the puddle. And while Luke Carr continues to sit next to me in art, he has mostly ignored me since the first day. So much so that I start to think I imagined that whisper.

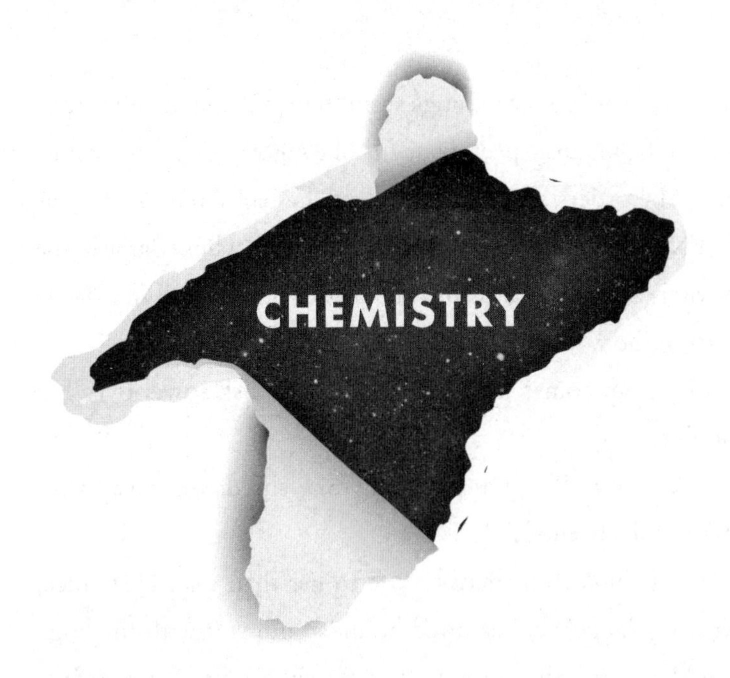

"ANYBODY GOT A MATCH?"

Katherine and I are watching an old movie that just started on WQED, called *To Have and Have Not*. It stars two actors who were famous in the forties—Humphrey Bogart and Lauren Bacall.

"It's Humphrey Bogart!" she exclaimed when I turned it on, and while I'm grateful that this got her to stop pacing and trying to open the front door to "go home," I'm also a little offended that she recognizes Humphrey Bogart as soon as he appears on screen, but not me, who actually lives with her.

So far, the movie has been a little slow. It's mainly about a bunch of people who hang out at this bar in Martinique while smoking about a million cigarettes. But now that the Lauren Bacall character has made her big entrance, asking for a match in a deep, sultry voice, things seem to be picking up. She steals wallets from unsuspecting men. She's got a cool nickname: Slim. She orders scotch and soda at the bar. And it's obvious she's already got Steve, the Bogart character (whose name in the movie is actually Harry, but she just decides to call him Steve because she wants to), wrapped around her little finger.

My mom comes in from the kitchen, dish towel over her shoulder.

"Oh, wow, Bogie and Bacall." She sits down next to us. "Wasn't she beautiful?"

Yes, I think. But there's more to her than that. Her voice, her body language, her fitted houndstooth suit with the huge shoulder pads—she doesn't ask for attention, she *commands* it.

The three of us keep watching, and at one point Slim just kind of out-of-the-blue plants herself in Steve's lap and surprises him with a kiss. When he asks her, "What did you do that for?" she answers, "I've been wondering whether I'd like it." Imagine that. Kissing someone you hardly even know just because you were wondering what it might be like. The thought gives me hives. Plus, you should probably ask first.

My mom tells me that Lauren Bacall and Humphrey Bogart fell in love in real life while making *To Have and Have Not* and I'm not surprised to hear this. You can tell that they've got something going on. Chemistry.

I spend the rest of the movie wondering:

A) How do you know when you have chemistry with someone?

B) What would I look like in a houndstooth jacket with shoulder pads? And . . .

C) Should I try to deepen my speaking voice?

When it's over, both Mom and Katherine are asleep on the sofa. Katherine is snoring softly, her purse next to her. Watching her sleep, I think about the photos I found of her in the hat box. It's weird. I've never really considered that she was once young like me, with her life stretched out far ahead. She was just my grandma, who took me to the park and baked pies. But now I wish I could ask her all kinds of questions. I wish I could ask about the cute guy with the sweet smile and dimples in her photographs and about the times she visited her sister in New York and about what it was like to be a teenager during the Great Depression and to live through a world war. I wish I had been able to ask more, to *know* more, so I could save some of her memories in my memory, for safekeeping, before it was too late.

I gently shake my mom's shoulder.

"Mom."

She opens her big brown eyes—a younger version of Katherine's, an older version of mine—and stares at me, disoriented, for a few seconds. Like she doesn't know where she is. I know it's only because my shoulder shake yanked her out of sleep too abruptly, but still, her momentary look of confusion rattles me. It's too similar to how Katherine looks most of the time. And it makes me think thoughts that I don't want to think. Thoughts that form into a tiny, tight ball of fear in the pit of my stomach. What if what's happening to Katherine happens to her someday? Or Jack? Or me? Who would I even *be* if I couldn't remember my own life?

I glance again at Katherine. The creases on her forehead smooth out a bit when she sleeps. I wonder, when she is awake, if she's aware anymore of what's happening to her. In the beginning, when it was just smaller things like forgetting to turn off the oven or her inability to call up a word she was looking for, it was obvious that she knew. And that she was scared. I wonder if it's better not to know.

"It's late," I tell my mom.

Hank follows the three of us up the stairs, and when I return from the bathroom after brushing my teeth, he's in his usual spot, stretched across my bed. "Move over, Hank." I try to push him aside, but he doesn't budge, so I squeeze in under the covers. I'll bet he'd move for Lauren Bacall. She'd just tell him what to do in between puffs of her cigarette and he'd do it.

Instead of turning out the light, I pick up the journal I found in Katherine's vanity and begin adding to the story I started on Labor Day. I haven't had much time to write in the two weeks since then.

> *I extract another cigarette from my case. He pulls a lighter from the pocket of his jacket. Army, I notice, wondering if he's shipping out soon.*
> *"May I?" he asks.*

I place the cigarette between my lips and cup his hand as he lights it for me. I lean back and study him as I smoke.

"You still haven't told me your name," he says.

"It's Grace. But my friends call me Slim."

I blow a ring of smoke, take another sip of champagne.

"I'm Luke," he says.

"I know."

He laughs.

"What are you, a spy?"

"Maybe," I respond.

I stamp my cigarette out.

"I've been wondering . . ." I say.

"What?" he asks.

"About you."

And then I get up, pick up my handbag, and leave the table without looking back, knowing he's going to follow.

The cuckoo clock sounds off down on the mantel, reminding me that yet again I've stayed up too late.

WHEN I TURN ONTO WILKINS, I SPOT TOM CHASING THE BUS again.

It's not raining today, but still. I feel like I should save him from being late. I pull over, slightly in front of him, and roll down the window.

"You should probably set your alarm earlier," I say.

He slows to a stop, panting. "I should, but the bus is demotivating." He takes a step toward the car and then stops. "You are offering me a ride, right?"

"Yes, Tom."

He opens the door and folds himself into the passenger seat. "Thanks."

"You're welcome."

His hair is damp, like he just got out of the shower, and he smells like shampoo and toothpaste. I pull away from the curb and adjust the volume on the radio.

"So . . ." He moves his seat back, making room for his grasshopper legs. "Do you have Rossi for English?"

"I do. Fourth period."

"I've got him second period. He has an excellent mustache, don't you think? Kind of Magnum P.I.-ish. I think he should get into Hawaiian shirts. Anyway. You know how we were supposed to read *A Tale of Two Cities* over the summer?"

"Uh-huh . . ."

"Well, I didn't quite get to it. Did you?" He's smiling big, like he's about to ask me for a favor. I notice there's a tiny gap between his two front teeth. Is it cute? It's kind of cute, I decide.

"I did."

"Ah, cool! I think we're supposed to be discussing it today and I was wondering if you could give me a quick summary."

Knew it.

"A quick summary? Of *A Tale of Two Cities*?"

"Yeah . . . you seem like you'd be a good summarizer."

"How so?" I say.

"It's just that your way of speaking is so *economical*."

"Hmm," I say. "Yours is . . . not."

He shrugs. "So I've been told."

"You do know about CliffsNotes?" I ask.

"Yeah, but I just remembered we are talking about it *this afternoon*," he says. "Plus, I trust you more than Cliffs." He acts like we've known each other for years instead of days.

"Well . . . *A Tale of Two Cities*, it's kind of involved."

"Is it?"

How does he not know this?

"Yes. I mean, there are a lot of characters, it switches between London and Paris . . ."

"Oh, London and Paris! Those are the two cities!"

"Oh my God."

"I guess I should know that . . . go on."

"It's set during the French Revolution."

"So: Storming of the Bastille, guillotines, rolling heads, et cetera."

"Yes, but that's only part of it. There's a lot of other stuff that happens."

Tom leans back toward the passenger-side window, making himself comfortable.

"Okay, what's the main theme? Teachers always want to know if you got the theme."

What *is* the theme?

"I think maybe it's duality?" I continue, wondering if I sound smart. "There are the two cities, right? *London* and *Paris*," I emphasize the names of each city. "And then the two main characters, Sydney Carton and Charles Darnay, look alike, so much so that Sydney takes Charles's place at the guillotine . . ."

"I knew heads were going to roll," he says. "Now you're making me *want* to read it."

"You should," I say. "It's actually a great book. But I don't think you have enough time to get to it before second period."

"Maybe I should just try and lay low and hope I don't get called on," he says.

"Probably the best plan." I think about mentioning Mina's strategic hand raise, but we've just arrived at the parking lot and don't really have time. The drive seemed short today. Maybe it felt longer the last time I picked him up because of the rain.

"Thanks for the summary anyway," Tom says as he reaches into the back seat for his backpack. "And if you ever need help in math"—he sings along with the radio, which is playing "I'm Your Man" by Wham!—"Not that I think you need help with math. I realize that's kind of sexist. But if you did. And not that I'm your man. Or anything. I was just singing the song . . ."

It's like he can't stop his mouth from moving.

"I get it," I say as I turn off the ignition. And then add: "You know, instead of you chasing the bus tomorrow, I can maybe just . . . give you a lift?"

"That would be excellent," says Tom. "What time?"

"Seven forty." I answer, which is ten minutes earlier than when we'd actually need to leave. Just to be safe.

"See you tomorrow," he says as we part inside the doors to the school.

"See you tomorrow."

I notice that I have no stomach bees today, or ants, or mosquitos.

In art class, we've started work on a mixed-media collage that's supposed to say something about who we are. I've settled on a collage of words. My idea is that the words will fill the profile of a silhouette I've drawn and maybe explode out of its mouth. I don't really know exactly how it's all going to come together yet, or really what it says about me, but for now, this is the plan. I'm leafing through a bunch of old magazines that Ms. Slater keeps stacked up on a shelf for people to use in their projects and as inspiration. So far, I've cut out the big block letters of *LIFE* from the cover of *Life* and the *You've come a long way, baby* slogan from a Virginia Slims cigarette ad.

Anybody got a match?

Luke Carr walks in and makes his way toward our drafting table. Today he's wearing a vintage military jacket. Army olive. Buttons open in the front. It looks *good* on him.

When he sits, I also am aware of something interesting. That anxious, awkward feeling I get whenever I'm around anyone I don't know very well is sort of absent today. Like, *gone*. It's kind of how I felt in the car with Tom this morning too.

"Cool jacket," I say.

"Thanks," he says while shrugging out of it, looking a little surprised that I spoke. He nods at my collage. "That's rad. I have no idea what to do. Collages feel like something from kindergarten. I wish she'd let us do something less conventional, you know?"

"Hmmm," I say. "Did you check the box?"

Ms. Slater has brought a bunch of random items in a box that people can use for their collage and Luke goes up to check it out, coming back with a couple of old Matchbox cars and a broken cassette tape. He shrugs.

I'm thinking about what he said about kindergarten.

"Maybe you could bring in some uncooked macaroni from home tomorrow," I say. "Use it to tell the story of your life. Macaroni art to . . . Matchbox cars to"—I glance at the cigarette pack in his jacket pocket—"Marlboro Lights. Though I don't know if Morewood High will approve of you putting cigarettes on your collage."

He breaks into a grin. "I'll tell Slater it was your idea."

"But not my cigarettes." I grin back.

We work in silence for a bit, but I'm experiencing this silence differently than I usually do. Usually silences make me feel anxious. Like there's this big, yawning chasm between me and other people and if I try to leap over it, I might just fall in, caught in a never-ending, stomach-churning free fall. But this silence makes me feel powerful in a way I really can't explain. I can sense his attention on me, even if he's not making it obvious. It's strange and unexpected and thrilling at the same time.

I paste a clear, glossy adhesive over the word *verisimilitude*.

"What does that even mean?" he asks.

I look at him. "Verisimilitude: something that only seems real. Kind of like a really vivid dream?"

He pauses, and the expression on his face is odd. Like I've reminded him of something. He pushes one of the Matchbox cars across the table. It rolls to a stop next to my collage.

Something strange is in the air. Maybe it's just static electricity.

"I don't mean this to sound creepy," he says, "But while we're talking about verisimil-whatever, I had this— " And then he *blushes* and shakes his head. "Nah, never mind."

Luke Carr does not seem like the kind of guy who would blush.

"Well, *now* I'm curious," I say, channeling my best Lauren Bacall.

"Okay, okay." He shrugs. "I had *such* a weird dream about you last night."

Luke Carr had a DREAM about me?

"You did?" I ask, trying to stay cool, as if this kind of thing happens to me all the time. Like I'm always showing up in people's dreams.

"Yeah, we were at this . . . nightclub or something? It was like in one of those cool old noir movies. We were drinking champagne and you were wearing this amazing satiny green dress."

Whoooaaaa.

And now I look directly at him just to make sure these are actual words coming out of his mouth.

He shakes his head and grins. "And you were smoking up a storm! Just blowing smoke rings all over the place. It seemed so *real* too." He laughs. "Wild, right?"

Number one: *What?*

Number two: *WHAT?*

What is happening right now? How is it possible that Luke

Carr had a dream that was *exactly the same* as the thing that I *wrote*? Like, exactly? Right down to the color of my dress? And the smoking? What the hell is going on?

I laugh too, almost hysterically, but keep it together enough to say: "Oh, yeah? And what did I say in this dream?"

"I can't remember exactly," he says. "Oh, wait, no . . . you told me your nickname was Slim."

Okay. I must be hallucinating. Is he some kind of mind reader? Does he *know* that I cast him as the lead in my story? The mere thought of this is embarrassing enough to completely evaporate my earlier swagger.

I'm staring at Luke, and his mouth is still moving, but I missed his last few sentences. His words have become abstract, like when the teachers are talking in the Charlie Brown holiday specials and just this *wa womp wa womp womp womp* sound comes out because, again, *WHAT IS GOING ON?*

I do catch the last part, however:

". . . anyway, we should hang out sometime," he says.

Hang out? Sometime?

"Sure." I nod. "Definitely." I don't know what else to say right now. My brain has completely short-circuited. Also, doesn't he have a girlfriend? Lisa from my front porch, college Lisa who seemed, like, a thousand times cooler than me?

Maybe he doesn't anymore. Maybe they broke up because she's dating some college guy.

"Cool," he says, turning back to his collage.

After the bell rings, he follows me out of the room and

walks with me through the halls until our paths diverge—he to whatever class he has next, and me to PE.

Fifteen minutes into PE, I'm not paying attention to anything that's actually going on in the dodgeball game that I am supposed to be participating in, because I'm still obsessing over what just happened. Have I somehow acquired special powers? Am I able to control Luke Carr's dream life with my Bic pen? Do I have ESP? Or did I just imagine that entire conversation?

Nope. It definitely happened. Otherwise I would also have had to imagine the note that I found tucked into the front pocket of my backpack when I changed in the locker room: *Hey, Slim. You really should skip seventh period sometime. With me.*

And then, *whack.* The red rubber ball we've been playing with smacks me hard, right in the face.

I hear a stifled laugh to my left. Brian Sullivan points to Christina Merlotti.

"Sorry," she says, smirking. "I swear I wasn't aiming for you."

That's clearly a lie, because it was a direct hit. She must have been saving that up since puddle day.

"Gracie, you're out!" Coach Gardener blows his whistle.

I walk over to the first row of bleachers and sit.

My face burns from the dodgeball, and it's probably going to leave a mark, but I don't care.

Because I think I might be magic.

"WHAT HAPPENED TO YOUR FACE?" MINA ASKS WHEN I WALK into French. She has completely changed her look this week, ditching the black in favor of head-to-toe neon. Even her socks.

"I got hit by a dodgeball."

"Worst game ever invented," she says. "It rewards sadists."

"Well, it at least rewards people who are mad at you because you accidentally drove through a puddle and splashed them in the school parking lot."

"I heard about that," says Mina.

"You did?" I ask, pulling my head from my cloud of thoughts about the similarities between the story I wrote in Katherine's journal and Luke Carr's dream. "From who?" I'm not sure if I'm concerned or pleased that I am somehow notable enough to be talked about.

"Tom Broder said she threatened you with her dry cleaning bill." Mina laughs. "She's ridiculous. Who dry-cleans their jeans?"

"You know Tom?" I don't know why I'm surprised by this. Tom seems to know *everybody*. Already. And we haven't even been in school for two full weeks yet.

She nods. "He's in my math class. Dude is so annoying—he can solve equations in his head. Doesn't even need to work it out on paper. I'm really going to have to up my game this year because I am not giving up my title as Morewood's reigning math champion."

From what I can tell so far, Mina is not just Morewood's reigning math champion, she's got just about every subject covered. I'm more of a specialist with English. As long as I don't get called on unexpectedly in class while daydreaming, that is.

"Tom's my neighbor. His mom teaches calculus at CMU."

"Aha!" Mina slaps her desk. "I guess that explains it. Because otherwise he seems fairly disorganized."

I picture him running for the bus. Backpack unzipped. No umbrella.

"Yeah, definitely disorganized," I agree. *But maybe in an endearing kind of way?* I want to ask Mina if she thinks so but then I worry that she'll read into it too much.

She squints at me. "You actually have an imprint of the dodgeball on your face."

I return my thoughts to Luke and the dream. *And the note! That he left in my backpack!*

"Do you know Luke Carr?" I ask, realizing too late that this abrupt conversational switch is sure to also prompt some "reading into."

"Not really," she says, looking *very* curious. "He's a senior. But I did hear he and his girlfriend, Lisa Kendrick, broke up. She graduated last year and they were like this school's Hollywood 'it couple.' I'm surprised paparazzi didn't follow them around."

They broke up.

"Why do you ask?" she adds, narrowing her eyes like she's waiting for me to share some juicy gossip.

"No reason, really," I say. "He sits next to me in art."

"Lucky you. He's smoking hot."

I shrug, as if I hadn't noticed. I like Mina, and I've been sitting with her and Daniel at lunch for a little more than a week now, but she's not someone I trust with all the details of my life, like Hannah. At least not yet. If I knew her better, maybe I'd tell her the rest: *And he dreamed the exact same story that I WROTE last night and I don't understand how that's even possible. Also, he said that we should "hang out."*

Not sure exactly what he means *specifically* by that, but hanging out sounds intriguing . . . more intriguing than anything else that's happened to me in recent memory. Where will we hang out? Will it be somewhere public? That's a little intimidating. Will it be somewhere not public? That seems even more intimidating. Will there be kissing? Am I good at kissing? I don't really know for sure.

I only kissed one other boy, sophomore year, at the first high school party I ever attended, and it's a story that still has the power to make me feel acute, immediate embarrassment whenever I think about it. Hannah and I were tagging along with her older sister, Denise, and the night had already gotten off to a weird start when Denise pulled her car behind a line of others on a dead-end road. I guess I'd been expecting a big house with lots of rooms and a pool table, like in the movies, but this party was in the woods. In February. When we arrived at a clearing where a bunch of kids crowded around an oil drum fire and a beer keg, someone handed me a full-to-the-brim red Solo cup. I drank it too fast because I was nervous, and when my cup was empty, someone else filled it up. I stuck close to Hannah most of the night, but at some point she ran into a friend from band and I really had to pee from all the beer. Denise handed me a small flashlight—"So you don't get lost"—and when I was walking back, the batteries crapped out. As I was frantically flailing around in the pitch dark, my hands crashed right into the very firm chest of a boy, who was also light-less. "There you are!" he said, putting his hand on my shoulder. "You okay?" I didn't recognize his voice, but he seemed to know me, so I figured that Hannah or Denise had sent him to find me. "I'm really cold," I whispered through chattering teeth. I was wearing black ballet flats—great for a house warmed by an actual furnace, terrible for the woods in February—and five minutes earlier had stepped into an icy puddle of slush. Or half-frozen mud. It was hard to tell. "Maybe this will warm you up," he said, and before I even knew what was happening, his other hand was on my waist and he was kissing me. The whole thing was so out of the blue and surreal that I wasn't sure what to do, so I just stood there. Plus, I was really cold and his lips were warm. "We should go back to my car," he said as he pulled away. As I was trying to catch my breath, a girl's voice materialized nearby. "Michael? Where *are* you?" The boy's hand was still at my waist, but I could feel his body freeze. A glint of flame from a lighter flickered through the trees. "Wait," he whispered. "Who are *you*?" But I didn't answer. As soon as I realized what was going on, I ran. I ran through the trees, branches scraping my face, until I was able to stop and listen for the sounds of the less-impressive-than-I-had-hoped party and orient myself in the right direction. "What happened to you?" Hannah asked, when I finally returned. Even though it was cold, my face was burning hot. "Nothing," I said. "The flashlight batteries ran out." I was too embarrassed to even tell my best friend the rest. My first real kiss was 100 percent accidental. It only happened because some guy named Michael thought I was someone else.

"*Hello?*" Mina waves her hand in front of my face. "You kind of zoned out there for a minute."

"Sorry," I say. "I do that sometimes." More like a *lot* of the time. But maybe that explains what happened earlier, with Luke. My highly overactive imagination is reading into everything when it was all just a big, weird coincidence.

The weirdest coincidence of my life.

"You're doing it again," says Mina.

"Am I?"

"Where do you *go*?" She laughs.

The door to our class swings open and Madame Linney sweeps in in true French fashion—*late*—and *shushes* us so she can begin class. *"Excusez-moi."* She looks directly at Mina and me. *"Nous devons commencer."* I think this is the first time I've ever been shushed. We open our books to the page that she writes on the board.

As I drive home from school, I go through the possible coincidental explanations for what happened today. Maybe Luke was watching *To Have and Have Not* last night too. It seems unlikely, but it's possible. Maybe he enjoys classic movies, just like Katherine. The cigarettes, the banter, all of it was right there. Maybe the movie simply triggered my story *and* his dream. But he was so specific about the green dress. That wasn't in the movie. And . . . I grip the steering wheel tight. There was also that army jacket he was wearing! That wasn't in the movie either. *I* wrote those things. They came directly out of *my* brain.

I shake my head no. The army jacket wasn't part of his dream—or if it was, he didn't mention it. He probably even wore that jacket before today, which means it was floating around in my subconscious, and *that's* how it ended up in my story.

I pull into the driveway, and as much as I want to run up to my room immediately and pull out the journal to confirm the details, I don't have time. Mom is working the late shift tonight, so I have to pick up Katherine at her new day care and get dinner started. Right after a quick check to make sure that Hank has been let out and that Jack, who gets home before me, has started his homework.

"Are you doing your homework?" I call to Jack as I drop my backpack on the bench by the front door. I peek into the front sitting room and he and Hank are sprawled together on the sofa, watching *Guiding Light*, an afternoon soap opera. A bag of Doritos is open next to them, and Jack is feeding one to Hank.

"*Oh my God*, Jack, stop feeding Hank people food."

"He really loves Doritos, though."

"Did you let him out?"

"Yep!" he says, his eyes still glued to the TV.

I'm not entirely convinced but let it slide. I'm also not seeing any open books. "It doesn't look like you're doing your homework."

"Fifteen more minutes," he says. "Then I'll start. I promise."

"It better be in progress when we get back," I call over my shoulder as I head back out. "And be careful with Hank around the front door!" We *still* need to fix the screen.

Katherine's day care is only a couple blocks away, and I decide to walk so that she can get some exercise on the way home. The place is in a large old house similar to ours. But unlike ours, as I discover when I arrive, the front gate includes a number of complicated latches that are a bit of a pain to get open. This, I realize, is probably to keep the seniors with dementia from wandering off and getting lost.

That's what happened to Katherine last winter. She got lost. And it's one of the things, in addition to her leaving the oven on, that convinced my mom that we would need to move in with her. It happened before my grandfather died. He was home with her, but must have fallen asleep reading or watching TV, and she'd left the house to go for a walk. Then she got confused about where she was. It was a sunny day, but really cold. She wasn't wearing a coat or gloves. My grandfather called my mom, frantic, and my mom had to notify the police. They found Katherine in the park, sitting on a bench, and she was almost hypothermic. They had to take her to the hospital to check for frostbite on her fingers and toes. My mom felt terrible, my grandfather felt terrible, but it really wasn't anyone's fault.

When I arrive at Park Manor, I say hello to the two ladies playing cards on the porch, as Susan, the woman who runs the place, greets me at the front door. "Gracie! So nice to see you again," she says as she lets me in. "Katherine did great today! She really seems to enjoy all the activities we do here—it's so good to keep their brains engaged." I look around the front room, where one of the residents, Reggie, is playing chess with a young-ish man I haven't met yet. I think he's an aide. A handful of seniors like Reggie live at Park Manor full time, but there are also others, like Katherine, who just come for the day because they can't be left at home alone. "Where's everyone else?" I ask.

"In the kitchen," says Susan. "Hiroko Nakamura's son Rob is a chef and owns a restaurant downtown. He stopped by today to make these Japanese dumplings—gyozas—with everyone. Anyway, it's complete chaos in there, but they are loving it. Come on in and check it out."

I follow her into the kitchen, which, unlike the kitchen at Katherine's, is large, with a giant counter in the middle. The first floor of this house must have been renovated. Katherine stands alongside a few other ladies, spooning filling into rolled-out disks of dough. She's very focused on her work and doesn't even notice me come in.

"Rob," says Susan. "This is Gracie, Katherine's granddaughter."

Rob looks up from where he's frying the dumplings in a pan. "Hey, Gracie! Would you like to try a gyoza?"

"Sure," I say.

He passes me one on a small plate, and as I take a bite (delicious), I watch Katherine across the counter. Her demeanor is more relaxed than usual, and she's even set down her purse. She looks like she's having fun.

The sun is getting lower in the sky as we walk home, and Katherine is moving slower than a turtle, stopping every few minutes to turn around, saying that she needs to go home. "Home is *this* way," I keep telling her as I turn her around and point her in the right direction. We stayed longer at Park Manor than I expected when picking her up, as I didn't want to pull her away from Rob, who was cheerful and patient with everyone in the kitchen, even the ones who got confused about what they were supposed to be doing or asked the same questions over and over. But now *I'm* getting a little impatient . . . I have homework. And dinner to start. I was also hoping to get in a walk for Hank, who hasn't had a good walk in days. *And* I'm also still dying to revisit the story I wrote last night in Katherine's journal.

When we turn the corner onto Shady Avenue, a flash of Hank's brindle coat catches my eye. Shit. *Not again.* He's dashing though the Broders' side yard. *Goddamnit, Jack,* I think. He had ONE job. I spot a flash of yellow fur right behind Hank. The Broders' golden retriever. I watch the retriever pause, paws out. And then Hank stops, twists, and faces her, his long front legs down on the ground, his butt up in the air. Both of their tails are wagging. Are they . . . *playing?* I almost can't believe my eyes. Based on his behavior, well, ever since we've owned him, I've always thought Hank didn't like *any* other dogs. Or even many other people, besides us. But there he is, frolicking with the Broders' dog. Seriously. *Frolicking.* Jack and the Broder twins emerge from their house, one of them tossing a ball into the air that the dogs race to catch.

I call to Jack with a reminder: "Homework!"

"Fifteen more minutes!" he calls back.

"I think I'll be going now," Katherine starts walking in the opposite direction again.

"This way." I steer her, again, toward the house and leave Jack with the twins and the dogs. Hopefully, he doesn't have much homework anyway. And at least Hank won't need a walk.

After I take Katherine to the bathroom and get her settled in front of the TV with *I Love Lucy*, I check the clock. It's nearly six. I should start dinner, but Katherine and I are still half-full of gyozas. Right when I'm about to head into the kitchen, the phone rings. I duck into the alcove underneath the stairs to pick it up.

"Hey Gracie! I was hoping to catch you."

I take a breath. It's my dad. He usually checks in on Sunday evenings, but I missed his last call when I was on an "avoid talking to Dad" trip to the grocery store.

We chat for a few minutes about mundane, surface-level things that neither one of us really cares about. We don't chat about anything that matters. And we definitely don't chat about all the things we haven't really resolved.

How's school? Fine.

How're things in the 'Burgh? Fine.

He doesn't really know what to ask anyway. Now that he and Kirsten and my new baby sister, Ashley, have moved to Bethesda, a suburb of Washington, DC, for his job, but also because Kirsten's family is there—he's not really up on the life and times of Gracie Byrne.

"How's Grandma Katherine?" he asks.

"She's okay. I mean, the same, but okay. Mom found her a day care place near us."

"Oh, that's good. Hopefully that takes the pressure off your mom a bit." He pauses, and the silence on the line feels so . . . *silent* . . . "How is she?"

How is my mom?

Tired? Anxious? Lonely? Sad? All of the above? None of which I say.

Why does he care anyway? None of this is his problem anymore. Especially not now that he's moved on to a new city, complete with new daughter, new wife, and new life.

"She's fine," I say.

"That's good. Well, anyway . . . I just wanted to check in with you about Thanksgiving. What do you think?"

He wants my brother and me to come down to Bethesda for Thanksgiving break. But that means my mom will be alone with Katherine for five or six days.

"Grandma and Grandpa said they can drive to Pittsburgh and pick you and Jack up and bring you down with them," he continues.

He's talking about Grandma and Grandpa Byrne, who still live in Altoona. I do want to see the two of them, but with Grandpa Byrne driving, that trip is also going to be *painfully* slow.

"Umm . . . I need to see what Jack wants to do."

"Jack wants to come! But he said I should check with you . . ."

Jack. He is definitely the forgiver and forgetter of the family.

There is an awkward silence on the line.

"Plus, don't you want to see Ashley?"

My cute, chubby-cheeked replacement? Can't wait. I wish I

could say I was above being annoyed by a baby, but that would be a lie.

"Can I let you know soon? Just want to make sure Mom will be okay here."

"Sure, sure," he says.

More awkward silence, which is the worst part about this situation with my dad. Before my parents split up, he used to be the person I talked to the most. We were close. When I was younger, *he* was the one who never pushed me to be different than I was. "Just let her be," he'd tell my mom whenever she was trying to orchestrate my social life or encouraging me to try out for some extrovert-y activity like debate club. "She'll find her place, in her own way."

But now I don't know. Maybe "let her be" was just his way of keeping his distance. Not engaging.

"I gotta go," I say. "Talk to you Sunday."

"I love you, Gracie," he says.

"Love you too."

I hang up. It's weird to love someone and also sometimes hate them at the same time.

By the time I actually do make it to my bedroom—after dinner, after Katherine is in bed, after my mom gets home—I'm exhausted. I make an attempt at my math homework but can't stop thinking about the journal under my bed and Luke's words, matching my story, burning a hole in my brain. *Forget math.*

I get the journal out and open it to the page that I marked with the black ribbon bookmark. I reread the passage I wrote last night. It's all there. The dress, the smoking. *Slim.* I stare at it for a few minutes and then close the journal, running my hand over the velvet cover. There's nothing that seems very mystical or magical about it, other than the fact that it's old. But . . . *could* it, somehow, give me some weird magical ability to infiltrate a person's dreams? Like Freddy Krueger in *A Nightmare on Elm Street*, but in a totally innocuous, not murder-y way? I laugh. This seems absolutely bonkers. But the details Luke recalled were so *specific* . . .

I rack my brain for other explanations. There's still the possibility that it could just be a very surreal coincidence. Or . . . I feel my stomach drop. *What if it's a joke?* What if . . . Luke somehow got ahold of the journal, read the entry, and for some reason has decided to play a practical joke on me and tomorrow at school everyone will be laughing at how gullible I am? I mean, he does know where I live. But he would also have had to have *broken into my house*. This seems about as far-fetched as magic. I don't know what to think. Maybe I'm just losing it.

My mind continues to churn as I open the journal again and study my words on the page. *Slim. Chartreuse dress. Cigarette. Champagne.* And then the obvious idea hits me. An experiment. I need to write a new entry. And then I'll pay really close attention and see what happens tomorrow. Probably nothing will, and I can officially chalk this all up to a case of Luke and me having some bizarre, noir-inspired mind meld.

I pick up my pen and turn to the next blank page. It almost seems to glow in the light of the lamp as I consider what to write. Should I continue the nightclub story? Should I write about Luke again? Or someone else? I lean my right cheek on my hand and then stop. It still hurts from where Christina Merlotti thumped me with the dodgeball in PE. Maybe I should go downstairs and get a bag of ice. Or maybe . . .

As the woman in the chartreuse dress wove her way through the crowd, a handsome Army lieutenant following close behind, Christina studied her intently. What was it about her? She was beautiful, yes, but there was more to her than that. There was something striking about her body language, and the confidence in her stride, that commanded the attention of the entire room. Christina glanced around the table she was sitting at—at Rebecca, her friend and fellow chorus line dancer, at the fresh-faced boys they'd picked up after the show, who were eager to buy them champagne—and none of them could take their eyes off her.

Christina stood up. "I'm going to the ladies' room."

I pause, pen poised above the page. *And then what?*

And that's where Christina found her. She was standing in the middle of the lounge area, adjusting the garter attached to her stocking, almost too . . .

Too . . . what? Too stunning? No. Too . . . magnificent? No, no. Too . . . *dazzling.*

That's it!

. . . too dazzling to look at up close. The woman in the chartreuse dress nodded hello, picked up her bag from the vanity counter, and turned to leave. She was almost out the door when Christina noticed the gold lipstick case she'd left behind. She picked it up and held it in her hand. For a moment, she thought about trying the color herself, and wondered if, in doing so, she might absorb some of the woman's mysterious aura. But instead she called out, "Wait! You left your lipstick!"

The woman returned for the lipstick, thanking Christina in a distinctive, velvety voice. And then she was gone, leaving the scent of gardenias in her wake.

Christina memorized the lipstick color—Cherries Jubilee—but was never able to find that particular shade.

I put down my pen and yawn. It's late. A first draft will have to do. For what, exactly, I'm not sure. I mark the page with the black ribbon, close the journal, and set it on my nightstand before drifting off to sleep.

CHERRIES JUBILEE

MORNING MAKES EVERYTHING LOOK DIFFERENT. EVERYTHING that seemed to glow in the soft light of my lamp late last night is now a gray shadow. Including the journal on my nightstand. It looks ordinary. Dull. I climb out from under the covers, put it back in the box under my bed, and roll my eyes at myself for being such a weirdo. Why is the fact that Luke Carr dreamed about me, *flirted* with me, so unbelievable that the only explanation I can come up with is that I somehow wrote it into his brain with a magical journal?

I look at the time. I need to stop obsessing about strange dreams and chartreuse dresses and cigarettes and get in the shower, or else I'm going to be late. It's a new day. Come what may or whatever.

* * *

Tom is leaning on the Seville when I come out, his long legs stretched out and crossed at the ankles.

"Wow, this lackadaisical attitude toward being on time seems very unlike you, Gracie Byrne."

Oops. I completely forgot that I told him to be here ten minutes earlier than he needed to be, because I didn't trust he wouldn't be late. But that was yesterday morning. And a lot of stuff happened in between. Also: *lackadaisical*. Nice.

"We should be fine," I say, unlocking the driver's side door. Once inside, I lean over and pop up the lock on the passenger side.

He climbs in, smelling all Pert-shampoo-y again, wet hair curling at the nape of his neck.

He squints at me. "Oh, I see."

"What?"

"I actually didn't need to be here at seven forty, did I?"

"Well," I say, my face heating a bit, "I only have your bus chasing to go on, so . . ."

"Okay, okay . . ." He nods. "I get it. My track record is not great thus far. But I am highly motivated to avoid the bus."

I put the Seville into reverse, look in the rearview, and feel myself getting a little self-conscious. I hate backing out of Katherine's driveway onto busy Shady Avenue on a normal day, and it's even worse when I have an audience sitting next to me. Cars whizz by behind us as I inch backward, looking over my shoulder.

"You have an opening . . ." he says.

I step on the gas.

"No, wait."

I slam on the brakes.

Tom winds down his window. "Okay . . . go. Wait, stop."

I stop and glare at him.

He laughs. "I'm sorry!"

"You are annoying today," I say. "If I don't get out of this driveway, we really are going to be late."

"I got you."

And then he hops out of the car, walks closer to the street where he can see around the Chevy Cavalier parked at the curb, and waves me out once he sees an opening.

"So," he says after he settles back in and I put the car in drive. "I hear our dogs are friends now."

"I know," I say. "A small miracle. At least where Hank is concerned."

"I knew Hypatia would have him eating out of her paw in no time," says Tom. "She's like a goodwill dog ambassador."

"Your dog's name is Hypatia?"

"Yeah," he laughs. "My mom named her after Hypatia of Alexandria. Apparently, she was one of the first female mathematicians. We're all named after mathematicians."

"You *all* are?

"Yeah, Leo is for Leonhard Euler," Tom says. "And Isaac is of course for Isaac Newton because she *had* to name at least one of us after the inventor of calculus. A little too obvious if you ask me, but my mom is not exactly subtle."

"Huh," I say. "I thought Newton invented gravity."

"That too," says Tom. "Well, not *invented,* I guess. Gravity just *is*. He invented the formula for universal gravitation."

"Right."

"And you probably won't guess my namesake, unless you are a math nerd like my mom."

"English is my strength."

"Ah, yes! Your synopsis of *A Tale of Two Cities* was spot-on, by the way. So anyway, I'm named for Thomas Bayes, who developed Bayes's theorem, which has to do with probability theory and statistics. It's this tool for analyzing information to understand why a particular outcome might be happening. But I'm more interested in using probability theory to predict outcomes, because that comes in handy for stuff like poker. Do you know how to play poker?" he asks.

"Nope," I say.

"I could teach you."

A thought flashes across my brain: *Gracie Byrne, card shark.*

"Speaking of theories," he says, "have you ever heard of Benford's law?"

"I haven't."

"So it's this mathematical concept that my mom was talking about last night and *holy shit*, it kind of blew my mind."

I laugh. "So you're *both* math nerds."

Tom does this funny shrug where he puts his whole body into it. He is hardly ever completely still.

"Yeah, but I'm not going to name my future kid after

Pythagoras or anything. Anyway, Benford's law states that in many naturally occurring collections of numbers, the leading digit is likely to be small. So, like, if you have a set of numbers—say populations of all the cities in the US, or the number of passes made during all professional football games during a season—and you graph them, the distribution of numbers starting with one will occur the most, then two, then three, and so on. A graph of the numbers will look like this curve with the highest point at numbers starting with one and the lowest point at numbers starting with nine."

"Uh-huh . . ." I say. I hate graphing but don't tell Tom this.

"Well, here's the cool thing: once you start graphing all kinds of data sets, this curve pattern appears *everywhere*, even with sets of numbers that you wouldn't expect to follow a pattern, like winning lottery jackpots, or measures of things in nature, like the lengths of rivers or the depths of earthquakes."

"I'm still not sure I understand why this is so mind blowing." But I'm surprised to discover that now I'm curious. Tom got me to be curious about *math*.

"Because"—he shifts in his seat toward me—"all these different sets of numbers measuring all kinds of different things follow the same curve. It's like there's this blueprint underneath everything—even stuff that seems like it should be random. I don't know." He shrugs again. "It just makes me feel like there must be some kind of mathematical order to the universe. Like it's not all chaos. Or something."

"Huh," I say, nodding. "That *is* kind of wild."

I'm realizing that Tom is definitely not just the goofy jock I thought he was when he first showed up in front of Katherine's house. And what's funny is that even though I can barely wrap my head around what he's talking about, I get it. I get being obsessed with something—something that you think about a lot. He's into numbers like I'm into words.

I turn into the school parking lot, my mind churning.

I can't decide whether I find the whole Benford's law thing comforting or suffocating. Like, *is* it cool that the universe is made up of all these repeating patterns, or does it mean we're all locked into a formula that we didn't choose and can't break free from? And if the universe somehow always mathematically makes sense—then why do so many terrible things happen? Like famine and war and genetic mutations that cause you to eventually lose all your memories? I mean, what the *hell*, universe? You know?

"Are you okay?" asks Tom. "Am I losing you? I do that sometimes with people, I'm sorry . . ."

I pull into a parking spot and turn off the ignition. I turn and look at Tom. Really look at him. He has dark brown eyes. A bump on the bridge of his nose. I wonder what he'd say if I shared my thoughts about Benford's law and mathematical patterns and how it's somehow disappointing to imagine that everything follows some predictable curve. But also, did he suddenly get cuter? His mouth is still too big for his face, but his lips do look very kissable.

Stop it, Gracie.

He's your neighbor. That would be awkward.

And Luke Carr wants to hang out sometime, remember?

I shake my head to clear it.

"Okay, but not everything can be graphed. Some things really *are* random."

Tom's entire face lights up. "Well, you'd be surprised. The note patterns in Mozart's compositions?"

"They follow Benford's law?" I ask. "*How?*"

"They just do!"

Tom seems to find this incredibly exciting, but . . . *really*? Even a genius like Mozart didn't break the mold?

"So *everything* follows this pattern? This formula?"

He shakes his head. "No, not everything. But it applies to more things than you'd think. Like Fibonacci numbers . . ."

"Wait. How do you spell that?" I ask, pulling my word notebook out of my bag.

"F-I-B-O-N-A-C-C-I . . . why?"

"I like that word. *Fibonacci.*"

"It's a name. Fibonacci . . . Italian mathematician."

I give him a suspicious look. "You don't have another brother named Fibonacci, do you?"

"*Ha,*" he says, and nods at the notebook. "So, what are all those words?"

"I sort of collect them? Words I like, or that sound funny or interesting or whatever. To prompt story ideas sometimes. I don't know, I guess it's kind of silly."

"It's not. Give me one."

"We should get to class," I say.

"I guess we should, but hit me up with some weird words on the way."

We get out of the car and walk together toward the school entrance.

"Okay," I say. "*Pareidolia*. It's this phenomenon where the mind thinks it sees a specific image or pattern where it does not actually exist. Like . . . a parade of elephants in the clouds."

"Ah, see, there's a great example of where Benford's law would probably not apply."

I stop walking. "I might have reached my math quota for the day."

"Okay." He laughs as we continue on. "What else you got?"

"*Petrichor*. The pleasant, earthy smell after rain."

"Oh, I love that."

"Me too," I say.

"Go on . . ."

"*Lackadaisical.*"

"You definitely stole that one from me."

"I did."

The first bell rings as we walk into the front lobby. "Crap," says Tom. "I gotta run to my locker before class. I left my Spanish assignment in there yesterday and need to get it done during first period."

"When do you have Spanish?" I ask.

"First period."

"Uh, better hurry, then."

He's already running down the East Wing hallway. "See you later, Gracie!"

I wave and head off in the other direction, and only then do I remember that I'm supposed to be paying attention today . . . keeping my eyes open for anything out of the ordinary that might be similar to what happened with Luke. Which is probably, almost definitely, not likely.

Christina Merlotti is at the center table with her usual group at lunch, and while I do get the odd feeling that she and her friend Becky are watching me as I weave through the room with my tray, I'm pretty sure it's because they are amusing each other with Christina's account of her direct dodgeball hit to my face yesterday in PE. I ignore the urge to look their way as Mina and I join Daniel.

Daniel nods approvingly when I sit down. "Wow Gracie, you look amazing today."

"Right?" says Mina. "That's what I told her." Which is funny, because Mina is more fashionable than me on my best day by a mile. For example: today I'm wearing jeans cuffed at the ankle, a Mickey Mouse T-shirt, and high-top Reeboks. Although I'm not really sure why this counts as amazing, it *is* one of my favorite outfits. And I am having an exceptionally good hair day, if I do say so myself. So instead of questioning the compliment or laughing it off with a *Yeah right, except for this new zit on my cheek!* I just say, "Thanks! I *feel* amazing too!" Because, for real? I kind of do.

"By the way," Mina adds, "nice job on the strategic hand raise in English. Mr. Rossi seemed duly impressed with your insightful take on *A Tale of Two Cities*."

"Why, thank you." I give a mock bow.

I glance across the cafeteria and immediately make eye contact with Tom. He smiles and waves. I lift a hand in return, my thoughts turning back to Benford's law.

"He's cute," says Mina, who, I realize, never misses anything.

"You think?"

"Yeah, in kind of a quirky way. Like John Cusack."

"But taller," adds Daniel.

"Also"—Mina makes a face—"why are Christina Merlotti and her minion staring at you?"

When I shift my focus to Christina and Becky, they both look away.

I shrug. "Probably plotting her next dodgeball attack," I say. "But honestly, I couldn't care less what the two of them are talking about."

Daniel high-fives me. "The best policy."

This isn't entirely true, however. Because now that Mina pointed it out, I am wondering. *Does* it have anything to do with the journal entry I wrote last night? Most likely not, but I have to admit I'm curious about how Christina will be in PE. And even more curious about how Luke will be in art.

After he walks into class, Luke pulls a plastic bag with uncooked macaroni out of his jacket pocket and shakes it at me.

"What's that?" I ask.

"Your idea! Macaroni to Marlboro Lights. For my collage."

I nod. Oh, yeah, I did suggest that.

Luke slides into his seat and rakes the fingers of his right hand through his thick dark hair, leaving it attractively disheveled. Then he looks at me in this way that sends goose bumps up and down my limbs. Like instead of a T-shirt and jeans, I'm wearing that clinging green dress. He has the vintage army jacket on again today. White T-shirt underneath.

"How's it going, Slim?" he asks in his sleepy-cat-toying-with-a-mouse voice.

"Amazing," I answer. *Slim.* He just called me *Slim.*

He laughs. "Cool. That makes two of us."

I can't be 100 percent sure, but it definitely feels like he's flirting with me. Again. Because that's what he was doing yesterday, wasn't he? Why else would he leave me that note? *Hey, Slim. You really should skip seventh period sometime. With me.*

We get to work on our collages, and I swear he's sitting closer to me than he was the day before. I can feel the warmth of him. It's distracting, but I try to focus on my project, pasting three new words into my silhouette:

Oneiros. Origin: Greek. A dream.

Toska. Origin: Russian. A vague restlessness.

Nefelibata. Origin: Portuguese. Cloud walker. Daydreamer. Person lost in the clouds of their imagination.

"Did I mention that that's a really cool idea?" he asks me, nodding at my collage.

"I think you mentioned it yesterday. But thanks again."

What Luke doesn't mention, however, is anything more about the dream he brought up yesterday. So maybe it all really was just a coincidence. Or maybe he already forgot about it? He also doesn't mention the note. But when the bell rings, he follows me out the door and walks with me all the way to PE.

Today we switch to volleyball. Only marginally less terrifying than dodgeball in my opinion, but, somehow, I manage a killer serve at a crucial moment, which wins my side the game. No fewer than four people give me a high five. Someone even slaps me on the back. Christina Merlotti is not far behind me as we file into the locker room but doesn't seem like she's about to pull me aside to share that she dreamed about a 1940s nightclub last night. One more data point in favor of the yesterday-with-Luke-was-a-coincidence theory.

And you know what? That's fine with me! Because I still feel *amazing*.

In the locker room, I'm careful not to mess with my good hair situation in the shower. I pull on and cuff my jeans, tuck in my T-shirt, and step back into my Reeboks. One quick glance in the mirror, and then I head for the door.

"Wait! You left your lipstick!"

That . . . is . . . definitely Christina's voice.

Before I can even wrap my head around the fact that those are the exact words I wrote last night, she's standing in front of me, holding out a gold tube. *Gold.* She smiles big. And it's not even fake. It's a real, genuine, please-won't-you-be-my-friend kind of smile. I'm momentarily stunned, but recover just enough to say, "Thanks."

"Love your outfit," she adds, still smiling like she thinks I'm the coolest person she's ever met, which is really throwing me off. All I can say again is, "Thanks."

"Nice serve today!"

I nod, because I *cannot* say thanks a third time.

She laughs. In almost a self-conscious way, like I make her nervous or something. "Well, I gotta get to class. See you around!"

Once she's gone, I turn the lipstick tube in my hand. It's sort of heavy—metal, not plastic, like it's a luxury brand. I look at the label on the bottom. The name of the shade is Cherries Jubilee.

Okay.

Wow.

Wow, wow, wow, wow.

This is . . . *not* what happened yesterday. This is not what happened with Luke. Christina did not just describe a dream, she handed me something *tangible*, and it's a FICTIONAL OBJECT THAT I MADE UP IN A STORY.

Like, *HOLY SHIT*?

But wait . . . I rewind my mind to twenty-four hours ago. There was the dream that Luke described, but *also*, he was *wearing* that army jacket. The one he's wearing today too. I just assumed he'd worn it before and I'd recorded the detail without realizing it, but what if . . . ? And what about the earrings and the cork that appeared on my nightstand after that first night I wrote in the journal? I thought Katherine left them there, but now I don't know . . . And now that I think about it, there were a lot of other things today. Slightly out of the ordinary things that maybe, sort of, in a way, echoed the *feel* of my story?

There was something striking about her body language, and the confidence in her stride, that commanded the attention of the entire room.

There was Mr. Rossi, so impressed with my *A Tale of Two Cities* analysis in English.

Daniel and Mina appreciating my *amazing* outfit at lunch.

Christina and Becky watching me from across the room.

Luke following me to PE.

All the high fives during the volleyball game.

And then, the lipstick. The lipstick!

It's like everyone was *noticing* me, like I was commanding attention right and left all day. I walk out into the hallway to make my way to French class, the halls already emptying because I spent so much time standing in the girls' locker room with the Cherries Jubilee lipstick in my hand. Brian Sullivan, the kid who laughed when Christina hit me in the face with the dodgeball yesterday, slams his locker door shut and takes off down the hall, but turns around as he runs to class and calls, "Killer serve, Gracie! You should try out for the team or something!"

Wow. I did not even think this kid knew my name.

This is batshit. This is not possible. This is too strange to believe. This is the wildest thing that's ever happened to me. This is (I think) totally breaking Benford's law. This is . . .

Pretty freaking *cool* . . .

Isn't it?

I'm still not sure, exactly, how it all works, but I am sure of one thing: I, Gracie Katherine Byrne, am fucking magic. Exactly *how* magic is to be determined, though. Time to run another experiment.

CONTROL STORY

I'VE RE-CREATED LAST NIGHT'S CONDITIONS: IT'S LATE. THE lamp on my nightstand casts that warm glow. I open the journal to the next blank page and pick up my pen.

This time, I need to write something different. Something wholly disconnected from my regular life. No characters or scenarios remotely similar to people I know. Or things on TV that someone else may have seen. Just so there's no question that *whatever happens* actually is coming from what I put down in the journal. Like a control group.

A control story.

Click, click. Click, click, click.

Of course this would be when I get writer's block.

I yawn and glance around the room, searching the artifacts

of my life for an idea. A pile of clothes rests on the floor in front of my open closet. A textbook lies open on my desk. Prince gazes at me from atop his motorcycle in the *Purple Rain* poster, surrounded by a cloud of lavender smoke. My eyes stop at the copy of a *National Geographic* magazine on my nightstand. I pulled it from the shelf in my grandfather's study a few days ago. On the cover, there's a close-up photo of a huge owl. According to the story inside, it's a Blakiston's fish owl, the largest species of owl on the planet. Apparently, they are super rare and hard to find, living only in remote forests on the east coast of Russia, parts of China, and on the island of Hokkaido in Japan. The story centers on this researcher who has spent most of her life trying to track one down in the hopes of getting a photograph of the world's most introverted bird . . .

> *Gracie Byrne, renowned ornithologist and National Geographic photographer, is the first to capture a Blakiston's fish owl on film. With a body the size of a small child and a wingspan of up to six feet, these extremely shy creatures have never been photographed in the wild, until now. Asked about the challenges involved in finding such a private bird, Ms. Byrne said, "Well, it required a lot of patience. I had to spend days being very still and quiet. In the end, that's what worked. This owl and I? Well, we just seemed to understand each other."*

Okay. I mean, that's about as far from my regular life as I can get. I put down my pen, mark the page with the black ribbon, close the journal, and put it back in the box. Phase two of my experiment is officially launched.

NOT LIKE OTHER GIRLS

I'M UP BEFORE MY ALARM, IMMEDIATELY CHECKING THE nightstand for . . . *something*. I'm not really sure exactly what I'm expecting. Feathers, maybe? A Polaroid of me and an actual owl? But nothing seems out of the ordinary. Besides my alarm clock, there isn't anything on my nightstand aside from the copy of *National Geographic*, the Blakiston's fish owl spreading its wings on the cover. Right where I left it last night.

After I shower, I dig the Cherries Jubilee lipstick from my backpack and stand in front of the mirror. It *is* real. I can feel the weight of it in my hand. *What if I . . . ?* Leaning closer to the mirror, I open the case, swipe the lipstick on and study the result. Contrasted against my fair skin and dark brown hair, the deep red color makes me look *waaay* different. Older. Glamorous. Like a femme fatale wanted for murder but who beats the rap because she seduces the detective working her case, or . . .

A shiver of recognition ripples through me.

Like Katherine in that photo in the hat box.

A *lot* like Katherine. The lipstick, which stands out in the same way as the one she wears in the photograph, makes me realize how much. I have the same mouth, same wavy hair, same dusting of freckles on my cheeks, and the same heart-shaped face.

"Gracie!" my mom is yelling from downstairs. "We're going! Don't forget about picking up your grandmother this afternoon!"

"Got it!" I yell back.

"See you tonight!"

"See you!"

I hear her and Katherine rustling around in the front entryway below, getting ready to head out. "Who's Gracie?" Katherine asks.

Who IS Gracie? I ask my reflection in the mirror. No answer.

Before I leave, I run to the bathroom, pull a few squares of toilet paper off the roll and quickly wipe my lips.

"Do you think a person could, like, *break* Benford's law?" I ask Tom on the way to school.

He gives me a sideways glance. "What do you mean by break it?"

"I don't know," I say. "Could someone maybe override the pattern or something?"

Tom nods and considers my question. He also seems delighted that I actually have questions for him related to his favorite math theory. "Yeah." He nods. "*Yeah* . . . so think about something like a tax return, right?"

"A tax return." I was hoping for something more about Mozart, or the heights of all the mountain ranges in the world or whatever, but I wait for him to continue.

"So when people are trying to cheat on their taxes, they fudge the numbers, right?"

"Uh-huh . . ."

He grins and waves his arms like he's about to say *ta-da!* "Well, that's breaking Benford's law."

"How so?"

"Okay, so tax data, like a lot of financial transaction data, tends to follow the first-digit law. So if you graphed the numbers reported on a return, it should look like Benford's curve, with more numbers at the top that start with one and so on, right?"

"Okay."

"But when random, *false* numbers are inserted into a tax return—when someone is trying to cook the books—those numbers break the pattern. In fact, Benford's law analysis is actually sometimes used to catch tax fraud. Auditors can apply it to spot data that's been manipulated."

I nod. "Oh, okay, I see. That makes sense." But inwardly,

I'm not really satisfied with Tom's answer. I'm not talking about manipulating tax numbers, I'm talking about changing the patterns that apply to . . . reality? I guess? But I can't tell him that, even though I'm practically vibrating with the need to tell *somebody*. A little part of me is curious what he would say if I did tell him—about Luke, and Christina, and the lipstick. Would he laugh?

I pull into a parking spot and turn off the engine, still thinking.

"You okay?" Tom asks. "You kind of zoned out there for a minute."

I shake my head and glance at him. He looks a little amused. "Yeah, sorry. I do that sometimes."

"Well, I *was* talking about taxes, which I now realize makes me sound like a very uncool middle-aged accountant."

I laugh. "Don't worry. I won't give away your secret uncool ways."

"Thanks," he says, getting out of the car. "Race you to the door!" And then he takes off running. I lock the car, hike my backpack over my shoulder, and try to catch him.

He's waiting at the top of the stairs when I approach the main entrance, gasping for air. "No fair," I say. "You had a head start. And your legs are like three feet longer than mine."

"Yeah, but now don't you feel invigorated? Ready for the day? That's the *real* reason you used to catch me running for the bus."

I roll my eyes at him when I reach the top stair. As we push through the school doors into the front lobby, he adds, "So you were checking out my legs?"

"What? No, I wasn't checking out your— " and then I stop talking. Because immediately, it's obvious that something is up. There's a big commotion near the entrance to the East Wing. A crowd is gathering there and I hear this metallic banging sound, like something large is repeatedly crashing into a locker door. The sound gets louder and louder and then the crowd starts to back up and move toward us. A girl runs by screaming and covering her head.

My heart starts to race.

Tom spots someone he knows. "Hey, Marcus!" Marcus nods in greeting and jogs over.

"What's going on?" asks Tom.

Marcus points a thumb back toward the East Wing. "There's a huge bird in here!" He laughs. "I think it might be an *owl.*"

"An *owl*?" says Tom.

AN. OWL.

A FUCKING OWL.

"Yeah. It just came out of *nowhere*."

And then . . . all hell breaks loose. The kids who were clogging the East Wing entrance start running by us, some ducking, making way their way to the opposite hall as the hugest bird I've ever seen comes flapping into the front lobby. Its wingspan must be at least . . . *six feet.* It weaves and swoops erratically, like it's trapped and doesn't know where to go. Some boy yells out, "*Eww* . . . I think it shit on me!"

"I heard that's good luck," Tom says to me and Marcus.

Marcus makes a face at Tom. "What is?"

"Getting shit on by a bird."

"I'm going to need everyone to clear this area!" Mr. Sweeney, our principal, is now in the lobby, trying to project his voice above all the commotion, but most people aren't listening. They want to see what's going to happen with the owl.

It flies up near the ceiling, and as it does, it knocks the glass cover off one of the light fixtures, which drops and shatters on the floor. Thankfully, no one appears to be hit. Before I can even think about where to go or what to do, Tom grabs my hand and pulls me away from the center of the room and the broken glass. We back up against the wall with all the football trophy cases and I look up just in time to see the owl diving straight toward us, like it's a fighter pilot from *Top Gun*.

And then it lands.

On my shoulder.

So now there's a ginormous owl. Just sitting on my shoulder.

I remain absolutely still.

Tom's face is as white as chalk, he's gripping my hand like a vise, and for once, he is speechless. Everyone is speechless, just staring at me and the owl. Only *I* can't quite get a good look at it, because it's ON MY FREAKING SHOULDER.

Tom regains his composure and our eyes lock.

"Uh, there's owl on your shoulder." He looks like someone put a spell on him.

I start laughing like a maniac. "I KNOW!"

I, Gracie Byrne, am not like other girls. Not anymore.

Somehow, I know exactly what to do. "Give me your sweatshirt."

"What?"

"Your sweatshirt. Also, you are breaking my fingers."

"Sorry." He lets go of my hand and pulls his University of Chicago sweatshirt over his head.

I am different. Unusual. Exceptional. Like the Great and Powerful Oz.

I hold as still as possible and, very slowly, wrap the sweatshirt around my lower arm. The owl hops from my shoulder to my arm, and for the first time I get a good look at it. It's flipping *magnificent*. Enormous neon yellow eyes. A mass of speckled brown-and-white feathers sticking out everywhere. Talons that look like they could tear a small cow apart. And holy shit, it's heavy.

Actually, I might be better than the Great and Powerful Oz, because, as Toto showed everyone when he pulled back the curtain, the Great and Powerful Oz wasn't actually great and powerful at all. He was a fraud. And I'm talking about real, unable-to-explain-it, maybe-lightning-bolts-will-start-coming-out-of-my-fingertips-next power here.

The owl and I stare at each other. It blinks its moonlike yellow eyes. I don't think I've ever been so close to something so extraordinary. For a few minutes, everything and everyone else just falls away and it feels like this otherworldly owl and I are the only living things in the universe.

I don't just live in reality, I MAKE reality.

"Gracie?" Tom is whispering, trying not to disturb the owl.

"Yeah?"

"You might just be the most fascinating person I've ever met."

But before I can respond to that, Principal Sweeney starts inching toward us, keeping his distance, but trying to reassure me at the same time. "Just stay still, uh . . ." He doesn't know my name.

"Gracie . . ." I offer helpfully, too caught up in the moment to remember my previous commitment to *Grace*.

He holds out his hand, as if to keep me still. "Help is on the way." I hear the sound of a siren blaring and getting louder, closer. Then I hear a truck screeching to a halt in the school parking lot. *Did he call the fire department? What the hell are they supposed to do about it?* It's not like this owl is on fire. The school's main entrance doors are flung open with a bang and two firefighters in full gear walk in. The owl shifts on my arm, inching closer to my shoulder again. I can feel it shaking. I think that maybe it's terrified.

"*Go.*" I whisper to it. "Now's your chance." And it's like it was waiting for my signal. It spreads its fabulous wings, pushes off from my arm, and flies toward the open door and the firefighters, making them duck. And then it's gone.

I feel someone's eyes on me from across the lobby. Luke Carr. And not just Luke Carr. *Everyone's* eyes are on me.

"Well, that was weird," says Tom. "I always thought owls were nocturnal."

"PEOPLE! THE BELL HAS RUNG!" NOW THAT THE OWL HAS departed, Mr. Sweeney is trying to regain control, walking around and herding students toward their classes. "Move along! Watch your step, move along."

One of the school's custodians has come to place a couple of those yellow "wet floor" signs out to keep people away from the mess of glass and feathers and owl poop in the front lobby. I study the man for a minute, thinking about how his day, like the owl's, has been turned upside down. It's going to be a huge job for him to clean everything up.

"Hey." Tom is still standing next to me. "Are you okay? I mean, it's not every day that something with razor-sharp talons lands on your shoulder." He pauses. "Is it? Honestly, for a few minutes there, you seemed like a professional owl . . . handler? Wrangler? Rustler?"

"I'm fine," I say, still watching the custodian as he begins to clean up. I almost feel like I should offer to help him.

"What's a person who trains owls called?" Tom asks.

"I don't think owls are especially trainable," I answer. "But maybe an experienced falconer could do it?" *What am I even saying right now?*

Tom studies me like he's trying to work a math problem out in his head.

Did he say I was fascinating?

"Do you want a ride home after school?" I ask.

"I have cross-country practice," he says, looking a little . . . *disappointed*? "Marcus gives me a lift home in the afternoons."

"Oh, okay. Cool."

Maybe I'm the one who's disappointed.

"I guess I'll see you tomorrow," he says. "Or, I don't know, maybe we could—"

"Gracie, was it?" Mr. Sweeney interrupts.

Maybe we could . . . what?

I look at Mr. Sweeney and nod.

His face is all red and sweaty. "Can you come with me to the office for a few minutes?"

"Um . . . sure. Did I . . . am I in trouble for something?"

"Oh!" Sweeney shakes his head. "No, no. But the fire department needs to fill out an incident report, we need to be sure you are not injured in any way, and your mother would like to speak with you on the phone."

"My mom wants to speak with me?"

"Yes, Assistant Principal Jenkins called her. We need to notify a parent any time a student has a safety incident on campus."

"A safety incident?" This is becoming such a production.

"We'll give you a late slip for first period."

"What about me? Can I get a late slip too?" asks Tom.

"You can go to class. Thank you."

Tom makes a disappointed face, waves, turns, and jogs down the hall.

I'm still holding his sweatshirt.

After getting quizzed by two firemen and the school nurse ("Are you injured? Do you have any cuts? Any scratches? Do you feel like you need to go home?") and my mom ("Gracie! *What* is going on? They called and told me you had been attacked by a *bird* at school?") and explaining to them all that I was fine, absolutely *fine*, I pocket my late slip, pretend like I'm going to class, but instead lock myself into a stall in the West Wing girls' bathroom so that I can freak out in peace.

OH. MY. GOD. WHAT JUST HAPPENED?

Did I just manifest a living creature out of thin air? Or did I teleport it here from somewhere else? What if that owl was happily sitting on a snowy tree branch somewhere in Eastern Russia, about to dive-bomb a fish, and then—poof!—all of a sudden it found itself trapped in the hallway of my high school with hundreds of screaming people, when all it wants is to be a recluse in the wilderness? And where did it go after it flew out the door? Can it get back to where it came from? Is it scared?

This is possibly a little more than I bargained for. Because what happened today was not just a shared dream or a . . . vibe . . . or even a lipstick in my backpack. It was way more than that, and seems to point to the journal I found in Katherine's drawer having some seriously intense reality-altering power.

Which brings up a lot of questions.

What do I do with it? Now that I know it works—although I'm not exactly sure how or why—what should I do with it? For instance, does this obligate me to be a force for good in the world? Like a superhero? Or a benevolent goddess? Should I start writing stories about curing cancer and ending the Cold War? I look down at my untied sneaker. What do I really know about cancer or the Cold War though? When was the last time I even watched or listened to the news? Perhaps I'm not the best person to be mucking around with any world-changing events. It would really suck if I inadvertently set off an international crisis. No. Think smaller, Gracie. Journals are personal, right? Meant to capture a writer's personal story, their personal thoughts. Aren't teachers always saying to write what you know?

I stare at the dented stall door in front of me. Someone has scratched a heart into the surface, and a name inside: *Robbie*. In another spot, a Sharpie writer has scrawled: *Holly Reese is a bitch.* I don't know anyone named Holly Reese, but wonder if it bothers her that her name is in here. I scan the rest of the graffiti: *Fuck you Laurie! I love Prince. Sweeney sucks.* It's funny to me. This is where people want to leave a mark? In the West Wing girls' bathroom at Morewood High? Prince is never going to know that some sophomore who recently changed her tampon in here also left him a tribute on the door. But what I have with the journal—it's the opposite of scribbling nonsense in a toilet stall.

Like, what would happen if I wrote a story about MEETING PRINCE? The possibilities are making my head spin. They're potentially life-changing. I can't waste this opportunity, right? It's a lot to think about. But first, I should probably try to catch the last fifteen minutes of first period.

The rest of the morning is weird. Everyone wants to talk to me about the owl. Even people who have yet to say a single word to me, which honestly is the majority. "Were you scared?" "Did it cut you with its talons?" "What did you say to it?" It's all a little overwhelming.

"Looks like I missed all the excitement this morning," Mina says when I slide into a seat next to her in English.

"Where were you?" I ask.

"Dentist appointment."

Today she's wearing a plaid blouse with puffed sleeves, white fringe boots, and a prairie skirt. Her hair is in French braids.

"That poor owl," she continues. "My mom had the news on

in the car and I heard that they've been chasing it all over town."

Oh, God.

"Who's *they*? Who is chasing it?"

"Um, I don't know exactly." She shrugs. "I think it was some naturalist or owl expert heading up things. Apparently, it's a super-rare species that only lives in *Russia* or something?"

"Blakiston's fish owl," I say.

"Yeah, that's it!" she says. "Did it really land on your shoulder?"

"It did," I say. Even Mina wants to talk about the owl. I don't know why I'm annoyed about this, but I am. "Have you started *The Catcher in the Rye* yet?" I ask, hoping to change the subject.

But before she can answer, Mr. Rossi steps to the board. He picks up a piece of chalk and writes: *The OWL as a symbol.*

Oh, for fuck's sake. I thought we were going to finish up our discussion of *A Tale of Two Cities*. I was on a roll yesterday.

He turns around and faces the class, making what I think he assumes is an ominous face.

"'Hark!—Peace. It was the owl that shrieked, the fatal bellman, which gives the stern'st good night.'" He pauses dramatically. "Anyone know what this line is from? Anyone?"

"Oh! I've got this." Mina grins at me while raising her hand.

"Yes! Ms. Amani!"

"It's from *Macbeth*," she says.

Rossi is beside himself with English teacher excitement

that someone in his class knows this. We aren't scheduled for Shakespeare until next month.

"Yes! The owl appears several times in the"—he lowers his voice—"*Scottish play*, symbolizing . . . ?"

"Death." Mina smiles.

I'm not surprised she's already read *Macbeth*. Judging from her love of Bauhaus, she seems to have a bit of a dark and gloomy side, despite her current prairie getup. And she's also mentioned, repeatedly, that she's in the drama club. I think she wants me to join. But while I love the *idea* of taking a bow to a standing ovation, in reality I wouldn't make it through an audition without vomiting from performance anxiety.

"Exactly!" Rossi is beaming. "The owl is used to *fore-shadow*, to *portend*, King Duncan's murder. In fact, we see the owl as a symbol of death in many examples from mythology, folklore, and literature." He looks very pleased with himself for tying his lesson into the morning's events.

"Anyway, I just couldn't let today's mysterious visit go by without mentioning Shakespeare! You can all look for the symbolism when we read . . . well, you know."

Mina rolls her eyes and whispers to me, "I think it's only bad luck to say *Macbeth* in an *actual* theater."

"The owl landed on Gracie's shoulder today," says a kid named Troy, who is sitting in front of me and Mina. He turns in his seat to face me. "Hopefully you won't drop dead tonight!" He seems to find this hilarious.

But Mr. Rossi's face, so triumphant just seconds ago, falls.

"Oh! Well, that's . . . The owl symbolizes other things too . . . wisdom . . . and . . . prophecy! In Greek mythology, the owl is frequently depicted as a companion of the goddess Athena."

I'm starting to feel bad that he feels bad. Plus, the attention of the entire class—it's like a spotlight. A hot, bright spotlight. The combination of both first- and secondhand embarrassment is making me sweat.

"That's . . . cool," I say.

But also, now that I think about it, and in light of the morning's events, should I be worried?

Mr. Rossi continues, "And the Welsh associate owls with fertility . . ."

I hear someone giggle.

Holy shit, Mr. Rossi, I think. Just. Stop. Talking.

I duck into the bathroom to collect myself and to apply some lip gloss before heading to art. So much has happened today, I'm not sure what to expect. Hopefully, Ms. Slater is not going to ask us to draw a goddamn owl. At lunch, I learned that *my* owl is still on the loose in the city. Daniel told us that his bio teacher let the class listen to updates on the news.

"Hey, Slim." Luke walks up to our drafting table as I pull out my chair. He's earlier than usual.

"Hey," I say.

"So, are you an owl whisperer now?"

"Apparently."

Is there anybody who isn't obsessed with this owl I conjured?

He puts down his books—Luke never carries a backpack—and sits. "You're a fascinating girl, Grace."

Wait, what?

Tom also said something like that this morning. When the owl was perched on my shoulder: *You might just be the most fascinating person I've ever met.*

The second time around, it seems less, I don't know—less surprising, maybe? Less like a flash of lightning? Like it's part of a book I've already read or a script I've already acted out.

I'm starting to feel a little queasy and light-headed. But maybe it's because I barely ate any lunch.

At the end of the day, I walk out the front door and am stopped in my tracks by a crowd gathering on the school steps. My stomach drops. *What now?*

There's a *news truck* in the parking lot.

A few steps down and to my left, Kimberly Cooke of KDKA News, in a red power suit with impressively large shoulder pads, is standing in front of a cameraman while holding a microphone in front of some kid's face. I don't know his name. She looks from him to the camera. "So when you walked through the East Wing hallway this morning, tell us what you saw."

Several other students are hovering behind the interviewee, hoping to get on TV. One flips the bird. Which is fitting, I guess. "Well," the kid says, clearly enjoying the attention, "I was getting some stuff out of my locker, and it just swooped by out of *nowhere . . .*"

A headache is starting to brew behind my left eye and I worry that it will gather into a full-blown migraine by dinnertime. I move to the edge of the crowd and hurry down the steps past the news crew, walking as fast as possible to my car. I need to get out of here before Kimberly Cooke of KDKA pounces on me next. I need an aspirin. I need to think. I also need to go pick up Katherine, which I'm glad about because at least she'll only talk to me about normal stuff, like where her imaginary letters might be.

As I pull out of the school lot, I turn on the radio. "*. . . and it's been spotted in several locations today, including Frick Park, in a tree at the University of Pittsburgh campus, and atop the roof at Soldiers and Sailors Memorial Hall. If you have any information, call our hotline at 1-800 . . .*" I turn off the radio.

Shit.

I have totally ruined this owl's life.

Katherine, thankfully, didn't mention anything about an owl when I picked her up at Park Manor. But Jack, along with Tom's brothers, is trying to catch it. They've set up a homemade trap in the tree next to the Broders' house and claim to have put a dead mouse inside to lure it. "It's a *fish* owl! That means it eats *fish*!" I yell to Jack as Katherine and I walk by, already deciding I'm not even going to bother hassling him about his homework this afternoon. Now that I have perhaps broken the space-time continuum or whatever, the status of Jack's homework really does seem like a petty concern.

At home, the headache that started behind my eye is now taking over half of my face.

I take an aspirin, put on *I Love Lucy* for Katherine, and collapse next to her on the sofa to regroup. That's when it occurs to me: I found this journal in *her* drawer. Has *she* ever used it before? There was no writing in it when I found it, but I feel like a dope for not considering *why* she had it locked away until now.

"Hey, Katherine," I touch her arm. "What's the deal with that journal you keep in your vanity?"

She turns and stares at me. "What journal? I don't know what you're talking about." I don't know why I bothered. Even if Katherine once had some answers about that journal, they're lost now.

She turns back to *I Love Lucy*. The episode we're watching is one of her favorites: Lucy and Ethel get jobs at a chocolate factory and they have to wrap chocolates coming by on a conveyor belt that keeps getting faster and faster and faster until they can't keep up. Katherine always laughs so hard at this, which usually makes me laugh too, but all I can think about this time as Lucy and Ethel start stuffing unwrapped chocolates down their shirts and into their mouths and hats is how quickly everything spins out of control. Like this entire fucking day.

* * *

When my mom walks in after seven, she immediately asks me to recap the "owl incident."

And I just can't. I'm done.

"It was nothing," I say. "I'm fine."

"What a strange thing!" she says, setting down a bag from Kentucky Fried Chicken.

"I know."

"It was on the news!"

"I know."

"Did you . . ."

I cut her off. "I think I'm going to go lie down."

Her brow furrows. "I picked up chicken. You don't want any dinner?" Then she crosses her arms and squints. I feel like she's seconds away from taking my temperature. "Are you okay, Gracie?"

"Yeah. It's just . . . I have a headache, and bad cramps."

Cramps. Always handy when you need an out.

"Oh. Okay. There's some Motrin in the medicine cabinet."

"Thanks," I say, getting up. I reassure her one more time. "I'm fine, really." She doesn't say anything more, but I can feel her watching me ascend the stairs. When I close the door of my room behind me, all I want to do—all I *can* do—is lie down. I don't even bother to go wash my face or brush my teeth. I just pull off my jeans and climb into bed in my T-shirt. Then I turn out the light, close my eyes, and let the events of the day drift through my head.

Benford's law.

Blakiston's fish owl.

Macbeth.

Magic.

Me.

Within seconds, I'm asleep.

NIGHT OWL

I WAKE IN THE NIGHT TO TAPPING AT MY WINDOW.

Tap, tap. Tap, tap, tap.

What the hell is that? I sit up, turn on the light, and nearly jump out of my skin. It's the owl. The Blakiston's fish owl that the entire city of Pittsburgh is trying to track down is currently perched on my windowsill, staring in at me with its spooky harbinger-of-death eyes.

This is it, I think. Any second now I'm probably going to drop dead.

Tap, tap.

Okay. Think, Gracie. What am I supposed to do here? Does it want in? I quickly look around the room to make sure Hank isn't sleeping somewhere on my floor. He must be with Jack tonight. But if this owl keeps tapping the window, Hank's dog ears are going to perk up, and then all hell is going to break loose. As for the owl, I suppose I do owe it a little help, even if it is large enough to possibly murder me.

I go to the window. It hits the glass again with its beak. I can see that it's shaking, just like it was when it perched on my shoulder this morning. I assume a slightly defensive posture, move closer, unfasten the window latch, and pull it open, quickly taking a step back. The owl hops into my window and onto my desk. Cool late September air wafts in behind it, along with a smell of pine sap, soil, and wet leaves.

My heart is hammering against my rib cage. The owl is so huge. Beautiful, but also terrifying. I look at its talons, sure it really *could* kill me if it wanted to. But I don't think it does. I think it just wants help. And what sucks is, even though I could probably rattle off a number of facts about the Blakiston's fish owl, I have no idea how to help it in this particular situation. Food, maybe? I wonder if it's had anything to eat. Was it able to catch some fish? Should I go look in the pantry for some canned tuna?

We lock eyes and slowly, so slowly, I reach out my hand and gently run my fingers over the feathers on the top of its head. They are velvety soft.

Now what?

I can't let this owl live in my bedroom, at least not indefinitely. I gaze past it out into the night, thinking. Light glows in the window directly across from mine, at the Broders' house. A figure moves across the room and then stops, as if they've just noticed me noticing them. Even though it's too far away to really see well, and the figure's face is in shadow, I know it's Tom. I recognize his tall, lanky frame. Our bedrooms must face each other. *We* are now facing each other, and it feels like both of us are frozen in place.

After what seems like an eternity, he walks closer to the window and raises a hand. Yes, it's definitely Tom. Okay. So he must also know it's me over here. I tentatively raise a hand in response, but my movement startles the owl. It hops back onto the sill, opens it wings, and flaps up to a nearby telephone pole.

And Tom has seen it all. He's sure to have questions about *this* in the morning.

He moves even closer to his window, opens it, rests his hands on the sill, and leans out, looking up at the owl on the pole, and then back at me. A breeze blows through my open window, sending a chill up my bare legs. Which in turn makes me acutely aware that I'm only wearing a cropped T-shirt and underwear, like the first girl to get killed in a horror movie. Mortified, I reach up for the cord attached to the roller blind and quickly yank it down.

Except I've yanked too hard, and the entire blind pops off the bracket and lands with a loud clunk on the floor.

Shit.

The barking has already started.

Hank is at my bedroom door in seconds, clawing to get in.

And a few seconds after that, I hear my mom's voice: "Gracie? What was that noise?"

I open the door and Hank rockets in, running around the room, sniffing every corner.

Mom is in the hallway, looking groggy, pulling on her fuzzy pink robe.

And then Katherine appears in her plaid flannel nightgown, hair wild, purse over her arm. "I think I need to go home now," she announces.

Mom sighs.

I grimace. "I'm sorry. I was pulling down the blind and it popped off the bracket."

"I thought you were asleep." Mom looks so exhausted.

"I was . . . but the moon was so bright it woke me up." I have no idea if the moon is even visible, let alone bright tonight, but I obviously am *not* going to tell my mom that the owl I manifested via a journal I found in Katherine's vanity was tapping on my window.

So.

"Let me help you get her back to bed," I add.

"It's okay," Mom says. "You have school in the morning."

"And you have work."

"Where did they put the letters?" Katherine asks.

By the time we get Katherine back to sleep and Hank calmed down, it's past one a.m. Moonlight streams into my bedroom window, or maybe it's the light from the streetlamp. I'm too tired to tell. The blind, crumpled on the floor, is ripped. Before climbing back into bed, I glance outside. The owl is no longer perched on the telephone pole, and Tom's window is dark.

It's hard to know how to process this day. The way my story about the owl manifested itself in real life was extraordinary. I'm beginning to realize that whatever special power that journal has . . . well, it's more intense than I ever could have imagined. But, at the moment, it feels less like some kind of magical gift and more like Pandora's box. And through it, I have become an agent of chaos.

An impulse grips me. I pull the hat box out from under my bed, get the journal, turn to the page where I wrote about the Blakiston's fish owl, and rip it out. For a few seconds, I hold my words in my hand.

This owl and I? Well, we just seemed to understand each other.

And then I crumple them up and throw them in the trash bin next to my desk.

It's a long while before I can fall back asleep.

WE'RE ALL GROUCHY, RUNNING LATE AND RUSHING TOO fast in the morning, which agitates Katherine. She's giving my mom a hard time about everything. Won't take her pills. Won't eat her Raisin Bran. Won't use the bathroom before they leave. Won't put on her sweater. Hank is agitated too, pacing back and forth between the entryway and the kitchen and whining, because he always starts to freak out when any of us are stressed. The only happy one is Jack. Mom got so tied up trying to get Katherine to eat her breakfast, she let Jack sleep in, and now he gets to have a Pop-Tart in the car. I grab a banana off the counter and nearly crash into a freshly showered Tom when I open the front door. He looks like he was just about to ring the bell.

"Hi," I say, face flushing immediately at the thought of me waving to him from the window in my underwear last night.

He grins. "So I'm starting to feel like you are less committed to punctuality than I originally thought." He doesn't, however, seem very bothered by the fact that we are probably going to be late. Or by anything else, for that matter.

"I'm sorry," I say. "We were— "

"NO, I WILL NOT!" Katherine is yelling from the hallway upstairs. Mom is trying one last time to get her to go to the bathroom.

"Uhhh . . . Is everything okay?" Tom glances in the direction of all the noise.

"We were all up too late," I finish, as my mind flashes to him watching the owl fly out of my bedroom window. Tom in a T-shirt and sweatpants. The two of us facing each other. "My grandma is a little out of sorts."

"Jack!" Now my mom is yelling too. "Get your backpack and get in the car! We are coming down right now!"

Tom looks back to his own house and then back at me. "You know, my mom is leaving with the twins right now. She could give Jack a ride. They're all at the same school, so it's no problem. Then your mom can just focus on your grandma."

He doesn't wait for my answer, just runs back down the front walk and stops his mom, who was pulling out of the driveway in the Volvo. I hear her say, "Oh! Of course!" She sounds enthusiastic about it even.

When Tom returns, Jack is ready with his backpack and

Pop-Tart in hand, excited to be driving to school with the twins.

"Tom, tell your mom thank you!" my mom calls from upstairs.

"Sure!" he says, then looks at me.

Just how much could he see from across the street?

"We should hit it," I say, and pick up my jacket and backpack.

Once we are in the Seville, I'm jittery. I don't know how I'm going to explain the owl being in my *flipping bedroom* last night. But at least I parked the car on the street, so I don't have to repeat yesterday's reverse-into-traffic maneuver. As I pull away from the curb, I am acutely aware of the smell of over-ripe banana filling up the entire space. *Why didn't I just grab a Pop-Tart like any other normal person would?* I wind down the driver's side window a few inches. Tom, meanwhile, is uncharacteristically quiet. I expected him to mention the owl flying out of my window as soon as I shut the car door. But maybe he's weirdly quiet *because* of the owl flying out of my window?

I click on the radio. There's a traffic report and the day's headlines, but no update on the owl search.

"Hey," he says.

Finally.

He shifts in his seat. "I got a word for you."

I turn onto Wilkins Avenue. "A word?"

"For your collection."

I guess he's not going to say anything about last night?

"Oh. Cool. What is it?"

"Grawlix."

"Grawlix," I repeat. "What does it mean?"

"Grawlixes are the string of symbols that comic artists use in the speech bubble when one of their characters is swearing."

"So, like, in place of an actual swear word."

"Exactly." Tom looks at me like he's waiting for more of a response.

"I like it," say glancing at him, quickly trying to decode his face for a hint about what else he may be thinking. "Thank you."

Didn't he say he played poker? Maybe this is his poker face.

"Is it going in the collection?" he asks.

"Collection?"

"Your word collection, that you keep in your notebook. Does it pass the weird word test?"

"Oh!" I nod. "Absolutely."

"Cool."

And . . . he's quiet again.

We're stopped at a traffic light. I turn the radio dial, looking for music, landing in the middle of Tiffany's "I Think We're Alone Now." It fades into George Michael's "I Want Your Sex."

I switch back to the news.

By the time we hit the next light, I can't stand it anymore. I have to say *something*.

"I guess you're a night owl too? No pun intended."

Tom gives me a curious look. "Uh . . . sometimes? You?"

"Sometimes." I nod again, tapping the steering wheel with my fingers.

Maybe it was too dark? Maybe he didn't see it?

Should I try to be more direct? "So . . ." I just go for it. "Did you see the owl?"

He looks at me and makes a face that is both amused and confused. "What owl?"

Okay. Okay, okay, okay.

Is it possible he doesn't remember what happened yesterday? But how could a rare owl from Russia landing on my shoulder at school *and* flying out of my bedroom window later that night be anything other than memorable?

Unless . . .

I ripped that story out of the journal. Does that mean it didn't happen?

HOLD THE PHONE.

Did I *erase* yesterday?

Holy shit.

"Oh," I say, frantically searching for a plausible explanation for why I'm asking him about owls. "There was a news story last night . . ." I trail off.

"About a missing owl?"

I picture a cartoon thought bubble above his head: *What the $%&* is up with this girl?*

"Yeah. Never mind. It was nothing. I think it got loose from the National Aviary or something."

And now I am completely making shit up.

Correction: Making more shit up on top of shit I already made up.

This morning is off to an amazing start.

In first period, we prep for tomorrow's trigonometry test. Nobody mentions the owl. Nobody mentions the owl in second or third period either. I get to English early so I can interrogate Mina before Mr. Rossi starts the class.

"Hey. Tell me something." I don't even wait until she's settled at her desk.

Mina sits and pulls out a notebook and her copy of *The Catcher in the Rye.* Today she's all Madonna-ish in a tight stretchy tube skirt, crop top, rosary beads, and about three hundred jelly bracelets.

"What do you want me to tell you?" She laughs.

"What did we talk about in this class yesterday?"

She stretches her arms above her head and yawns, showing off the bottom of her purple lace bra. "Uhhhh . . . English stuff?"

"Like, what English stuff *specifically*?"

Mina's face gets this faraway look, like she's thinking. Or lost. I can almost see the gears grinding in her brain. She sighs and shrugs. "I don't know? Didn't we talk about *A Tale of Two Cities*?"

NO! I want to scream. *No, Mina, we did not! We talked about the symbolism of the owl in literature and you were very excited about Mr. Rossi's* Macbeth *reference! Don't you remember this?*

I glance at the board, and although it has been erased, I think I can see the ghost of yesterday's lesson. And I swear it looks like there was a list there titled: *A Tale of Two Cities—Themes.*

So I guess it's official.

I've wiped an entire damn day from everyone's minds.

Tom. Marcus. Mr. Sweeney. Mina. Mr. Rossi. Luke. Christina Merlotti. Kimberly Cooke of KDKA-TV. Jack. My mom.

Everyone at school? Everyone in Pittsburgh? The world?

How far does this go?

The good news is that the Blakiston's fish owl is back where it's supposed to be, I guess. I hope. The bad news is . . . well, I don't know. What are the ramifications of deleting a day from everyone's memory? Do they just not remember the owl? Or did they forget *everything*?

So.

Hundreds of people didn't see a giant-ass bird land on my shoulder in the school lobby yesterday.

Mr. Rossi didn't teach his lesson on symbolism.

Mina didn't answer the question about *Macbeth*.

Luke didn't call me an owl whisperer.

KDKA-TV did not do a news report.

And finally, Tom didn't wave to me from his bedroom window in the middle of the night.

What about our conversation in the car yesterday morning about tax fraud and breaking Benford's law? Was that erased too? What about both him *and* Luke telling me I was fascinating?

I guess I'm going to have to wait and see how the rest of this day unfolds to find out.

Lunch was so chaotic yesterday that I hardly registered anything that was going on outside of my newfound owl-girl fame. But as Mina, Daniel, and I settle in at our table on the periphery today, I sense immediately that the status-quo has returned.

Tom and his friend Marcus walk in with their lunch trays and join the center-table crowd. And while Mina and Daniel gossip about something that's going on in drama club, I get caught up in watching them all interact, like I'm a sociological researcher and they are my test subjects.

Marcus, who is handsome, athletic, as well as super laid-back, draws a lot of attention from everyone, especially girls. Jessica Shaffer's popularity is tempered by a layer of aloofness that suggests she's only biding her time here in high school with everybody else. Gina Russo, I've heard, throws the best parties. And Tom appears to be the one who makes people laugh. Amy Taylor, from my and Mina's French class, has joined their group and squeezed a chair in next to Tom. She's already cracking up at whatever it is he's saying.

How does he do it?

Cool guys like Marcus want to be his friend. Cute girls like Amy laugh at his jokes. My mom already loves him and she's only met him twice. Jack, of course, thinks he's awesome. Even

Mina, who normally rolls her eyes at anything having to do with the center-table crowd, seems to like him.

That's because Tom has a way of winning over *everybody*. He has this uncorked, effervescent energy that people are drawn to. I watch the way he moves. How his whole body gets involved when he talks. But also, he *listens*. He makes people feel comfortable, like he's really interested in what they have to say.

So, even if he said it (and then forgot because I wiped it from his brain), I am *definitely* not the most fascinating person he ever met.

Not that I thought I was.

In art, Luke doesn't mention the owl either. But now that I've figured out what's going on, this is not surprising. He does call me Slim, however. And I realize that's because he *hasn't* forgotten the green dress dream. Because I didn't rip that story out. The nightclub, the champagne, the flirting, the banter—it all must still be there, or at least the memory of it is. Although, here, today, in the real-not-dream world, he doesn't have much else to say. Neither do I, so I keep working on my collage, pasting more words into the speech bubble that comes out of my silhouette's mouth:

Ephemeral. Origin: English. Transitory; fleeting; short-lived.

Novaturient. Origin: Latin. Longing for change.

Dépaysement. Origin: French. The feeling of being an outsider, out of your element, a fish out of water.

I sneak a peek at Luke working next to me. He's leaning on his left elbow, hand threaded through his hair to keep it out of his eyes as he works. Today he's wearing an olive T-shirt, jeans cuffed at the ankles over black motorcycle boots, and a leather bracelet. Three tiny hoop earrings line his right ear.

Aside from the fact that he has an excellent sense of style and that he has recently broken up with his girlfriend, I don't really know much about Luke. We only have this one class together, and because he's a senior, we aren't in the same lunch period. I wonder who he sits with. Who his friends are. Does he have any weird theories about how the universe is organized? A favorite band or a favorite author?

I see that his copy of *The Catcher in the Rye* has been replaced by a new book: *On the Road* by Jack Kerouac. Maybe I should ask him about it. Maybe I should ask him what he liked about *The Catcher in the Rye* since I'm reading it now too. Or at least trying to. It's not really grabbing me like *A Tale of Two Cities* did. But every time I open my mouth to speak, all I can think about is everything that went down yesterday and the fact that my version of yesterday and everyone else's version of yesterday are no longer aligned. What if I say something that makes no sense because he forgot about it, like me and Tom and the "night owl" thing in the car this morning?

Hey, Slim. You really should skip seventh period sometime. With me.

Does Luke even remember the note he left in my backpack on Monday? If he does, he's giving no indication. *God*, how has my life become so weird in the space of twenty-four hours?

The bell rings, jolting me from my thoughts. He gets up. "See you tomorrow, Slim." And then he picks up his books and heads out the door.

I walk to PE alone.

When I arrive to pick up Katherine at Park Manor, I pass through the front door and step into another era. Big band music is playing on the stereo, the staff has moved all the chairs back against the walls in the main sitting room, and a number of the seniors, including Katherine, are *dancing*.

"It's the Lindy Hop," says Susan, as I move to the archway between the entrance and the sitting room so I can watch them. "They always love it."

Katherine spins with an older gentleman who can usually be found seated at the card table with the jigsaw puzzles. But not today. Puzzle Man swings her out and back in again as they hop from side to side, shaking their hips. She raises one arm above her head, waves her hand at us, and laughs. *Wow.* They both have *moves*. I had no idea she was such a good dancer. I had no idea she'd even be able to remember the complicated steps she's currently busting out.

There are several other couples on the floor, including Betty and Laverne, the two ladies who normally bicker with each other over card games.

It reminds me of that movie *Cocoon*, where the old people get rejuvenated by aliens.

"Pretty amazing, right?" says Susan. "It's like they're all teenagers again."

Watching them makes me happy, but it also makes me sad, because I wish they could be like this all the time.

"Well, that sure was a lot of fun." As we walk home, Katherine's conversation is much more coherent than usual. She remembers what she was doing twenty minutes ago, for one, which hardly ever happens anymore. It's a brilliant fall day, with the sky a deep cobalt blue and clouds like cotton candy. She talks about the weather and how pretty the leaves on the trees are. She waves to a baby in a stroller passing by, saying, "Oh, isn't she sweet!" to the baby's mother. She *doesn't* ask where "they" put the letters. And then she sings a line from "Don't Sit Under the Apple Tree (with Anyone Else but Me)," one of the songs that Susan was playing at Park Manor.

"Henry loves that song," she says. "Sometimes I hear him singing it in the shower."

I don't know who Henry is—my grandfather's name was Charles, and Katherine's brother was Frank—but it seems like the song has called up a buried memory about him. My mom has mentioned this about Alzheimer's patients—that music sometimes unlocks something in their brains that words can't. It definitely unlocked some dance steps for Katherine, so I guess it makes sense that it could bring back other memories as well. Of someone named Henry. In the SHOWER.

"Who was Henry?" I ask.

She gets this delighted, girlish look on her face, as if she's about to tell me a secret, and says, "We're engaged."

I don't point out that she is not currently engaged, or that the man she ended up marrying wasn't named Henry. She's so happy this afternoon, so I just say, "Congratulations."

Later that night, I take the old photos out of the hat box and bring them to Katherine's room. I want to show them to her before she goes to bed. Just like the music, I'm thinking that they might light a little spark in her brain. A spark that might even shake loose a memory about the journal.

I crawl in the bed next to her and we sit up against the pillows.

First, I show her the photograph of her and her brother and sisters, from when they were kids. "That's all of us at the old house," she says, running her arthritic finger over the faces. "Frank, Caroline, me, and Anna." Next, I show her the photo taken in New York City. "Me," she says, pointing to herself, "and Anna."

I smile, happy that the names of her siblings are still there. For a few seconds, it even feels like we are having a regular grandmother-granddaughter conversation and that any minute now she's going to ask me how school is going and if I might like her to make an apple pie this weekend.

But then she turns to me and studies my face. "Are you Anna?"

I think about putting the lipstick on the other morning and

how much I resembled Katherine, not Anna, in the photo I am currently holding in my hand.

"No," I say. "I'm Gracie."

"Oh," she says. "Gracie."

And although I can tell by the blank expression on her face that my name is not ringing a bell, I still like hearing her say it. I nestle deeper into her pillows and lean my head on her shoulder. Shuffling through the photos, I come to the one of her in the satiny dress with the flutter sleeves. The one with the restaurant table and the champagne flutes. With Katherine and the dimpled boy in the army uniform looking into each other's eyes and laughing.

"Oh!" She smiles and places her hands on her cheeks. "That's the time we went to . . ." And then she trails off, her eyes clouding over in confusion. "That place . . ." She looks to me for help. "What was it called?"

I wish I could help her, but I don't know what the place was called either. Was it a restaurant? A nightclub?

"Was this Henry?" I ask, pointing to the photo. I also show her the other one—the one where he's leaning against a wall and she sits behind him with her chin on his shoulder and her arms around his chest.

And then she gets this look on her face. Like she's concentrating really hard, so hard that it physically hurts. I can see her trying to find the memory of the day the photo was taken, and I can see her frustration that she can't locate it and call it up. I've noticed her doing this before, especially around the time when she was first diagnosed, but less often recently. It's painful to watch. It's painful to sit next to her, helpless, while she struggles with an awareness of the fact that she can't remember. She *wants* so much to remember.

Where were they that day?

What were they talking about?

Who were they with?

What a fucking awful disease. Even though my grandfather's death was sudden and sooner than any of us expected, I sometimes think he was the lucky one. He didn't have to feel his sense of self slowly slip away over months and years. He left us as he always was. A serious man who read a lot of books and newspapers, who liked to drink whiskey, who didn't hug and rarely said much. But he was, up until the end of his life, himself.

"Where did they put the letters?" Katherine asks me, back to her usual pattern.

"They're downstairs on the table," I say. "I'll take them to the post office tomorrow."

"Oh, that would be nice." She smiles and yawns. She's tired from all the dancing.

I collect the photos off the bed and climb out. "Good night, Katherine."

"Good night." Her eyes are drooping like a toddler's. I turn off the lamp next to her bed and tiptoe out the door.

Back in my room, I put the photos back in the box, sit down on my bed, and hold it in my lap, thinking.

Our memories. They're what make us who we are, aren't they? Our experiences, our connections, the things we've learned, the people we've loved, the mistakes we've made? They're the scenes that make up the story of our lives. Alzheimer's is stealing Katherine's life away, one memory at a time.

My stomach lurches. I've stolen people's memories too. Me. With the journal. I didn't mean to, because I didn't really understand what ripping out those pages would do, but I did it nonetheless. I wiped seconds, minutes, possibly hours from their lives.

Tom.

Mina.

Luke.

My mom.

Everybody.

Mina's face from earlier today flashes though my mind. The way she looked when I asked her what we talked about in English class yesterday and she couldn't remember. She looked confused. A little frustrated. Lost.

I can't do that again. Not ever. I get up and push the box with the journal as far under my bed as I can—back with all the dust bunnies, where I can barely reach. Until I've really thought it through, until I understand all of the possible ramifications, it's probably not something I should mess with. For now, at least, I'm just going to go back to being normal, boring old Gracie. That will have to be enough.

I STARE AT THE NUMBERS AND SYMBOLS UNTIL THEY DISSOLVE into a meaningless blur. I have no idea how to solve the equation in front of me because I did not take the practice test last night. I also did not go to Mrs. Drazkowski's tutorial session for students who need extra help yesterday after school. Everything is exactly like that dream I routinely have about showing up for a test that I've forgotten to study for only, in this case, it's not a dream. It's real. And I'm screwed.

I need to get my shit together. Get my head back in the game of real life. Even if real life is struggling in trig and constantly answering nonsensical questions about letters and always apologizing for Hank and feeling like I never know the right thing to say most of the time, instead of smoky nightclubs and rare, majestic owls.

According to the clock on the wall above the blackboard, I've got fifteen minutes left. I frantically scan the test for some problem, any problem, that looks doable. There are a lot of graphing equations, which, I think with a hint of annoyance, Tom is probably going to breeze right through.

He was vibrating on a slightly higher frequency than usual when we drove to school this morning, jumping from one topic to the next, fiddling with the radio dial, rooting around in his backpack as if he was looking for something. I noticed it was full of loose papers. Not a folder in sight.

"Did you forget something?" I finally asked.

Tom leaned back in his seat. "I feel like I have, but I'm not sure what it is."

That made me feel guilty about everything with the journal all over again. Like his backpack angst was just a subconscious manifestation of all the memory holes that must now exist in his brain because I—inadvertently!—wiped out most of Wednesday.

"Don't you hate that?" he asked.

I replied, "What?" But I also silently answered him in my head: *Do I hate feeling guilty? Yes. Yes, I do. It sucks.*

"That feeling," said Tom, "where you're sure there was something you were supposed to do or remember?" Then he shrugged. "It's probably nothing. My fault for never writing anything down."

And that's when it hit me. The trig test first period. That's what *I* forgot.

"Shit!"

I almost drove us straight through a red light.

Tom was quiet for a minute after I slammed on the brakes, probably saying a silent prayer of thanks that we hadn't died in a hideous collision on the way to school, and then he asked me: "Just a wild guess, but did *you* forget something?"

I shook my head at myself in disgust. "I have a trig test first period. I didn't study. I didn't even do the practice test."

"Aha! That's it!" Tom clapped his hands together. "The trig test! Same here. Well, it's third period for me, but . . . whew! Okay. This is *not* a disaster. I thought it was something I needed to turn *in*. Don't worry. We've got this."

"We do?" I failed to understand how "we" had anything.

"Just stay calm, skip over anything you aren't absolutely sure of, and then go back and try to deal with the trickier problems once you handle everything else. It'll be fine. But even if it's not, it's just a test, and the good news is we didn't get T-boned by that delivery truck. Also"—he pointed ahead—"the light is now green."

The car behind us laid on the horn, and I stepped on the gas, annoyed. I knew he was only trying to make me feel better, but Tom "my mom is a math professor who named me after a mathematician" Broder obviously has enough trigonometry in his genes that *he'll* probably be fine even when winging it. As for me, my mom has already made it more than clear that she is not the person to turn to if I need help with my math homework. And my dad, well, my dad is not really available to help with much of anything. Plus, math is not like English. You can't bullshit your way through an equation you don't know how to solve.

We continued on in silence for a few more minutes, me ruminating about the test, Tom likely relieved he hadn't forgotten about a book report, until he said, "Hey."

I glanced over at him. "Yeah?"

"Got another word for you."

Words were the last thing I was thinking about at that moment, but it was at least a distraction from my math panic.

"What is it?" I asked.

"Googolplex," he said.

I'd never heard that word before. It honestly sounded made up. But according to Tom, *googolplex* is a number that is so enormous, it's impossible to write out and counting to it would take longer than all the time in the universe. So a math word, which brought me right back to stressing about the trig test . . .

I nearly jump out of my seat when Mrs. Drazkowski announces, "Time's up. Put down your pencils." As she collects our papers, she glances at the number of problems I didn't finish and quietly asks me, "Is everything okay, Gracie?"

Automatically, I nod, but she doesn't look convinced. I'm not convinced either.

I took Tom's advice and skipped anything I wasn't sure of to focus on the equations that I knew I could answer. The only problem was, what I wasn't sure of was most of the test. And when I came back to try and work out the problems I skipped . . . well, that's when everything dissolved into a meaningless blur.

So here's the only thing I'm pretty certain about: I'm going to fail.

At lunch, Amy Taylor is sitting next to Tom again. Whenever he talks, she laughs. She's also wearing a really cute outfit. Is she flirting? Is he? Are they flirting with each other? I feel like I'm kind of bad at flirting, so it's hard to read the signs.

"I heard she wants to ask him to homecoming." Mina's voice breaks through the cafeteria chatter. She has obviously noticed me noticing them.

"Who wants to what?" I turn to her, trying to pretend I was just randomly spacing out, which, for me, is not completely out of character.

She nods her head toward the center tables. "Amy. From our French class. Wants to ask Tom."

"Really?" I try to make my voice as light and breezy as possible.

Homecoming is next month, but with everything else that's been going on, it hasn't really been on my radar.

"Tom doesn't seem like the kind of guy she'd go for," I say, although I have no idea why he wouldn't be.

Amy Taylor is one of those girls you wish you could hate but you can't. She is popular but also genuinely nice. Pretty, but not full of herself. A cheerleader but also an A student. Why *wouldn't* Tom accept her homecoming invite, if she ends up asking?

"Why not?" asks Mina.

"I don't know." I shrug.

Mina studies them for a minute and then turns back to me. "He may talk too much and be a little bit of a goofball, but a sense of humor goes a long way," she says.

"It does," agrees Daniel.

Yeah. It does.

And then Mina gets this look on her face like a light bulb appeared above her head and shoves me in the arm. "Wait! Oh my *God*! Do *you* like Tom? Why don't you ask him? Don't you drive him to school?"

I like Tom.

But do I *like* Tom?

I like that he always has things to talk about and I don't have to guess what he's thinking.

I like that he has ideas about how the universe is organized and that he contributes words like *googolplex* to my collection.

I like that he makes me laugh.

I like the way he smells when he gets into my car in the mornings, all damp and freshly showered. That combination of minty toothpaste and shampoo and clothes that seem like they just came out of the dryer . . .

I can feel my face heating up but try to hide it by shaking my head.

"No, no. He's my *neighbor*," I say. "That would be weird. Don't you think? Especially since we carpool."

Plus, the thought of me asking anyone to homecoming, even Tom, sends my brain into full meltdown territory.

Mina waves her fork at me like a symphony conductor. "Or, it could be like a movie! You falling for the boy next door!"

"He doesn't live next door. He lives across the street."

Mina narrows her eyes. "Close enough. You can pine for each other from your bedroom windows!"

"Talk to each other using tin cans attached to a long string," adds Daniel.

I roll my eyes and don't dare mention the other night. Me and Tom standing in our windows, facing each other. And then I remember that "the other night" didn't even happen anymore. And least for Tom it didn't.

I change the subject. "What about you guys? Are you asking anyone to homecoming?"

Mina laughs. "Duh, we're going together."

"Oh!" I didn't realize they were a couple. She and Daniel seem more like friends.

"As *friends*," she says, noting my confusion. "Daniel and I have a pact."

He explains: "Unless we happen to meet our soulmates—which, c'mon, this is high school, we are *not* going to meet our soulmates here—we are each other's dates."

"We're going to dress as Brad and Janet from *The Rocky Horror Picture Show*," Mina adds.

"Damn it, Janet." Daniel puts his hands over his heart and gazes at Mina. "I love you."

"Is it a costume theme?" I ask.

Mina laughs. "No, but why wear the same boring Gunne Sax dress that everyone else is going to wear when I can be *Janet*, you know?"

Daniel adds, "If you don't ask Tom, you can come with us."

"I'm *not* going to ask To— "

"Oooh, should she be Magenta or Columbia?" Daniel asks.

"Hmmm . . ." Mina studies me. "Magenta, I think." Then she looks at Daniel. "Or maybe *she* should be Janet and I should be Magenta. I've always wanted to wear a French maid costume."

I have no idea what they are talking about.

"I've never seen *The Rocky Horror Picture Show*," I say.

"WHAT?" They both slap the table at once, shaking the plates and silverware on our lunch trays.

Mina claps her hands together. "Oh my God, Gracie, we are taking you to the midnight show at Kings Court this weekend!"

"Okay, sure . . ." I say, my attention drifting back to the center of the cafeteria, even though I try not to look like I'm looking. "What time?" I ask.

"It's at midnight!" Mina rolls her eyes. "Pay attention, space cadet."

And right at that moment, my eyes meet Tom's. He waves. Like a goofball. Then he mouths words that look like *Math test?* and alternates between giving me a thumbs-up and a thumbs-down sign.

I make an exaggerated *I don't know* shrug, even though I'm pretty sure my grade is not going to be anything close to a thumbs-up.

"See what I mean?" Mina asks Daniel. "She should definitely ask him."

"Not going to happen," I say. "Plus, didn't you just tell me that what's-her-name over there wants to go with him?"

"Amy Taylor," she says. "Not if you ask first! You gotta make your move, Gracie Byrne!"

I roll my eyes at her to make it clear that this is all just joking around.

Plus, I don't have any moves.

And it would be weird to go with Tom.

Wouldn't it?

I glance across the cafeteria one last time, and right at that moment, I see Amy Taylor ripping out a piece of notebook paper, writing something down, and giving it to Tom. It must be her number.

I tell myself I'm cool with that.

Later that night, I lie in my bed, staring, yet again, at the crack on my ceiling. Now that homecoming *is* on my radar, I can't stop thinking about it. Will I go? Probably not. I mean, I wasn't expecting to. Was I? I doubt anyone is going to ask,

I'm *not* going to be the ask*er*, and I don't really want to be Mina and Daniel's third wheel, even if they are just going as friends. But still. It would be fun to get dressed up. To be a part of things.

I assess my options. I know exactly three boys at my school: Daniel, who is going with Mina. Tom, who Amy Taylor may or may not have already asked and who lives across the street, which sort of would make it awkward? Maybe? And then there is Luke, who wants to "hang out," whatever that means. But today in art class, he barely spoke to me. It's almost as if the spell of the story with the dress and champagne and the smoking has worn off, even if he keeps calling me Slim.

Gah, everything would be so much easier if I were more like Mina, who doesn't seem to overthink every word that comes out of her mouth. Or like Tom, who can apparently start up a conversation with anybody. If I were more confident or funny or quick-witted or even mysteriously aloof. If I were just *more.*

But I *could* be more.

There was something striking about her body language, and the confidence in her stride, that commanded the attention of the entire room.

More confident. More mysterious. More *fascinating* . . .

That journal is still under my bed.

And right now I'm trying to avoid thinking about it so much that it's all I *can* think about. *No.* I need to leave that thing alone. Who knows what endangered species I would further endanger the next time around?

In a fit of vague restlessness, I throw my covers off and get out of bed. Should I go downstairs and watch some late-night TV until I get sleepy again? Get a glass of water, or maybe warm milk? Isn't that supposed to help when you have insomnia? Honestly, warm milk sounds gross.

Instead, I walk to the window and look out. Tom's light is on and I see him walk across his room. I'm in a T-shirt and underwear again, so instinctively, I reach for the string on the blind, and am stopped by the realization that it's back in place, where it's supposed to be, instead of in a pile on the floor where it fell the other night. And not only is it back where it's supposed to be, it's not ripped. Because the owl, Tom seeing it, me pulling down the blind—it all no longer happened.

Tom moves closer to his window and instead of closing the blind, which would alert him to my presence, I step back to make sure that I'm standing in the dark. He rests one hand on the window frame above his head and looks out.

He really is quite tall. And lean. And because of the way he's standing, his shirt is kind of riding up . . .

Gracie, don't be a creep, I think, aware of the irony that I am peeping *on* Tom. I return to my bed, climb under the covers, and pull them over my head.

ON SATURDAY NIGHT, MINA ANSWERS HER FRONT DOOR IN a short, bubblegum-pink dress and a white sweater, her dark hair pulled back from her face with barrettes.

Her house is large and one of the more modern types of houses in our neighborhood. The living room has lots of beige furniture. The dining room table is glass. I follow her up a spiral staircase.

Daniel is lying on Mina's bed and sorting through a box of cassettes when I walk in. He's wearing gray dress slacks, a tan zip-up windbreaker, and thick-framed Elvis Costello glasses, which is all very different from his usual style.

They must be in costume.

"You didn't tell me we were supposed to dress up," I say, glancing back and forth between them. Mina's room looks like a cyclone has torn through, scattering clothes and shoes everywhere. Also hats and jewelry and wigs and jackets.

"That's the whole point!" says Mina.

"Mina, how was she supposed to know?" says Daniel. He makes an *Awwww, you're so cute!* face at me. "She's our little *Rocky Horror* virgin!"

"What?" As I start to worry that there's something about me that screams virgin, Mina laughs.

"Because it's your first time at the *show*. But don't stress—I've got you covered."

She goes digging around her closet and pulls out what looks like a French maid costume on a hanger. "I was going to be Magenta, because I've been dying to wear this, but Daniel and I discussed—and this is a sign of my heartfelt friendship, Gracie—I really think *you* should be her tonight. Your wavy hair is perfect."

"She does have the hair for it," Daniel agrees.

"Plus"—Mina grins—"I think we need to see you get a little wild!"

She thrusts the costume at me and I hold it up to inspect it. It's super short. "Mina, I don't know . . ." I say.

But she ignores me and claps her hands. "Okay, what else do we need for Gracie?"

"Boots!" Daniel says.

She goes back to the closet, pulls out a pair of high-heeled black ankle boots, and tosses them to me. I drop one.

Daniel again: "Stockings!"

Mina opens a drawer where stockings, socks, and leggings spill out like one of those joke cans of silly snakes.

"One," she calls out as a thigh-high black stocking sails through the air. "And two . . ." Then another.

I catch them both and stand there holding everything, except for the boot I dropped.

"Ummm . . . you know," I say, "this outfit really isn't me."

Mina laughs. "Again, that's the point! Be someone other than you! Don't worry. You are going to look awesome."

"Try it on! Try it on!" Daniel chants.

Mina picks up a brown bottle from her dresser and pours some peach schnapps into a shot glass. "Here, have some liquid courage first." She hands it to me and I down it in one gulp. It's sweet and syrupy and kind of disgusting, but I guess I can't be picky at the moment. When I turn twenty-one, I'm only going to order glamorous drinks, like martinis, but I guess in high school you need to take what you can get. Which in my case so far has consisted of cheap beer from a keg at the embarrassingly short list of parties Hannah and I knew about and attended sophomore year; Bartles & Jaymes wine coolers, purchased by Hannah's sister, Denise, who has a fake ID (drunk at a sleepover in Hannah's game room); and now Mina's schnapps.

I go into Mina's enormous closet while she and Daniel debate music options for a few seconds, until the beat of New Order's "Blue Monday" takes over the room. Combined with the schnapps, it gets me moving. I step out of my jeans and pull my chunky sweater over my head. I step into the maid uniform and then roll on the stockings—sheer black with a solid seam running up the back—one at a time. Then I pull on the boots, which make me about four inches taller, and come out just as "Temptation" starts playing.

"*Holy shit,*" says Daniel.

"OKAAAY!" says Mina, clapping and jumping up and down. She and Daniel cheer each other, clinking their own shots of schnapps, and then she sets her glass back down.

"The boots are a little big," I say.

She goes back to her drawer, digs something else out, and throws it to me. It's a pair of thick socks. "Wear those with the boots," she says. "Okay. Now. Makeup."

"I have lipstick . . ." I brought the tube of Cherries Jubilee. It's in the pocket of the jeans I left crumpled on the floor of Mina's closet.

"Break it out!" she says. "And then come over here so I can do your eyes."

She dumps a pile of clothes and a bright red phone that looks like a pair of lips off a fluffy swivel chair next to a mirror. I find the lipstick and sit. Mina spends an eternity putting black mascara and eyeliner on me, but she won't let me look. Daniel ejects New Order and pops another cassette into Mina's giant silver boom box.

"Okay, give me the lipstick," she says, finally, while Daniel plays Echo & the Bunnymen's "Lips Like Sugar." It's like they're choreographing the whole thing.

I hand it over and she puts it on my lips and stands back,

nodding with approval. "*Damn*, I'm good," she says, grabbing my hands and pulling me out of the chair. "Okay, now lean over and let your hair hang down." I do as she asks and she sprays my head with hairspray. "Now flip it up." I stand up, toss my hair back, and cough. Mina fluffs it all over and gives it a couple more sprays for good measure. The entire room is a haze of Aqua Net. Then she turns me around so I can face the mirror.

And . . . *wow*. Mina *is* good. I look flipping amazing. Wild and sexy and slightly intimidating with all the black eyeliner. Not like myself *at all*. My mom would probably have a heart attack if she knew I was going out dressed like this. But, as Mina said, that's the point. Tonight I can be someone else. Someone fiercer, with retro-red lips. It occurs to me that maybe this is why Mina never sticks with the same look. She gets to try on a new self *every* day. I hadn't considered it could be this easy. Maybe I don't need an all-powerful journal to experiment with different versions of me. Maybe all I need is a new outfit. And *possibly* magical lipstick.

Mina pulls on a red wig. She checks herself in the mirror, spins around, and says, "How do I look?"

"Even better than Susan Sarandon," says Daniel.

"Perfect," she says, glancing back and forth between us. "Brad. Magenta. It's time."

"We should gather the supplies." Daniel hops off the bed and picks up his backpack. "I brought a lighter, toilet paper, and the rubber gloves."

Mina holds up a shopping bag. "I've got rice, squirt bottles, toast, and newspapers. I think we're all set."

Toast? *Rubber gloves?* I must look confused, or possibly alarmed, because she immediately adds, "You'll see when we get there. It's all very *interactive*. When something happens in the movie, the audience plays along with the props."

"For example," says Daniel. "When Brad and Janet go to the wedding, we all throw rice."

Mina takes one of the newspapers out of the bag.

"And when they get caught in the rain, you hold the newspaper over your head, like this . . ." She demonstrates.

"Okay," I say. "I think I get it."

We all do one more shot before pulling on our jackets. When I step out the front door, I feel kind of fearless . . . and *hot*. But I'm not entirely sure if it's because of my costume or because of the schnapps. Maybe it's a bit of both.

There's a line outside the Kings Court theater when we arrive, and about two-thirds or more of the crowd are dressed up in a costume. There are lots of Brads and Janets, a few other Magentas, several people in glittery outfits with top hats, others who look like they're dressed as blond vampires, maybe—I'm not sure—and one or two wearing blue hospital gowns with fishnets and stilettos. It's like a very wild Halloween party.

Daniel whispers in my direction, "Pretty awesome, right?"

I nod and continue taking in the scene. Mina seems to know a lot of people here. She's hugging friends in line, waving hello.

They all seem to know each other, in fact, like this is something they do on a regular basis.

The front doors open, so we pay for our tickets and file into the lobby of the theater.

"I'm going to grab us some seats," Mina says. Daniel and I agree to get popcorn, which takes about a million years because it's so crowded. We're making our way toward the doors to the main seating area when I hear a familiar gravelly voice behind me.

"Is that *you*, Slim?"

I turn and find myself face to face with Luke.

He's not in a costume. Instead, he's wearing jeans and the motorcycle boots again. And the army jacket, but tonight it's buttoned up and he's got a maroon scarf wrapped around his neck. Like he came straight from a café in Paris. As usual, he looks *good*.

And in my sexy Magenta outfit, I feel a little less awkward than I usually do around him. Also tall.

"Yes, it's me," I say. "Well"—I look at Daniel—"actually, I guess it's Magenta. For tonight. Whoever she is. It's my first time seeing this show."

"*Rocky Horror* virgin," Daniel explains.

The corner of Luke's mouth twitches. "I see."

"This is my friend Daniel," I add, being sure to emphasize the word *friend*. "Daniel, Luke."

Luke nods, and then he looks me up and down in the way that he did when he was talking about me in the dream. Like

I'm hardly wearing any clothes, which, in this case, is somewhat true.

"You look"—he breaks into a half smile—"different. Nice stockings."

And then a girl appears at his side. And not just any girl: Lisa Kendrick. From the sidewalk in front of my house. From what seems like a million years ago, even though it's only been about three weeks since then. She tucks her arm inside of his.

Now I don't know what to say. The inside of my brain is just a running monologue: *Didn't they break up? I heard they broke up. Mina told me they broke up. The rumor at school is that they broke up.*

"Remember Grace?" he says to her. "You almost fainted in front of her house."

She looks confused for a minute, biting her glossy hot-pink lip. And then something must ring a bell. "Oh! The *toe* girl!"

Daniel gives me a look, like, *What?*

And suddenly, I'm right back on that sidewalk, sweaty and tongue-tied and mortified. I can almost hear Hank barking. All traces of my inner Magenta have left the building.

"Ha, yes, that's me." I let out a weird laugh. That is also too loud. The lobby is clearing out. "I think we need to grab our seats."

"Yeah, us too," he says. "Enjoy the show."

Luke and Lisa make their way to the theater doors on the right, and Daniel and I follow a couple of Brads and Janets and a person in a fishnet/stiletto combination toward the center entrance. Before we go through, I look across the lobby in Luke and Lisa's direction, searching for a sign that might tell me whether they are back together or just catching up as friends. Or maybe they never broke up in the first place and the rumors were all wrong? And then, right before they disappear into the theater, Luke looks over his shoulder, scanning the lobby until his eyes lock on me. He does that half grin again.

What does it mean?

Enigmatic. Mysterious. Difficult to read.

That's what he is.

"Soooo," Daniel says as we walk down the aisle of the theater. "What was *that*?"

It's like he can read my mind.

"I don't know." I shrug. "We sit next to each other in art."

"Well, he looked like he wanted to trade Blondie for Magenta."

Like we're accessories, I think.

"I don't know about that," I say.

"Maybe you aren't truly understanding your Magenta power here tonight," he says. "Also, I thought they broke up."

Yes, Daniel. So did I.

So did I.

We spot Mina waving at us near the front, make our way to her, and sit down. The lights dim, and a giant pair of red lips appears on the screen.

JOURNAL, BLAKISTON'S FISH OWL, KATHERINE, TRIG TEST, Luke, Lisa, homecoming—none of it matters today. Because today I get to hang out with Hannah. Hannah, who I've known since I was five, when her family moved in down the block from ours. Hannah, who's been my closest friend through elementary school and middle school and half of high school, whose house has felt more like home than my house even, and certainly more like home than Katherine's. Hannah, who I can just relax around, without worrying whether I've said something weird or I have poppy seeds from my morning bagel in my teeth. (She'd tell me, immediately.) Being with someone who you've known forever is like curling up on the sofa with your favorite blanket and a VHS copy of *Grease*. It's warm and comforting and just . . . easy. Unlike constantly worrying about fitting in when you don't yet belong, which is exhausting. At Morewood, a lot of the time I still feel as if I'm trying to sing along to songs I've never heard before in my life.

Hannah's driving in from Altoona, and we're going to spend the day at the Century III Mall on Route 51. As I wait for her to arrive at our designated meeting spot—the center court fountain—I come up with a potential itinerary: we can goof off for a while at Spencer Gifts, shop for some funny socks, get Orange Juliuses and soft pretzels, and then maybe check out that new movie with Molly Ringwald and Robert Downey Jr. Either way, I can't think of a better way to spend a Sunday. I keep my eyes on the crowd, and just as the colored lights in the fountain switch from turquoise to violet, I spot Hannah walking my way. As usual, her white Keds are spotless. I stand and wave.

"So," Hannah says, after we get all the hugging and complimenting each other's outfits out of the way. "I need you . . . to help me find a homecoming dress!" She grins. "Jason Yost asked me."

She has a date for homecoming already?

Ugh. I'd hoped today would be my escape from all talk of dances and prospective dates, but perhaps that was a silly assumption. Of course my old school has a homecoming dance. And why wouldn't Hannah go? I try to conjure up an image of Jason Yost. I think he was in my bio class last year. He's nice enough, I guess. So if Hannah's excited, I'm going to be excited. Or at least try.

"That's great!" I say. "Where do you want to go first?"

"Hmmm . . ." Hannah thinks. "How about Express?"

"Let's do it." We pass by Spencer's on the way, but don't go in. And just like that, my imaginary mall itinerary is rearranged: instead of popcorn and a movie, it looks like we will be on a quest. A quest to find Hannah the perfect homecoming dress.

"What about you, Gracie?" she asks in the dressing room at Kaufmann's, as I zip her up in a satiny purple dress with an enormous bow on the butt. A dozen discarded options lie in a heap on the floor. "Don't you want to try anything?"

She asked me this at Express too. But trying without any intention of buying seems kind of pointless.

"There have got to be some cute guys at your new school," she adds. "Any possibilities?"

I guess I could tell her about Luke—about art class and the whisper and the note he left in my backpack and seeing him in the lobby of Kings Court—but everything with the journal and the Slim dream has made the whole thing kind of difficult to explain. Plus, he and Lisa Kendrick looked very much together last night, so I think he's probably off the "possibilities" list for now. And then there was the whole conversation at lunch the other day when Mina was being so annoying about Tom. But that seems even more far-fetched than Luke. Doesn't it?

So I just shrug and say, "Nobody yet."

"Well," Hannah says, and her voice takes on that tone she

gets when she's trying to sound upbeat, which, at the moment, annoys me. "There's still plenty of time . . ." She examines the dress in the mirror. "I don't know. It's a little too . . . purple. What do you think?"

I think I should have brought some snacks, because this is going to take one hundred years.

After we hit all of Century III's flagship department stores, as well as several smaller shops and a bridal boutique, Hannah appears to be settling on a burgundy velvet Gunne Sax dress. I think the sleeves are a little too puffy, but don't dare say a word about it.

"It's PERFECT!" I affirm, perhaps a bit too enthusiastically.

"You think?" she asks. "Really?"

"Totally."

I'm wearing a tight black crop top with a sweetheart neckline. I tried it on while Hannah was getting into the Gunne Sax dress, just to have something to do.

"Wow, that's a new look for you," she says, once she takes a good look at me.

"Well . . . that's the point," I respond, channeling Mina. "A new me."

"You should get it."

"And *you* should get that dress before we both pass out from a lack of nourishment."

To be honest, I don't really know if the crop top *is* my style. But I buy it anyway.

We make our purchases, move on to the food court to get some fries and Orange Juliuses (one win for my itinerary!), and catch up on anything we didn't get to catch up on over the course of seven dressing rooms. Hannah fills me in on Jason. They kissed for the first time at a house party two weekends ago. I tell her about Mina and Daniel and our costumes for *Rocky Horror*. Hannah is excited for an upcoming band trip to DC. I tell her about Hank and my toe and we laugh about it, although I wish we could have laughed about it the day it happened, which now feels like long ago. And then it's time for Hannah to head out.

"My mom is so annoying," she says. "She wants me on the road before it's dark."

We hug again at the fountain, and I watch as she blends into the Sunday afternoon crowd. We probably won't see each other again until Christmastime.

I feel a little melancholy as I make my way to the exit near where I parked. The day hasn't been as relaxing as I'd hoped. It's probably—mostly—because Hannah and I covered at least five miles chasing down homecoming dresses. But also, the easy rapport we've always had with each other felt a little less easy. Perhaps the physical distance between us has complicated the comfortable language of our friendship. Which makes sense, I guess. We don't see the same people every day. We don't have the same stories or inside jokes anymore. Even though we promised each other before I moved that we'd talk on the phone every day, we haven't been able to keep it up. She's been busy with band and mock trial. And I've been busy rewriting reality. Then erasing it. And manifesting owls and invading people's dreams. None of which I told Hannah. Mainly because I haven't told anybody. But also, I don't know if she'd even believe me . . . I mean, who would?

But if I can't talk to Hannah, who *can* I talk to?

When I walk in the front door around six thirty, the house is abnormally quiet. Jack is not in front of the TV. In fact, he, my mom, and Katherine are nowhere to be found, even though mom's car is in the carport. Hank doesn't appear to greet me with his tail whipping at my legs. All I hear is the clock ticking on the mantel and the muffled sound of cars passing by on the street outside.

This is weird. Where is everyone? Maybe they all went out for a walk? That never happens, but maybe?

I hang my coat on the rack and walk through the dining room and into the kitchen.

There's nobody in here either, but there is a note on the butcher block. It's from my mom.

> *Gracie — The Broders invited us for an impromptu Sunday dinner. Come over when you get home. I told them you would join us!*
>
> *—Mom*

That's just like my mom. Signing me up for a social gathering that I did not sign up for myself. I'm tired from last night and from the day at the mall with Hannah. I have some homework due tomorrow. But still. It would be rude not to go over there now, right? Plus, I'm kind of curious about Tom's family. I've only seen them coming in and out of the house, really. Tom's mom always waves hello from the carport when she sees me, especially now that she gives Jack a lift to school with the twins. She looks kind of like Tom. And sometimes I see Tom's dad leaving early in the morning or returning in the evening on his bike. He must ride it to work. But I haven't officially met either of them, even though my brother practically lives at their place at this point. *And why is Hank not here?* Did my mom and Jack bring him to the Broders' house too? If everyone in my family, even the *dog*, is over there right now, it's going to look especially impolite if I don't show up.

I'm not sure I like what I'm wearing, though. And I need to brush my teeth. I run upstairs with my shopping bag and take out my new crop top and pull it over my head, study myself in the mirror, and then take it off again, certain it's not appropriate for dinner at the neighbors'. Like, noticeably so. But the shirt I had on today is blah. I settle on an oversized boatneck sweater and leggings with ballet flats.

I dig around in my bag for the Cherries Jubilee lipstick that I wore last night and swipe it on in front of the bathroom mirror. I wipe it off again. Somehow it worked when I was Magenta but it's not working now. Gloss. Gloss is better. I roll on a layer of gloss, shake my hair, and study my reflection. What am I even doing right now? I'm just going to the neighbors' house. It's just dinner. It's just *Tom.*

In many ways, the Broders' house is a mirror of Katherine's—wide porch, front door flanked by windows—but here, the windows around the door are stained glass. I take a second to catch my breath and then ring the doorbell, hearing it chime inside. There are muffled footsteps on the hardwood floor. A shadow behind the stained glass. My heart is beating fast. It must be from jogging across the street.

It's not Tom who answers. It's his dad. They don't look much alike. Mr. Broder is medium height and stocky where Tom is tall and lean. His hair is dark while Tom's is an ash blond-brown. His dad also has a beard.

"You must be Gracie."

His voice is soft and warm and it puts me at ease. At least a little.

"Yes," I say, still a little breathless. "Nice to meet you."

"Welcome," he says. "Can I take your jacket?"

"Sure." I hand him the blazer I threw on before I left the house.

As he takes it and hangs it on a rack in their entryway, I look around. The space is littered with jackets and sweatshirts and soccer cleats. Running shoes and backpacks. There are also moving boxes that still need to be unpacked, and more in the living room to my right.

I hear a thump above our heads.

"The boys are upstairs playing Atari." He nods toward the stairs as Hank and Hypatia run into the entryway to greet me. "The rest of us are in the dining room. Come meet Trish, and then feel free to head on up there if you'd like." Looks like they are a call-us-parents-by-our-first-names kind of house.

Another thump. He smiles. "Or stay in the dining room with us, where it's perhaps a little more civilized."

I follow him into the dining room, which is noisy with conversation and my mom laughing louder than usual, a glass of red wine in her hand. Katherine sits next to her. The dogs are right behind us, tails wagging, and they circle the table, which is lit up with votive candles that have been placed in mason jars. I scan the room for Tom—he's not there—as Mrs. Broder jumps up from her seat to greet me.

"Gracie!" She throws her arms around me like I'm her long-lost niece and then she steps back to take me in. "Aren't you adorable! It is *so* nice to meet you finally. We've been meaning to have you all over for a while now, but it's been so busy with school starting and getting everything unpacked! Which, as you can see, we are still working on." She laughs. "So I just told Alan, '*Who cares* about the boxes? Let's have a dinner party!' We're glad you could make it!"

"Thanks for having us," I say, slightly overwhelmed by her exuberance.

She continues, "We all *adore* Jack and have been looking forward to meeting you and your mom and Katherine. And it's so nice of you to give Tom a lift to school! Hopefully, he can return the favor sometime. We've been looking for an inexpensive used car. You are single-handedly saving that boy from having to sprint to the bus every morning. I guess the extra ten minutes of sleep are inspiring him to be on time!" She laughs again and pulls out a chair. "Here, have a seat. You can call me Trish."

I sit down, and she rests her hands on my shoulders.

"So, what can we get you to drink? Water? Soda? A glass of wine?" She turns to my mom. "A little wine is okay, right, Maggie?

My mom shrugs, saying, "Fine with me," and I'm surprised to see her so *whatever* about it, which leads me to conclude she must be at least a little drunk.

"*Mom.* Boundaries."

I turn to see Tom in the entryway to the dining room and . . . something is different. It's . . . glasses. He's wearing thick-framed tortoiseshell glasses.

Mrs. Broder makes an exasperated face at him but lifts her hands off my shoulders. "Oh, there you are. How about a hello?"

"Hello, Gracie," he says.

There's *something* about guys with glasses. For me, anyway. I've never understood why Lois Lane preferred Superman to Clark Kent. In Tom's case, they make him look like an adorable librarian who is able to reach the highest shelves for a book. My stomach flips. Then flops.

"Hi," I say. And then I turn to his mom. "Water is great." I'm still recovering from the schnapps last night.

Are his cheeks a deeper shade of rosy than usual?

Are mine?

Maybe it's just warm in here.

"I'll get it," says Tom, and he lifts the empty glass pitcher off the table and disappears through the swinging door that leads to the kitchen.

While he's gone, Mrs. Broder—I mean *Trish*—sits down next to me. I watch my mom top off her wine. Jeez. She's acting like she never gets out. But I guess that's because she never does.

"How was your shopping trip with Hannah?" she asks.

"It was fun."

Katherine is between my mom and Mr. Broder—am I supposed to call him Alan?—and seems to be enjoying herself. She's also sipping a glass of wine and has even set her purse aside, instead of keeping it in a vise grip on her lap. Tom's dad appears to be the only quiet one in this family, which makes me feel a sort of affection for him, even though we just met.

"So your mom tells us you're new at Morewood this year too," Trish says. "How's it all going?"

"It's good," I say. And I realize that even though I just said "it's good" automatically, it is, in fact, not terrible. I've made a few new friends that I really like. I'm no longer eating lunch alone in the library. I may not be the most fascinating person at Morewood High—not anymore, at least—but things are not as bad as I originally imagined they would be.

Tom reappears with a full pitcher of water and fills a glass for me.

"Do you play football, Tom?" my mom asks. "Gracie says you have practice after school."

Why does she have to tell anybody what I've been saying about anything?

"*Noooooo,*" says Tom, shaking his head. "I'm on cross-country. I like to run fast *without* huge guys tackling me. And I play basketball in the winter."

"And what about you, Gracie?" Trish asks. "Do you play a sport?"

"No." I say. "I just . . . go to school."

Tom nudges my chair. "So you want to stay down here so they can grill us about our college plans next or go upstairs and crash that Atari game?"

"Let's crash the Atari game," I say, because 1) I have no idea what my college plans are going to be (*should I?*) and 2) I'd rather play Pac-Man than sit at the table with our parents and feel like we are on some old-timey chaperoned dinner date.

"I'm going to steal this Chex Mix," Tom says as we leave.

"Take it!" Trish says. "We'll call you kids when dinner is ready."

I follow Tom past more stacks of moving boxes in various stages of disarray. We climb the stairs, the dogs right behind us, and stop in the second floor hallway.

"Good thing our parents are a little drunk, otherwise my mom would insist on giving you the house tour," he says.

Hypatia licks my hand and I scratch her behind her ears. Hank isn't even jealous.

"So . . . Hypatia is named after the first woman mathematician. Did I get that right?"

Tom rolls his eyes and laughs. "Yeah. Hypatia of Alexandria. She was also an astronomer, writer, and philosopher . . . or so my mom says."

"A polymath."

He raises an eyebrow behind his glasses. "Okay, word woman, are you going to tell me what that means?"

"A person of wide-ranging knowledge or learning."

"Exactly!" he says, nodding. "Though *our* Hypatia is probably not any of those things because she's a dog. I mean, *maybe* she's a little philosophical, I don't know. But sadly, the real Hypatia was eventually killed by a mob of Christian zealots for her scientific and mathematical views. Mom continues to be outraged on her behalf."

"Yikes," I say. "That's horrible."

"I know, right? Imagine getting murdered for *math*. At least now all people want to do is copy your homework." Tom moves on to the first open doorway. "This is what my mom refers to as the rumpus room."

Inside, Jack, Isaac, and Leo are all sitting on huge bean bag chairs in front of a television and an Atari console, playing *Space Invaders*. They don't even notice us. Even when the dogs run in.

"So what else is on the tour?"

He laughs. "You want the Trish tour?"

"Well," I say, "now I'm curious about what's so tour-worthy."

Tom walks over to our brothers, sets the bowl of Chex Mix between them, and comes back out to the hallway.

"Do you think they saw me?" he asks.

"I don't think so. They're fully hypnotized. Just like my mom suspects."

Tom makes a fake static sound and holds a pretend tour bus mic up to his face. "Welcome to the Broder family house tour. Please keep your hands and head inside the vehicle at all times. As your guide, I'm happy to answer any questions . . ."

I trail him down the hallway until he stops and pulls open an old-fashioned laundry chute.

"Do you have one of these?" he asks.

"Yep. I think a lot of the old houses in this neighborhood have them."

"The twins think it's awesome. They drop stuff down there all the time. Everything *except* laundry. I'm just glad they're big enough that they can't fit in it themselves or we might have a problem."

"Jack drops dog treats down to see if Hank is smart enough to go find them in the basement."

"Oh, wow. We'll have to try that with Hypatia."

"Well, she *is* a polymath . . ."

"Right." He nods, makes the static sound again, holds the fake mic to his mouth, and keeps walking. "If you look to the left, we have . . . my parents' room. It's wine time, so they are out of their enclosure right now." I glance in and see lots of books on nightstands as Tom continues on. "And up ahead we have the bathroom . . . where you will see . . . a clawfoot tub. And this is me," he says, stopping at the next open door. His room. Which I already know faces mine. Because of the night with the owl. Which he doesn't remember.

I stand next to Tom in the doorway but don't cross the threshold. I don't know why, but it feels like if I go in there, I'll break through some kind of magical force field that will put us in another dimension where we are not just neighbors who carpool. But what *would* we be then? Friends who hang out in each other's rooms? I hang out in Mina's room, so this shouldn't seem like a big deal. But it feels different.

Tom's room is surprisingly neat. The bed is made. There aren't any clothes on the floor. Based on the state of his backpack, I expected disorder or even chaos. Instead, it looks like a place you'd want to hang out. His walls are covered with concert posters and album art. Talking Heads. Elvis Costello. David Bowie. The Pretenders.

"Your room faces mine," I say, as my brain flashes back to me standing in the dark a few nights ago, watching him look out the window.

Why did I say this? Why? My face flushes.

"I know," he says.

Oh, shit.

Did he see me?

And then he quickly adds, "I mean . . . I figured."

He looks at me, and I could be imagining it, but is he blushing too? The light is dim in the hallway, so it's hard to tell.

"Okay," he says, in this confessional tone like he's in an interrogation room and I'm the detective. "I saw you walk past your window maybe once, but that's *only* because I just happened to be looking out *randomly* and your light was on. It's not like I have binoculars and sit here spying on my neighbors like the guy in that Hitchcock movie . . ."

"Jimmy Stewart. *Rear Window*," I say, relieved to have something else to talk about.

"Yeah, that's the one. Cool movie, though."

"It's one of my favorites."

"I like it too," he says. "But I do feel like disposing of a body via suitcase would be much messier than it's made out to be."

"Maybe the murderer wrapped everything in Saran Wrap first."

Tom makes a disgusted face. "And what was the dog digging up in the garden?"

"I think it was probably the wife's head. He couldn't fit it in the suitcase."

"That's pretty dark, Gracie."

"I'm sorry." I shrug. "I have a vivid imagination."

We stand there silently for a minute. Tom adjusts his glasses. I lean against the door frame.

"Did you just get those glasses?" I say.

"Nah, I've had them a while. I usually wear contacts to school." He leans against the frame too, so that we face each other. I notice that he has a tiny scar on his chin.

"I like them," I say. "They make you look like a librarian. Or an absent-minded math professor."

He smiles. "I guess I'll take the librarian thing as a compliment, since you like books."

What if I just stepped over the threshold right now? What if I broke the magical force field, just to see what happens next?

But a voice from below pierces the weird bubble of *whatever* that was just in the air.

"Kids! Dinner!"

"Aaaand . . . that concludes our tour." Does he look . . . *irritated*? Or maybe disappointed? "Get ready for my mom to quiz you about everything under the sun," he adds. "She's incredibly nosy."

We walk back to the rumpus room, disconnect our brothers from the Atari, and follow them downstairs.

I carry the empty bowl that held the Chex Mix.

I think the dogs ate most of it.

"Such a great family," my mom says as we walk into the house later. She tries to hang up her sweater, but misses the hook. I pick it up.

"Why don't you go to bed, Mom. I'll get Katherine down."

"You have school tomorrow," she says.

"It's okay. I got it."

She doesn't object a second time. I can tell she's tired. We all are.

Thankfully, Katherine does not fight bedtime. She goes to

the bathroom. She puts her dentures in the cup where they soak overnight. I help her pull her plaid flannel nightgown over her head.

Once she's all tucked in, I ask her the question that's been on my mind all night.

"Do you think . . . I should ask Tom to homecoming?"

And instead of saying *Who is Tom?* like I expected her to, or *Where did they put the letters?*, she smiles a big smile at me and says, "Oh, *yes.*"

Before I turn out the lamp on my nightstand, I walk to my desk and glance out the window, already back to my *Rear Window* ways. (Even if, technically, my window is front facing.) Tom's light is on too, and I see his silhouette move through the room. Moments later, he appears at his window.

He waves.

Quickly, without overthinking, I wave back.

And for once, I don't want to change anything. Not one little bit.

ENIGMATIC

AMY TAYLOR IS NOT AT TOM'S TABLE THIS MONDAY. MAYBE she's out sick? Maybe she has the flu. Or it could be mono. I heard that's been going around. Maybe she'll be out of school so long that she'll have to miss homecoming entirely.

Gracie, stop, I tell myself. It is bad to wish mono on anybody. Especially someone who is perfectly nice. I watch Tom, who is wearing a Champion sweatshirt that smelled fresh out of the dryer this morning, deep in conversation with Marcus about something. Marcus is making the same face that I sometimes do when Tom has gone off on a tangent.

"Oh my *God*, Gracie." Mina throws a balled up napkin at me. "Ask that boy to homecoming already. Make your move before it's too late!"

I turn to her in an attempt to head off further discussion.

"Mina. I've told you. He's my neighbor. My brother is friends with his brothers. If we actually went to homecoming together and the whole night ended up being awkward, I'd still have to see him *every day*. So I'm not making any moves here. We are *just* friends. And, it's like, *weeks away*."

But I don't tell her what I'm really thinking—that, after last night, I was actually considering it. The cute glasses might have helped. And Katherine said I should. But then he was SO quiet in the car this morning. Something felt off. Or maybe it just felt off because he wasn't wearing the glasses.

"I'm just saying. You two are always checking in on each other when you think the other one isn't looking."

"We are?" *Is he?*

"Well," Daniel chimes in, "if she doesn't ask Tom, she might have another option . . ."

Mina narrows her eyes at me. "Who?"

"Luke Carr was one hundred percent looking her up and down in the Kings Court lobby on Saturday night."

Mina crosses her arms. "And how come you didn't mention this on Saturday, Gracie Byrne?"

"The movie was starting," I say. "Plus, he was not checking me out—"

"Yes, he totally was," Daniel interrupts me. "And why does he call you Slim? Because I feel like if you two are on a nickname basis, there has definitely been some flirting going on."

“It’s nothing. It’s . . .” Instead of explaining Slim, which I really can’t explain, I just add, “Also, I think he’s back with his girlfriend. They were there together.”

“Uh, I wouldn’t worry about that,” says Mina. “They’re always on and off. Plus, she’s in college! What does she want with a high school guy anyway?”

But that’s the thing. I’m not worrying about it. In the last twenty-four hours, I haven’t been thinking that much about Luke Carr. At all. But maybe I should be? Everything is so confusing.

“You know,” Mina says to Daniel, “I have an idea. Instead of Brad and Janet, maybe we do something more glam for homecoming.”

She goes on to describe a gold lamé dress she found in a thrift store that reminds her of an outfit that Bianca Jagger wore once to Studio 54. Daniel is in favor of the idea.

Homecoming. Homecoming. *Homecoming.* It’s all anyone wants to talk about.

Except for Luke, who, to my surprise, wants to talk about this past weekend.

“No French maid outfit today?” he asks the minute I sit down in art.

“No,” I say. “That’s, uh, only for special occasions.”

“Hmmm . . .” he says, squinting at me. “What *kind* of special occasions?”

I laugh nervously and get up from my seat. "Midnight movies. I'm going to go get a box of pastels. You want one?"

We've finished our mixed media collages and are now doing still lifes.

"Sure, thanks," he says.

I can feel his attention on me again as I walk to the supply shelves, or at least on the version of me that he saw in the Kings Court lobby on Saturday night. Which is not *really* me. It was just a character. And it wasn't even my outfit. I wonder what he actually thinks about *me*, Gracie Byrne. I try to recall. We've been sitting next to each other for nearly a month now. Has he asked me one personal question related to my thoughts about . . . anything? I'm not sure. Although it's not as if I've asked him anything personal, either. Maybe that's because I've been too caught up in the 1940s nightclub fantasy version of our interactions.

Tom asks a *lot* of questions. But Tom seems to have a curious personality. And, I mean, it's okay to *not* be curious, right? Some people are curious and ask a lot of questions and some people don't. Maybe Luke is one of those still-waters-run-deep kind of guys. Enigmatic. Maybe he's been burned too many times by a cold-hearted older woman (Lisa Kendrick) and is afraid to trust anyone again. Or maybe he has a tragic past, or difficult parents. Like Mr. Rochester from *Jane Eyre*. Or Dallas from *The Outsiders*. Plus, he's always carrying a book around, so he must *read*.

I watch him as he blends black and brown for the outline of a skull.

He just needs the right person to bring out his more—talkative? engaging? interesting?—side.

"What did you think of *The Catcher in the Rye*?" I ask.

"It was cool," he says, nodding without looking up.

He doesn't elaborate.

We work in silence until the bell rings, but when it does, he waits for me to gather my things and walks with me again to PE.

I stop in front of a row of lockers when we get to the entrance to the gym.

"Well . . . this is me . . ." I say.

Luke doesn't make a move to leave. Instead, he places his hand on the locker door behind me and leans in so that we are face-to-face, ridiculously close.

He grins. "Sure you don't want blow it off and get high in the parking lot?"

Oh, wow. This is . . . I mean, it's not as *cinematic* as a 1940s nightclub, but . . .

I feel like a butterfly pinned to a specimen board. The heat of his proximity is making me flush. "I can't," I blurt. "Today, I mean! I have something after school. A lot of homework."

Ooof. Could I sound like a bigger dork?

Out of the corner of my eye, I catch a familiar figure walking by in the class-changing crowd. Tom. Briefly, our eyes meet, and I flush harder. What is he doing *here*? Right *now*? I've never seen him in the hallway on my way to PE before. I try to back up a bit, so it doesn't look like I've been sucking face with Luke, but there's nowhere to go.

Two seconds later, Luke pushes away from the locker and gives me an amused smile, like he 100 percent expected my not-very-cool-girl response. "Okay, Slim. Some other time."

"Yeah." I nod. "Some other time."

I glance down the hallway, but Tom has disappeared into the crowd.

IT'S WEDNESDAY. MID-OCTOBER. ONE WEEK AND THREE days until homecoming.

There are posters in the halls. Tickets are being sold at a card table set up in the cafeteria. Mina and Daniel can't stop talking about their outfits.

It's raining today, and as I click on the windshield wipers on the way to school, I think back to that day when I picked Tom up as he was running for the bus. How he remembered my name. And then he asked me *so* many questions. Which, weirdly, made me feel more at ease. He wanted to know how my first week of school was going and where I had moved from. He asked about Katherine. He asked me to remind him what Pittsburgh's three rivers were called and told me his favorite was the Monongahela, because he liked the way it sounded.

Monongahela, Monongahela, Monongahela.

We hit the red light on Wilkins. I tap the steering wheel and look straight ahead at the cars whizzing through the intersection, but just about every other one of my five senses is tuned to his presence. I hear him shift in his seat because his long legs never quite seem to fit. I feel the warmth of him, just inches away from me. I wonder what it would taste like to kiss him. And as usual, he smells amazing.

"You're *especially* thoughtful this morning," says Tom. "Did you forget another test or something?"

"No." I shake my head.

Get it together, Gracie.

"I wonder if Drazkowski is going to be back today," he continues, in reference to our trig teacher, who has been out for a few weeks due to a particularly bad case of chicken pox, making my wait for what is sure to be a terrible test grade even more agonizing. "That test was harder than I expected. I honestly don't know—"

"Do you maybe want to go to homecoming together?" I ask.

And as soon as I say it, I wish I could reach out and stuff the words back in my mouth, but it's too late now. They float in the air like a fart. Impossible to ignore in such a small space.

The light turns green. I step on the gas and keep talking.

"I mean, it wouldn't be, like, a *date* . . . Mina and Daniel are going together as friends and I thought it would be fun for a group of us to go and I know you know Mina from math. *Anyhow*, they are dressing up as . . . originally it was going to be Brad and Janet from *The Rocky Horror Picture Show* but now I think Mina said something about Bianca Jagger? But homecoming doesn't *actually* have a costume theme, they just want to do that for some reason. We could completely wear normal clothes."

Tom is quiet for a *loooong* minute.

Oh, God. What the hell did I just say? It didn't even make sense to me.

More quiet.

I feel like I'm in a roller coaster car, the gears *clank*, *clank*, *clanking* as we reach the top, my stomach clenching in anticipation of the drop. And part of the track is missing.

I need to back this car up.

Now.

"You know, scratch that. You probably have other plans, right? It was just an idea since you hadn't mentioned if you were going or not and I—"

"I'm sorry," he says. "You just . . . kind of caught me off guard. I wasn't . . . Umm . . . yeah. I mean, yes. I do have other plans. I'm going with Amy Taylor?" He plays around with the radio dial, switching from news to music, back to news again.

I'm officially in free fall. And, yes, there is a huge, gaping hole in the track.

Of course he has other plans. I have been watching those plans unfold in front of my eyes in the cafeteria for *weeks* now. But I guess I thought he would maybe mention it? And if he hadn't mentioned it, then maybe they weren't plans . . . yet?

Why, why, *why* did I ever think this was a good idea?

I nod and keep nodding and nodding and nodding and nodding.

And then I say, "Amy Taylor! That's great! She's in my French class. She's great. She's really . . . *great.*"

That's three *greats*. In a row. Tom looks so uncomfortable. Like he wants to jump out of the car.

Meanwhile, I can't seem to stop talking about how *great* it is that Tom is going to homecoming with Amy. "Anyhow," I say. "That's really cool. You guys make a nice couple."

He finally looks up from the radio. "Well, I mean, it's not . . . we're not, a *couple*. Marcus is taking Amy's friend Samantha, and they suggested Amy and I join them. We're all going together."

"Well, you *should* be a couple." I laugh. Like a hyena. Who is possibly also on hallucinogenic drugs. "She's a great girl. And you're great . . . so it would just be—"

". . . great?" Tom tunes the radio to music again. Whitney Houston is singing "I Wanna Dance with Somebody." Of course.

Shut up, shut up, shut up, I say to myself. *Or at least find something else, ANYTHING else to talk about.*

He switches back to the news. The newscaster is talking about the Dow Jones Industrial Average and "market volatility." It sounds like me and the stock market are on this roller coaster together.

"Wow, that's terrible about the Dow Jones," I say.

Tom makes a confused face. "Do you own stocks?"

"No." I shake my head. "But all this volatility can't be good for the economy." Like I've ever opined about the economy in my life. I clamp my mouth shut.

The rest of the drive feels like it takes *googolplex* years.

For the first time since the start of school, I hide out in the library at lunch. I don't want to talk about my failed homecoming ask with Mina and Daniel, and I definitely don't want to watch Amy flirt with Tom at the cool table. And I even more definitely don't want, in any way, shape, or form, to make eye contact with Tom. If that were to happen, I feel like I might spontaneously combust. What on earth was I thinking? I'm already dreading the drive to school tomorrow and am frantically trying to devise a way to get out of it. Can I pretend I have a morning dentist appointment? But then I'd need to talk to him again *today* to tell him he'll need to take the bus in the morning, which . . . *no*. I keep replaying my hyena laugh over and over and over in my head. *She's great! So great!*

Great, great, great, great, great.

And then I recall that thought I had, when Tom's mom asked me how it was going at school. How, in that moment, I really had felt that things were not as bad as I originally imagined they would be. It's like I jinxed myself.

Because now? Everything suuuucks.

The bell rings and I pull my backpack over my shoulders. Three more classes to go before I can go home and bury myself under my covers for all eternity.

Wait. No. I can't even do that because I have to pick up Katherine.

In art, Luke is back to his aloof setting today, barely acknowledging my existence. Which, you know, of course. Of course on the one day that the ego boost of this guy's attention might make me feel a little less pathetic, he's going to be all mercurial. But his fickleness makes me think: there's a reason he only talks to me when I'm stalking his dreams in a slinky satin dress or wearing a French maid costume as Magenta. It's because the real me, the everyday me, the me without cigarettes and champagne or thigh-high black stockings or a huge honking owl perched on my shoulder, is clearly not enough to spark his interest. To spark anyone's interest.

The truth of the matter is this: regular old boring Gracie is not cutting it.

I am 100 percent lost at sea here.

And I need to turn this ship around.

WRITE WHAT YOU KNOW.

The journal sits open on my lap. I'm still not sure what I'm going to do with it yet. All I do know is that for most of the day, I haven't been able to think of much else aside from this: I wish that I could just wipe this morning from Tom Broder's brain. And then tomorrow, we could go back to normal—talking about words and books and math theorems and Hitchcock movies in the car. Nothing would have to be awkward or weird between us. Knowing that I potentially have the power to make this wish come true is . . . well, it's a lot. But I swore I wouldn't do that again. I swore that I wouldn't wipe anyone's memories. Especially because the first time I did it, it was basically an accident. This time, it would be on purpose.

I can't.

I won't.

As much as I want to.

I run my hand over the blank pages in front of me. There must be a reason I found this journal, right? Maybe the universe has somehow recognized that I just can't seem to get out of my own way without a *little* help. Most people wouldn't even think twice about using this to their advantage, so what am I so afraid of? I just need to be more thoughtful about how. I won't go overboard. I won't put any rare animals in danger or erase anyone's memories. Which means: deleting this morning's conversation with Tom is off the table. I'm just going to have to suffer through the ensuing awkwardness between us. What's done is done on that count. But things don't have to *continue* to suck, do they? I don't necessarily have to spend homecoming alone in my room, as Tom's mom snaps photos of him and Amy Taylor in their front yard. I don't even have to spend it as Mina and Daniel's sidekick. I have other options. *Hot* options. Options that maybe just need a little *nudge* in the right direction.

I pick up my pen from the nightstand.

Write what you know.

I still have a note in my backpack that reads: *Hey, Slim. You really should skip seventh period sometime. With me.*

This is what I know. So I write a single sentence on the blank page.

> On Thursday, October 15, Luke Carr asks Gracie Byrne to skip seventh period with him.

That's it. That's all I'm going to do. I'm not screwing with elements I can't control, I'm not erasing anything, or making anyone do something that they normally wouldn't. I'm just going to use this journal to *remind* Luke of what he was going to do anyway. What he had *already* asked me, in fact. So it's not even like I'm putting a new idea in his head. I'm just helping the idea that he *already* had come back out. Instead of saying it, I'm writing it. That's all.

I lock eyes with Hank, who is watching me from the spot where he is curled up at the foot of my bed. One of his ears is sticking straight up, like an antenna.

"Don't judge. It's fine," I say.

Really.

I reread what I've written one more time. Simple. Elegant. To the point. Once this little spark gets things moving, I really won't even need to touch this journal again. I'll put it back under the bed with the dust bunnies.

But instead of closing the journal, I stare at the sentence I wrote, thinking. My pen hovers above the page.

There is *one* other thing, though.

Because Mrs. D has been out sick, we still haven't received our grades for that hideous trig test I forgot to study for.

And . . . that test counts for a third of our grade this semester. I *know* I blew that test. But it was due to circumstances beyond my control. Well, okay . . . there were circumstances. That I didn't really know I was controlling, at least not at first. However. A bad grade in trig can really screw things up for me, from a college preparatory perspective. And it's not like I *wouldn't* have studied if I'd remembered. I just forgot. I didn't *intentionally* blow off the test.

So I also write: *Gracie doesn't fail her trig test.*

It's fine.

Really.

It's not like I'm even asking for an A or anything.

Quickly, I also scribble: *or get a D.*

Because a D could really screw things up too.

Okay. That's all.

I shake out my hands and close the journal.

I'll let the universe take it from here.

BASOREXIA

I WAKE UP WITH A STOMACH FULL OF BUTTERFLIES. AND birds. And a hive of bees. There may even be a bat flying around in there too. I'm not really sure what is going to happen today, but I know *something* will. And I'm already starting to have second thoughts. What if everything goes off the rails, like with the owl?

No, I tell myself in the mirror as I blow-dry my hair. *No second thoughts. You didn't understand how it worked before. Now you do. You've got this.*

I mean, maybe I've got it. My hope is that since I kept it really, really limited this time, without any fantastical embellishments, nothing too chaotic is going happen. Plus, there's no sense in worrying about it now. The words are already on the page and I'm not about to mess around with ripping them out.

I toss my hair and try to convince myself that I should be doing the exact opposite of worrying. Calm, cool, and collected people do not worry, right? In fact, journal or no journal, I should spend the rest of this day doing the exact opposite of anything "regular" Gracie Byrne would do, because it really feels like my primary problem is . . . me.

Step one. I'm going to channel my inner Mina and wear something *amazing*. I open my closet. Do I have anything amazing? Not especially so. What about something . . . black? Black is sophisticated. Chic. *Wait a second* . . . the crop top I bought at the mall with Hannah! It's still in the bag on the floor of my closet. I fish it out of the bag, pull off the tags, and yank it over my head. It's very . . . cropped. *Don't overthink it, Gracie.* I pair it with my tightest jeans and gold hoop earrings. And I still have Mina's high-heeled boots that I need to return from the night we went to *The Rocky Horror Picture Show*. I can wear those.

But maybe I should call and ask her first?

No! What am I saying? Opposite Gracie would not ask *permission*. Plus, Mina won't care.

I pull on a thick pair of socks and the boots, and then step in front of my mirror for the final touch: Cherries Jubilee lips.

Now I just need to get through the drive to school.

Mom and Katherine are still in the entryway getting ready to leave when I come down the stairs. "I was just about to yell for you to come down," my mom says as she shrugs on her coat. "You are going to be late. Tom's already waiting by your car."

Let him wait, I think. That's what Opposite Gracie would do. She'd be fashionably late.

I help Katherine zip up her windbreaker while my mom gathers the rest of her things.

"Wish me luck, Katherine," I whisper.

She doesn't say anything.

My mom gives me a closer look, and I can tell she's contemplating whether she should say anything about the (very cropped) crop top. "Don't break your ankle in those boots. Let's go, Katherine." She takes her hand and opens the door.

And then Katherine turns her head at the threshold and says, "Good luck!"

I smile. Katherine actually wishing me luck is even luckier than a four-leaf clover.

I inhale a deep, cleansing breath, throw on my coat, grab my backpack, and step out onto the porch.

Let's do this.

I take my time walking to the car. Mainly because I can't really hurry in Mina's boots.

Tom is standing on the sidewalk, waiting.

"Uh . . . hi," he says. "I was just about to ring your bell."

"Sorry," I say, as I unlock the door. "I slept in."

Wait, would Opposite Gracie apologize for being late? Probably not, but it's fine.

I lean over and pop the lock on the passenger side so he can get in.

"Hi," he says again as he sits, and I can't be sure, but it feels like he has paused to take in my new look. I glance into the rearview mirror to check my Cherries Jubilee lips.

"Hi," I say, trying on my most nonchalant smile as I fight the urge to apologize a second time for being late. I start the car, pull out onto the road, and tune the radio to the news so it's not so uncomfortably quiet. Also, the news seems safer than music because most songs are either about love or sex. Or both.

A reporter is talking about Baby Jessica—this little girl who fell into a well yesterday in Texas. There's a massive rescue effort underway.

"Wow," I say. "I sure hope they're able to get Baby Jessica out of the well."

"Yeah," says Tom.

And then neither one of us speaks for the rest of the drive. It's excruciating. I almost cry tears of relief as I pull into a spot in the school parking lot and turn off the ignition. But as I'm gathering up my things, Tom stays still. He looks like he's psyching himself up to say something.

"Gracie," he says.

Oh, no. No, no, no.

"Can we talk about yesterday?"

I'm going to have to put a stop to this discussion, pronto. What I need to project is that yesterday was no big deal, I've already forgotten about it, and he should too.

"Tom. There's nothing to talk about. Really!"

"But—"

"I think I hear the bell," I say, as I fling the car door open. "I can't be late to trig. See you tomorrow!"

I take off across the parking lot as fast as possible before he's even out of his seat.

I stumble into trig five minutes after the bell rings, feeling like I've run a marathon. Mrs. Drazkowski is back and finally passing out our graded tests. "Seems like a lot of you needed to review the practice problems a few more times," she says as she walks down one of the aisles, dropping bombs on people right and left. "We only had one A in this class."

Paige Dunn holds her test in her hands and looks like she's about to cry. And I mean, c'mon. I'm sure she's the A, but she's probably upset that it's an A–.

I slide into my seat just as she gets to me.

"You're late, Gracie."

"I'm sorry," I answer, my voice all breathless. "Do you want me to go back to the office for a late slip?"

She sighs. "No. Let's just let it slide today." And then she puts my test face down on top of the desk. "Nice job," she says.

As she moves on to her next victim, I flip over my test.

I got a 98 percent. The best score I've received on any high school math test, ever. And I studied for all the rest.

Don't feel guilty about it, I say to myself as I stuff the test into my backpack before anyone can see my score. Opposite Gracie does not feel any guilt.

The universe has selected 98 percent on your behalf.

* * *

"Nice boots," Mina says when I walk into English.

"Thanks," I answer absently, before I remember they are hers. "You don't mind, do you?"

"Of course not," she says, and then adds, "Are you okay? You seem a little . . ." She waves her arms around to indicate how I seem.

Like a jellyfish?

Like someone on drugs?

Like a drowning swimmer calling for help?

"I'm fine," I say. "*Great*, in fact." What is it with me and *great* right now? It's like I've forgotten all the superior vocabulary words at my disposal.

"Cool," she says. "But . . . you did hear about Tom and Amy Taylor, right?"

"Of course!" I smile big. "He told me."

"I still say you should have asked him. Amy Taylor is boring."

I don't tell her that I did. And that I was too late. And now everything is weird.

"Hey," I say. "I need to do some research in the library at lunch again today, so I'll see you in French." I really need to avoid the cafeteria situation until things calm down. Mina gives me a look like she doesn't quite believe me, but she says, "Sure. See you in French."

In the library, I watch the clock ticking. Forty-five minutes until art class. Forty-five minutes until whatever is going to happen with Luke happens. I try to do some of my trig homework, but the numbers dissolve in front of me just like they did on the day of the test that I have now scored a magical 98 percent on. I switch to *Macbeth*, which my entire class is reading for English, but all I can think about is the lesson on the Owl as a Symbol that Mr. Rossi taught that nobody remembers.

Ten minutes before sixth period, I swipe on another coat of Cherries Jubilee.

It's time.

The second I walk into the art studio, it's like the temperature has changed. I feel warm and weirdly exposed, like I'm underneath a spotlight.

Luke's eyes are on me immediately. "Nice boots," he says as I sit down. Just what Mina said, only the delivery is different. Mina was appreciating the boots. Luke is appreciating me in the boots.

"Thanks," I say.

He gives me one of his slow, enigmatic smiles. I'm tempted to look away, slightly uncomfortable in the Luke spotlight, but instead I hold his gaze. Opposite Gracie. Opposite *Grace*.

He gets up from his seat. "Want me to grab you a set of paints?"

"Sure."

We're now working on watercolor landscapes. I'm doing autumn leaves. He's doing a stormy sea. Near the end of class, he leans close to me—*so* close—to look.

"Seems a shame to be missing the real thing while we're stuck in here." His breath tickles my ear.

"The real thing?"

"The leaves," he says. "Outside. It's a beautiful day."

My heart rate picks up. *On Thursday, October 15, Luke Carr asks Gracie Byrne to skip seventh period with him.*

The bell rings. We put our paintings and paints away. Luke follows me out the door and walks with me down the hall until we get close to the entrance to the gym.

"Well, see you tomorrow," I say, wondering if I've misunderstood the rules of this confounding journal yet again. Except I did get a 98 percent on that test . . .

But then he stops and says, "Hey."

Here it comes, here it comes, here it comes . . .

I lean against the same set of lockers where he previously asked me if I wanted to get high in the parking lot and cross my boots.

"Want to bail?" He runs a hand through his sumptuous hair, something I'm beginning to notice that he does a lot.

I try to look surprised. "Bail?"

"Yeah, blow off seventh period. Go for a drive."

Boring Gracie does not skip class, but Opposite Gracie *totally* does.

"Okay," I say. "Let's go."

Together, we walk past the entrance to the gym, past all our boring classmates walking by on their way to boring seventh period, and push out a side exit door. My eyes are temporarily blinded by the bright October sun.

The doors clang shut behind us.

"This way," Luke says, and he leads me to his car—a black Jeep Cherokee.

He opens the door for me and I settle into the passenger seat. There's a shoebox full of cassette tapes on the floor, and I pick it up and start looking through them, just to have something to focus on.

"Your choice," he says, once he's behind the wheel.

I randomly pull a cassette from the box and hand it to him. It's The Cure's *Kiss Me, Kiss Me, Kiss Me* album.

"Cute," he says.

Oh, God. Does he think I picked that on purpose?

No. Stop, I tell myself. Opposite Gracie does not care.

Luke pushes in the cassette and swings out of the parking lot while winding his window down. I wind mine down too. The wind whips my hair everywhere as houses and telephone poles and trees whizz by in a blur.

He slows along the perimeter of Frick Park and pulls into an open space. We get out of the car.

"C'mon," he says. "I'll show you my favorite spot."

The two of us crunch through fallen leaves, me doing my best to maneuver the park trail in high-heeled boots. After a bit, Luke turns down a branching path that snakes through a tunnel of trees. It's shaded and almost dark in the tunnel, aside from the tiny beams of sunlight that break through the canopy. Leaves drift down on our heads. It feels like we are walking at a slight incline, and eventually we emerge into a tiny clearing at the edge of a ravine. All around us is an explosion of color. Red. Yellow. Gold. Orange. Crimson. Cornsilk. Amber. Flame.

Luke sits down on a bench and I sit next to him. *Now what?* I really have no idea because I just wrote that single line: *On Thursday, October 15, Luke Carr asks Gracie Byrne to skip seventh period with him.*

The rest I'm going to have to improvise. And I'm realizing now that thinking fast and being cool, calm, and collected in the moment are not really my strengths.

He pulls something out of his jacket pocket. A cigarette? It's hand-rolled. A joint.

"Want some?" he asks, after he lights it and takes a hit.

I've never actually smoked a joint before.

"Sure," I say, going along with my new commitment to do the opposite of what I usually do. Though the issue is, I don't know what I'm doing. At all. Which is embarrassing.

I hold the joint in my lips but must clearly look confused about the mechanics because he laughs.

"Inhale slowly," he explains. "Hold it in for a minute, *then* blow it out."

I do what he says, but I inhale a little too hard and get bits of it in my mouth. I cough so hard that I imagine I must sound like someone with tuberculosis.

Luke laughs again. "You are so adorable."

And I'm struck by a feeling of annoyance at that, because I don't think I want to be adorable. Mysterious, maybe. Intriguing. *Enigmatic.*

We sit in silence for a few minutes, looking out at the view while I wait to feel the effects of the joint. Problem is, I don't really know what I'm waiting for. Am I supposed to feel different? Happier? More relaxed? More *something*?

"I don't feel anything," I say.

"Try again." He takes another hit and passes it back.

I try it again, this time concentrating on getting the process right: inhale slowly, hold it in, let it out. A long stream of smoke comes out this time, but I still don't think I'm doing it right.

He laughs and watches me go a few more times. Inhale. Hold it in. Exhale. Cough.

"Maybe it doesn't work on me," I say.

"You have to give it a few minutes."

He seems content to sit in silence, but I need to find something to talk about, mainly so I can shut out my racing thoughts. "I like your jacket," I say, running my finger down the sleeve of the army jacket he's been wearing ever since I cast him in my swanky nightclub story. "It looks vintage."

"Thanks." Luke looks at the jacket like he just realized he was wearing it. "Yeah, I think it is."

"Where did you get it?"

And then he gets this look on his face, like Mina when I

asked her about what happened in English class on the day of the owl. He shrugs.

"I don't remember, really. I've had it for a while."

I wonder if it just appeared in his closet the morning after I wrote that story.

I don't just live in reality, I MAKE reality!

Luke runs a hand through his hair again, and looks me up and down. He does his signature half grin. He has full, almost pouty lips.

I can feel my palms getting sweaty because now that I've covered the jacket, I've run out of things to talk about. My mind churns. I need to channel some of that Magenta energy I was feeling that night at Kings Court. So what would Magenta do? Based on the plot of *The Rocky Horror Picture Show*, which honestly was pretty chaotic, she'd possibly either murder him or have sex with him. *So, okay, maybe not either of those.* What would Slim do? Slim, I think, would kiss him, just to see what it was like.

There's a word for that.

Basorexia: A sudden urge to kiss someone.

Since my last (and only) kiss was an accident, I'm not sure how to get things started.

Maybe I should just be direct.

"So," I say, "Are we going to kiss or what?"

My face immediately goes crimson. Luke looks . . . surprised? Slightly intrigued? Maybe?

I had this idea that I was going to be all bold and confident, but it just came out *weird*. Like I couldn't keep my inner monologue under wraps.

But then he says, "Go for it."

So I do.

I slide closer to him on the bench. I raise my lips to his and, just like that, we're *kissing*. And it's 100 percent on purpose. He tastes a lot like the joint we've been smoking, and a little like Big Red gum. As I wonder if I'm even doing it right, or I guess *well*, he maneuvers me so that I'm in his lap on the bench. His hands squeeze my hips. His tongue pushes into my mouth. Somehow, this is not exactly what I expected. I expected it to be more like a movie. I expected there to be more chemistry. Like Bogart and Bacall. Like the idea of it in my head when I was wearing a clinging satin chartreuse dress and chandelier earrings and he was in an army uniform. When I could blow smoke rings like a pro and he sent me a bottle of champagne. Which brings up some interesting questions: Like, is it normal to daydream about your fantasy of a person while you are actually kissing that person in real life? Is it normal to feel as though you are watching yourself do something instead of feeling as though you are an active participant? Somehow, I'm floating outside myself again, wondering if I'll ever feel right *inside* myself. If I'll ever feel totally at ease just being me.

Luke keeps kissing me but there's something niggling at the edges of my consciousness. *Kiss me, kiss me, kiss me.*

They kissed.

Ils se sont embrassés.

That's it. I have a French test this afternoon.

I pull back. "I have a test in French."

"Right now?"

"Well . . . soon," I say, catching my breath. "Eighth period."

He lets out a short laugh. "Well, we can't have you miss your French test, can we? Let's get you back to school where you belong, Grace."

I thought he'd be annoyed, but he doesn't seem to mind. If anything, he seems slightly amused.

But maybe that's because of the pot.

As Luke drives us back to school, I start to feel kind of weird, like my lips have gone numb. Was it from the kissing? Like a delayed chemical reaction? I don't know. But I can't worry about that at the moment because I'm worried about Luke's driving, which seems erratic. I hold on tight to the hand rest and try to focus on the road ahead. It appears to be coming at me like a freight train. "Slow down!" I say, but he shakes his head and laughs.

"I'm going *under* the speed limit right now."

Is he?

He lets me out near the East Wing entrance of the school and I make it to French class without a minute to spare. Mina stares at me when I walk in.

"You don't look so good," she says. The room is spinning as I sit.

Two minutes later, I throw up. I don't even make it to the trash can. I throw up right on the floor. In front of everybody, including Amy Taylor, Tom's date for homecoming.

AGENT OF CHAOS

I'M SENT TO THE SCHOOL NURSE, WHO IS NOW LOOKING AT me disapprovingly. I think she knows that I am chemically altered (not from the kiss, but from the pot), but she is thankfully going to go along with my story that I must have eaten something bad at lunch. "I'm going to have to call your mother to come pick you up."

"No, no . . . don't do that," I tell her. Mom will be furious if I cause her to miss a shift at work. And I don't want her to see me like this. She'll probably guess what's up. And she's got enough to worry about already—Katherine, money, a to-do list that never seems to get done—so I'd rather her not have to add her daughter's "brain on drugs" to the list.

I'm panicking. I need to get this figured out, fast. "What if . . . I get a ride with a friend?" Not Luke. I don't even think he returned to school after dropping me off. And Mina and Daniel take the bus, so that leaves . . . "Tom Broder!" I say. "He's my neighbor. He can give me a ride home. Tom Broder. He can drive my car."

"Do you know where he is this period?" she asks.

No, I don't.

"Somewhere . . ." I say weakly.

She looks at me disapprovingly one more time. "Let me see what I can do. But we'll still have to call your mom to make sure it's okay." And then she walks out the door.

There are no windows in the nurse's room and it's stressing me out. I feel like I'm stuck in a prison cell. *What the hell is wrong with my face?* I touch it to make sure it's still there. As soon as I start to wonder if the nurse forgot about me in here, I hear her voice in the hallway.

"She's not feeling well and her mother is at work. She says you might be able to drive her home."

"Yeah, no problem," another voice says. Tom. Thank God. I just want to go home. Right now.

The door opens.

"He can take you home," she says. "I will call your mother to let her know."

I pick up my backpack and meet Tom in the hallway.

"You got sick?" he asks.

"Uh-huh," I say, using every ounce of effort at my disposal to try and sound normal. "*Thank you* for taking me home."

Eighth period is still in session so the halls are empty. I stop at the first water fountain I see.

"Need some water," I tell Tom.

"Okay." He leans against the wall while I drink.

I feel like I could down a gallon of water, I'm so thirsty.

"You . . . done?" He pushes back from the wall as I wipe my lips.

"Uh-huh."

We continue on to the parking lot.

"You do know how to drive, right?" I ask, as we walk to my car.

"Yes," he says, making a face.

I hand him the keys and Tom opens the door for me.

He gets in on the other side and studies my face, like he's trying to figure something out. I watch the corners of his lips twitch.

"Oh, wow," he says.

"What?" I ask.

"You are *so* high."

"No, no, no, I ate something bad. Bad lunch."

"Uh-huh," he says.

He steers the car out of the parking lot and I clutch the arm rest.

Why can't anybody just drive normally today?

After we pull into Katherine's driveway, Tom helps me out of my seat. He helps me unlock the front door. He puts my backpack on the bench in the entryway.

"Tom," I say. "I think I'm having a stroke. I can't feel my face."

He laughs. "You are not having a stroke. You are just really, really high."

"Uggggggh . . ." I hang my head in disappointment. "Tom, this *sucks.* I thought being high was supposed to make you happy! I thought that it was supposed to be fun."

"Maybe not when you smoke *way* too much? Where did you get it from anyway? You don't strike me as a get-high-at-school-in-the-middle-of-the-day kind of person."

"Luke Carr. We skipped seventh period."

"That guy? The one who looks like he's from *21 Jump Street*?"

Now it's my turn to make a face. "He gives me more of a Matt Dillon vibe, but anyway. We're in art class together."

"Okay, well, maybe sit down." He leads me toward the sofa in the sitting room and I curl up on it.

I still do *not* feel good.

"I'm so thirsty, Tom. Everything is spinning."

"Put one foot on the floor."

"This is scary."

"It will wear off."

He disappears for a minute and comes back with a glass of water. "Drink this," he says.

"I'm so thirsty," I say again.

"I know. You've mentioned it."

I look at the clock on the mantel in the sitting room. It's three forty-five.

Shit.

"Tom! I have to get Katherine at day care. At four."

"Hmm," he says. "I don't know if you can do that right now."

"I have to!" I say.

"Where's your phone?" he asks.

"The hallway. In the alcove under the stairs."

He disappears into the hallway but then his head reappears, the yellow spiral cord of the phone stretched as far as it will go. "What's your mom's number at work?"

"It's 867-5309." I start laughing about the fact that I've given him the number from that song. And . . . now I can't stop . . . laughing . . . Is *this* the fun part? I laugh and laugh. Oh my God. I can barely breathe.

"Gracie, for real. What's her number? For real? Focus."

I give it to him. "That's the main nurse's station at Mercy Hospital. Ask for Margaret Byrne."

"I'll be right back."

"But *shhhhhh* . . . Don't tell her about this, Tom."

"I've got it covered," he says as he disappears back into the hallway.

I sing a few bars of the 867-5309 song to myself while I wait.

Tom is gone for like an hour. Or maybe five minutes.

What is time anyway?

Is it a construct?

He comes back into the sitting room.

"Okay. It's all worked out. Your mom called the day care

place. Katherine can stay till six when your mom gets off work. I told her you were still feeling sick."

"Oh, thank you, thank you, thank you," I say.

"C'mon," he says pulling me up by the hands from the sofa. "You just need a long nap and everything will be fine when you wake up."

And now all I can think about is the fact that our hands are touching. In a way that's more like I'm a toddler and he's my parent, but still. I follow him up the creaky stairs.

"Do you think time is just a social construct?" I ask him when we reach the landing.

"I think you've entered the philosophical phase of this little trip," he says as he pulls me up the remaining stairs.

"What trip?" I ask. "We're talking about *time*."

He shakes his head like he's exasperated. Like I've exasperated him. "Okay. Well. Einstein determined that time is relative—the rate in which it passes depends on your frame of reference. So, for example, right now our frames of reference might be a *little* different because I drank a Coke forty-five minutes ago to get through eighth period and you are really, really high."

"HAAAAA," I say. We *finally* get to the top of the stairs. I tug at the string on his sweatshirt.

"Why do you always have to smell so good?"

And at that, he is speechless. We stand there for a minute at the top of the stairs, so close.

I'm too close. I have so much basorexia right now, I don't know what to do. I want to know what it's like to kiss *him*. What if . . . I kissed two boys on the same day? That would be pretty freaking Opposite Gracie of me, wouldn't it? But our frames of reference or whatever he was just talking about aren't even on the same planet right now. Plus, he's going to homecoming with Amy Taylor. And *I*, I suddenly realize with horror, most likely have vomit breath.

"Gracie . . ." Tom says.

But I cut him off by stumbling down the hall. "Want to see my room?" I ask.

He follows me down the hall but stays in the doorway. "Wow, you are messy," he says as I pull off Mina's boots one at a time and drop them with a *clunk* on the hardwood floor.

"I'm an agent of CHAOS!" I tell him. "You don't even *know*." And then I collapse on my bed, laughing.

"Okay, Spicoli," he says. "I gotta go."

I don't want him to go.

"Tom, I think I'm dying of thirst."

"You are not dying," he says.

He turns toward the hallway.

"Tom!"

"Yeah?"

"Say *Monongahela* three times fast!"

He rolls his eyes and then squints at me. "Only if you do it first."

"I can't. I don't think I can even say it once."

And then he smiles big enough that I can see the adorable little gap between his two front teeth. His smile is lopsided, imperfect, but I think that's what makes it so absolutely perfect.

"You just did. Try to sleep, Gracie."

I close my eyes and say a prayer that my face will be back to normal soon.

When I wake up around seven p.m., my room is dark. There is a tall glass of water on the nightstand next to my bed. I pick it up and drink the entire thing. The shade of my blind is pulled all the way down to the windowsill. I hear the TV on downstairs and plates rattling in the kitchen. Hank barks a few times and then stops. Slowly, painfully, the rest of the day comes back to me. Kissing Luke Carr in Frick Park. Throwing up on the floor in French class. Tom driving me home. I sit up in bed with a jolt. Me asking him . . . *why he always smelled so good?*

Oh, God. I am such a complete disaster.

I hear my mom's footsteps on the stairs and the light from the hallway spills into my room when she opens my door.

"Gracie?"

She walks in and sits on my bed, reaching over to turn on the lamp on my nightstand. She's still in her hospital scrubs. "How are you feeling?"

"I think I'm okay now," I tell her. Other than my mouth feeling like the Sahara Desert.

She puts her hand on my forehead. "Doesn't seem like you have a fever, so that's good." She studies me.

I do my best to conjure up a food-poisoning face. "I think I just ate something that didn't agree with me at lunch."

Not sure if she buys it.

"Well, it was nice of Tom to drive you home."

I can feel my face heating. *What else did I do or say that was totally embarrassing*? Everything. Probably everything.

"I'm sorry about Katherine," I say.

"It's okay," she says. "It all worked out. Mrs. Nakamura's son was there cooking with them and she really seemed to be having fun. Did you know he's a chef downtown?"

"Yeah," I say. "He makes these amazing gyozas."

My mom nods. "It seems like she's really doing well over there. She's much more relaxed in the evenings now."

"I know."

"I just wish it wasn't so expensive," she says.

"Is it really expensive?" I guess I hadn't thought much about the costs.

She rubs her eyes. "Anything like that is. But a few extra hours won't make a big difference," she says. "I don't even think Susan will charge me. I just worry about what might happen when she needs full-time care."

Full-time care. That's the thing about Katherine's needs. They are only going to get more . . . needy.

"Can I get you anything?" Mom asks. "A little toast? Are

you hungry? Jack and I are making breakfast for dinner if you think you can handle some scrambled eggs."

I'm starving.

"I think so," I say. I know so, but I'm trying to keep up my recovering-from-food-poisoning cover. "I'll be down in a minute."

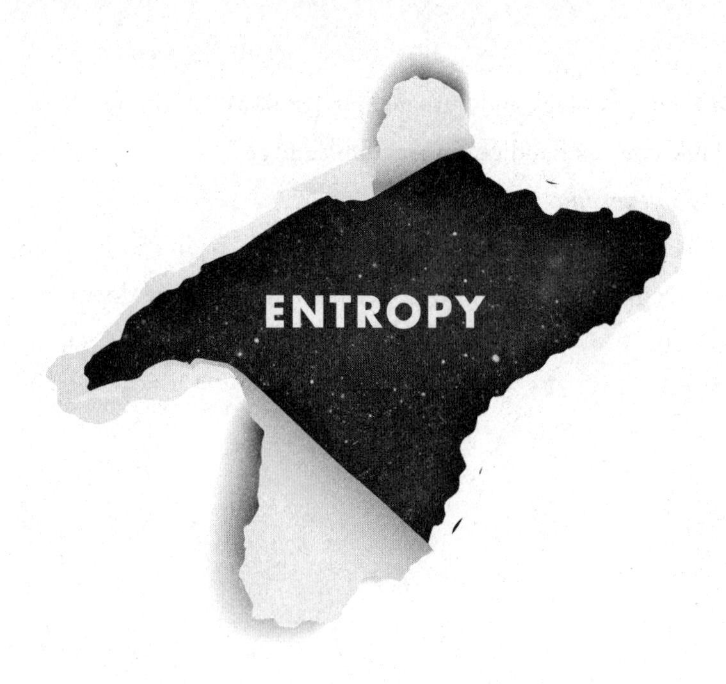

ENTROPY

IN THE MORNING, I CONVINCE MY MOM THAT I'M STILL FEELing sick and she lets me stay home, even though I suspect that *she* suspects that I'm faking it at this point. Maybe she senses that I just need a day off. I hear her in the alcove below the stairs as she calls the Broders to let them know I won't be able to drive Tom.

After she, Katherine, and Jack leave, the house is quiet. I hear the clock ticking on the mantel downstairs and lie back in my bed, staring up at the crack on the ceiling.

Maybe I can be homeschooled and I'll never have to go back at all.

I sigh. *Right.* Who would homeschool me? I'd have to homeschool myself. There's no getting around it—on Monday, I will have to go back. My blind is still pulled down and the room is dim and shadowy. I wonder if Tom took the bus today, and if he was late. I wonder if people are talking about me throwing up in French, and if Luke is curious about why I'm not at school.

Stop, I say to myself. *Stop. Just stop thinking about it.*

A long weekend is just what I need to get my head back on straight.

It's been so long since I've had an entire day alone in the house by myself that I don't even know what to do. I go downstairs and eat a bowl of Honey Nut Cheerios. I camp out at the big desk in the study and try to get up to speed on *passé composé* and *imparfait* for the French test that I will have to make up on Monday. Then I pull out a couple volumes of my grandfather's old unabridged dictionary, as well as a few of his other books, looking for words. I find a few good ones: *ambiguphobia*: fear of being misunderstood that leads to excessive explanations (been there!); *crapulous*: the crappy feeling one gets from overindulging in food or drink (been *there* too!); *entropy*: breaking down, collapsing into disorder; and *hiraeth*: a Welsh word that means a homesickness or longing for a place you can't return to, or that never was.

Hiraeth is the one that really stands out. It feels like a magical word.

A home you can't return to.

I picture our old house—the one we lived in when my parents were together. It was smaller than Katherine's but more comfortable. It didn't smell like dust. It didn't have ancient radiators that clanked and hissed. The kitchen was updated. I revisit memories of my dad making pancakes on Saturdays for breakfast. The day that Jack and I built a snow fort in the backyard. Afternoons with Hannah in my room, listening to Casey Kasem's *American Top 40* radio show on my pink boom box, waiting for just the right moment to record our favorite songs. Now everything is so different. So mixed up.

I put the books back on the shelf and go to the kitchen to get another bowl of Cheerios. I take it with me to the sitting room sofa, turn on the TV, wrap myself in a blanket, and settle in as Hank jumps up to join me.

The news is on. Baby Jessica is still stuck in the well. She's been down there, alone and scared, for almost two full days now.

A thought occurs to me.

Maybe I should write something about Baby Jessica tonight? Maybe I can use the journal to, somehow, help her get unstuck? Maybe—

No. I think what my recent owl fiasco proved is that I still need a *lot* more practice figuring that journal out. First of all, I probably shouldn't mess with big, high-stakes events because the transition from words on the page to actual, real-world results still feels a little . . . unpredictable. I mean, yesterday was an interesting experiment, to be sure. It seems like keeping it personal and *very* limited is best, but everything went off the rails as soon as I had to improvise. Maybe whatever I write shouldn't be too open-ended? Satisfying stories should have more than a beginning; they need a middle and end, right?

I sigh. I'm just guessing. I don't really know. And the one person who could possibly explain it to me—Katherine—doesn't remember. I sigh.

Days of Our Lives is just starting when I change the channel. I slurp a big spoonful of Honey Nut Cheerios as the voiceover intones: "*Like sands through the hourglass, so are the days of our lives.*"

SONDER

I'M LYING IN THE GRASS, LOOKING UP THROUGH THE yellow-orange leaves of the maple tree in Katherine's backyard and thinking about this word I found in one of my grandfather's books: *sonder*. *Sonder* is the realization that everyone—people we know as well as strangers we've never met—is living their own story. But we aren't really aware of those other stories, because we only ever get to experience our own. I wonder if this means that—no matter how hard we try—we can never truly understand one another? It sure feels that way sometimes. What a lonely idea.

"Are you trying to hear the highway breathing?" A voice to my left startles me out of my thoughts.

I perch up on my elbows and see Tom standing at the back gate. *What is he doing here?*

My mind flashes to Thursday afternoon, when I asked him why he always smelled so good and who knows what else. And then I try not to think about what else, because the story in *my* head right now is already 100 percent humiliation. I try to appear normal.

"I'm sorry, what?"

"Talking Heads. 'And She Was.'"

A little shiver runs up my spine. "And She Was" is my favorite Talking Heads song. It's about a dreamy girl who is lying in the grass, listening to the sounds of the nearby highway, and then she floats up in the air and drifts around all over town. This has always seemed thrilling to me: to not be bound by the laws of gravity, like an astronaut. In fact, I wish I could lift up off the ground and float away right now. But I can't. I'm not going anywhere. And Tom is still standing at my back gate, so I guess I need to talk to him.

"Ah, yes. I forgot how much you like the music of my uncle, David Byrne."

"I *knew* you were related." He smiles.

There's an awkward silence until Hank bangs out the door and starts going bananas at the gate, his tail ticking back and forth like a whip. But he doesn't bark. He hasn't barked at Tom in a while now. Lately, Hank more or less throws himself at him with embarrassing, obsessive devotion.

"Can I come in?" Tom asks.

"Sure," I say, sitting up cross-legged and brushing leaves off of the sleeves of my sweater. Hank runs circles around Tom as he walks over and sits down next to me in the grass. He's wearing those damn glasses again, clearly unaware that they're my kryptonite.

"Hi," he says.

"Hi."

Tom gives Hank's ears a scratch. "Just wanted to make sure you were okay. Since you weren't at school on Friday."

"Oh. I'm fine," I say. "Just had to keep up the food poisoning ruse for my mom. Plus, I wasn't quite ready to make up the French test I missed."

He nods.

"Thank you," I add. "For bringing me home and sorting everything out with my mom and Katherine. I hope you didn't miss anything important eighth period."

He shakes his head no. "Don't worry about it. I think I owe you more than a few favors after all those rides to school. *And* for getting me out of eighth period. That was a bonus, actually."

I pick up a leaf and start stripping pieces of it away from the middle stem.

"Plus," he adds. "It was all, sort of . . . entertaining?" His eyes meet mine and I flush.

I do not want to rehash my high times, so I stop him there. "Okay, but we don't have to reminisce about it. *Please.*"

"As you wish."

We both sit in silence for another minute, or maybe an hour, until Tom breaks it.

"Anyway, while we are on the subject of driving to school, guess what?"

"What?" I ask.

"I got a VW Beetle. We picked it up yesterday."

He got a car.

That's why he's here. To tell me he doesn't need me to drive him anymore. Oh, God, did he go out and buy a car just to avoid any more weird encounters with me?

"Ah, cool . . ." I say. "What color?"

"Green. It kind of looks like an M&M. And the inside door handle on the passenger side is broken, so you have to wind down the window and open it from the outside. But it was cheap, at least. All that my summer camp counselor savings could afford."

"Sounds great." There I go with *great* again.

"Anyhow, I don't know, maybe we can still carpool, just take turns or something?"

This, I suspect, he's just throwing in to be nice. Plus, even if he does mean it, I don't think I can handle being trapped in the car with Tom after the combined awkwardness of me asking him to homecoming, Thursday with Luke, and whatever else I might have said when I was stoned out of my mind.

I'll let him off the hook.

"Don't you still have cross-country practice after school?"

"Yeah," he says. "Until Thanksgiving. And then basketball practice starts."

"Probably best if we just take our own cars then, don't you think?"

He nods. "Yeah, probably. But come over and check it out sometime." He pauses and then nudges my knee with his leg. "I'll miss the Seville, though. And our morning conversations. And you spraying Christina Merlotti with muddy water. I don't think the Beetle will be able to cause the same amount of chaos."

"Ha," I say. *That's me: agent of chaos.*

"So . . ." He looks like he's searching for words. "No longer fellow carpoolers, but still friends?"

"Still friends," I say.

Friends is really for the best, even if it stings.

Tom gets up and brushes off his pants.

"Hey, how'd you do on that math test anyway? I only got an eighty-six. And I heard some asshole in your class ruined the curve for everyone."

Me, Tom, I think. *That asshole would be me.*

"I did okay," I say, without going into specifics.

"Cool, cool." He nods several times. And, it could be my imagination, but does he also seem kind of . . . nervous? Jumpy? Or maybe just a little overly caffeinated. But I guess that's really just his normal setting.

"Well, see you tomorrow. Not first thing in the morning. I mean . . . at school."

I get it. We are not carpooling.

"See you at school."

When he's almost to the gate, he turns around. "I don't know why, but that Talking Heads song kind of reminds me of you."

The shiver that ran up my spine earlier is back. Why does he say stuff like this? It's like he gets me on this subconscious level, but *consciously*, he's completely unaware of it.

I brush his comment off with a joke. "Didn't you know? Uncle David wrote it for me."

"Aha," he says. "Now it all makes sense."

Once he's gone, I lie back in the grass and imagine myself lifting off the ground, floating in the sky, light as air, defying gravity.

ADORABLE

ON MONDAY, I DRIVE TO SCHOOL ALONE. TOM'S NEW-OLD Beetle is still in the Broders' carport when I pull out onto Shady Avenue, and I wonder if he will be late. I make up my French test at lunch, so manage to avoid the cafeteria entirely. I also consider skipping out on Art, *and* PE, *and* French, but I already missed school on Friday, and while I can avoid lunch for days if need be, I do have to go to my actual classes eventually, so I might as well bite the bullet.

Luke says, "Hey," when he sits down next to me and I don't think I've ever felt more awkward for forty-five minutes straight. (And I feel awkward a lot of the time.) Does he know I threw up in French after our Frick Park outing? And the kissing . . . it was *off*. Wasn't it? I mean, I don't have a lot of data points to compare it to, but still.

After the bell rings, Luke surprises me by walking me to PE, but maybe it's just habit? When we get to the gym, I expect him to keep going. But instead, he stops and rests his hand against the locker behind me just like he did that day that Tom walked by and saw us, and now all I can think of is: *What if Tom walks by again?* But Tom and I are "just friends" so I guess it doesn't even matter.

Luke's voice snaps me out of it. "It's a really nice day again . . ."

I thought it was kind of windy this morning, but I just nod and say, "Yeah."

"Want to go to our spot?"

Our spot?

In this case, I just say what I'm thinking, but without the mental emphasis on *our*: "Our spot?"

"Yeah, I hit up my guy over the weekend and got some good shit."

Okay, obviously he does not know about me throwing up in French. And about my face practically melting off and Tom driving me home and . . . I flash to the two of us on the stairs: *Why do you always have to smell so good?*

Oh, God. I still cringe thinking about it.

"I can't," I say. "I have a test."

"You have a test in PE?"

It was the first thing that came to mind.

"Yes," I say. "A . . . fitness test."

He shrugs and laughs. "You are so adorable. Maybe tomorrow?"

There he goes again with *adorable.* Like I'm a puppy or something.

"Maybe!" And then I duck out from under his arm and head into the gym.

In the locker room, Christina Merlotti tells me she loves my outfit.

ON TUESDAY, MINA AND DANIEL TEAM UP TO PEPPER ME WITH questions about what happened before French class last week, but I stick to my "bad lunch" guns. They both back off when I finally say, "*Please.* I do not want to talk about it," even though I can tell that Mina is not satisfied with my explanation. She notices too much. Like when I glance across the cafeteria, and Tom—*of course*—happens to look up at exactly the same moment. He waves a "just friends" wave, which just about kills me.

In art, Luke watches me paint for a bit and then says, "How did your fitness test go?"

"It was great," I say. *Great.*

"Cool," he says. "Let's bail the rest of this afternoon then, yeah?"

I look up to see him giving me that half grin. Several locks of hair fall over his eyes. And those cheekbones . . . *whew*. It's like he's been assembled in some hot guy lab by John freaking Hughes himself. But something that I've been thinking about lately—all I *can* think about since last week—is the fact that I want more than an attractive cover. I want, *need*, to like the whole book. Luke . . . is just not the right genre for me.

I panic and blurt out complete nonsense again. "I can't. I have a test in French."

"Again? Didn't you just have one on Thursday?"

"Madame Linney gives us a *lot* of tests."

By Wednesday, I'm starting to feel like I'm trapped in some weird time loop, where even though the calendar keeps moving forward, the same scene keeps repeating with Luke. He asks me to go get high in Frick Park. I think of some excuse to say no. But despite three "nos" in a row, he seems undeterred. It's almost as if that journal entry from last week got stuck on *Luke Carr asks Gracie Byrne to skip seventh period with him,* like a broken record. Or maybe he's just not used to rejection and I'm going to have to be very, very blunt the next time he asks. Which is a problem, because I'm terrible at being very, very blunt.

On Thursday, as I catch sight of Amy Taylor sitting next to Tom again at lunch, I half-heartedly imagine writing a story in Katherine's journal about me getting swallowed up by a black hole, but figure that would very tough to undo. Then I imagine writing a story about both Amy Taylor *and* Luke Carr getting swallowed up by a black hole, eliminating all my current problems in one fell swoop. But I guess that technically would be murder, so I should probably skip that idea too. In fact, I should probably skip writing anything at all related to black holes.

On Friday, I count the seconds until I can finally get the hell out of homecomingland, which is what the halls of our school have become. Posters are everywhere, cheering on the Morewood Bobcats in the school colors: navy and black. The cafeteria is buzzing with chatter about multiple parties tonight, where cars that will carry candidates for the homecoming court will be decorated with tissue-paper flowers. Mina and Daniel make a final lunchtime pitch for me to come along with them to the dance. Mina says: "I've got this off-the-shoulder Halstonesque dress that would look perfect on you."

"I can't," I tell her. "My mom needs help with my grandma."

Which is exactly what I told Luke yesterday afternoon, when he asked me to homecoming, just after I politely declined (yet again) to accompany him to Frick Park to get stoned. He asked me to *homecoming*, which is what I hoped he might do a little more than a week ago, but I suddenly felt like the dog who catches the car. Now that I had it, I wasn't sure anymore why I wanted it so much in the first place. I tried as hard as I could to be very, very blunt when I turned him down, but "My mom needs help with my grandma" was the best I could do under pressure.

And, after lunch, instead of facing up to another possible round of *Luke Carr asks Gracie Byrne to skip seventh period with him*, I reacquaint myself with Opposite Gracie and skip art.

And PE.

And French.

MINA AND DANIEL CONVINCE ME TO AT LEAST GO TO THE football game on Saturday afternoon. The homecoming court parades in their tissue-paper-flower cars, the Bobcats win, *rah rah*, and as we pile into the Seville to go home, it starts to rain.

"Are you *sure* you don't want to come with us tonight?" Mina asks when I pull to the curb in front of her house, after we've dropped off Daniel. Today she is the epitome of school spirit, all decked out in navy and black like a peppy cheerleader, even though she and Daniel barely paid attention to the game. They spent most of the afternoon critiquing the lack of imagination that went into the homecoming pageantry.

"I can't," I say. "Thank you, though. Have a great time."

She squints at me. "Is everything okay, Gracie?"

"Oh, totally," I say.

"You know, friends don't have to pretend everything is okay if it isn't."

"I know," I say. But what I *don't* know is this: What does *okay* even feel like? I'm not sure. How do I explain this to Mina? How could I explain to someone who always seems to feel so at ease with herself that I never do? That most of the time I feel like I'm a sidekick, not just to her and Daniel, but also a sidekick in the story of my own life?

"I'll call you for the recap tomorrow," I tell her.

By the time I get home, the light rain has picked up volume and speed. I feel slightly glad that this probably means no homecoming photos will be snapped in the Broders' front yard, and then I feel slightly guilty for feeling glad.

"Oh, there you are," my mom says as I walk in the door. She looks . . . different. She's wearing eye makeup, for one. And a nice outfit, accented by a long string of pearls. "Would you mind looking after Katherine tonight?"

"Um, sure," I say. "Did you . . . get called in for a shift?" She definitely doesn't look like she's going to work, though.

"Well . . . no. I'm going out to dinner."

"You're going out to dinner?"

My mom *never* goes out.

"Yes." She hesitates for a minute. "You remember Rob, Mrs. Nakamura's son, from Park Manor? He invited me to dinner at his restaurant."

Wait. My mom has a *date*?

"Oh, wow. Sure. I don't have any plans."

I don't think my mom remembers that it's homecoming weekend. Which is fine. At least she's not going to badger me about why I'm not going to the dance. But also: *My mom* has a date on homecoming. And I don't.

Cool.

"Where's Jack?" I ask.

"He's going out for pizza with the Broders. It's Leo and Isaac's birthday," she says as she puts on her coat. "Trish said something about wanting to get a photo of Tom before he left somewhere and then they were heading out. Is there something going on at school?"

Oh my God!

"Nope," I say. There is no way I'm going to mention homecoming now and then have her get all weird about not knowing—and me not going—before her first date in like three years. "Have fun."

"Thanks," she says. "There's half a tuna casserole you can heat up for you and Katherine in the fridge. How do I look?"

She looks a little nervous. But she also looks good.

"You look great, Mom."

Katherine is in the sitting room, watching *I Love Lucy*. Not in any hurry to heat up leftover tuna casserole, I join her. It's the episode where Lucy is in Italy and takes a job stomping wine grapes and gets in a fight with another woman stomping grapes and they both start throwing smooshed-up grapes at each other. Which sounds like it shouldn't be *that* funny, but somehow it is. I hear a honking horn outside and, from where

I'm sitting, I can see that a car has pulled up across the street. It's Marcus, who I assume must be picking up Tom before they continue on to pick up Amy and Samantha. The porch light goes on, and Tom emerges from his house in a suit. Does it make him look . . . kind of hot? Yes, damn it. He runs to the car in the pouring rain. Without an umbrella. *What does he have against umbrellas?* I wonder. *Does he not own one?* The car door slams and Hank runs to the window, barking as they drive away. He continues to bark well after they are gone.

"Quiet down!" Katherine yells at Hank. "Who let that dog in here?"

"He's our dog," I tell her, getting up. "He lives here. You want some dinner?" I ask Hank. He immediately changes gears after hearing the D-word, abandoning his post by the window and trotting over to me, tail wagging. I turn to Katherine. "Are you ready for some tuna casserole?" She keeps watching the TV and laughs without answering. Lucy can keep her busy while I get the three of us dinner.

After I feed Hank, I take the leftover tuna casserole out of the fridge. I fill two plates that I can pop in the microwave, and because there's nothing in the fridge resembling a vegetable at the moment, I also slice an apple at the counter. While I wait for the first plate to heat, I absently stare out the window above the sink, which, in daylight, offers a view of the maple tree I was lying under in the sun last weekend. Tonight, rivulets of rain run down the glass and I can barely make out the silhouette of the tree in the dark.

I take plate number one out of the microwave, add a few slices of apple to it, and put in plate number two to heat as my mind drifts to what might be going on at the dance. Are they playing good music? Does Mina look amazing in her gold lamé dress? Will Tom kiss Amy? Why is it that I so often feel like I'm outside of everything that's going on around me? Lost on the fringes of a party. Kissing total strangers by accident. Watching things happen from a distance, like the girl in that Talking Heads song.

A random thought strikes me. What would happen if I copied the lyrics of "And She Was" into Katherine's journal? Would I have a weird-yet-cool adventure, or would I just float away into space, never to be seen or heard from again? Based on my track record so far, probably the latter. Which leads me to the following conclusion: maybe I should just get rid of that journal. Take it out with the trash or burn it up in the fireplace. The fact of it, and the fact that I can't quite crack its code, is really starting to mess with my mind. Things were much simpler when I wrote stories in a regular old spiral-bound notebook. When there were really no stakes involved because they were just that: stories.

Hank scratches at the back door. "It's raining," I tell him as I open the door. "You must really have to go." He's not a big fan of getting wet.

The microwave timer dings. I take the second plate out and find two forks in the cutlery drawer. We're out of napkins, so I rip two paper towels from the roll next to the sink. It's just me and Katherine, so I decide we can eat our dinners in front of the TV. I pick up the plates, push open the swinging kitchen door with my foot, walk through the dining room to the sitting room where *I Love Lucy* is still playing on the VCR, and . . . she's not there. The spot where she was sitting on the sofa is empty. My pulse immediately starts to race. Did she go up to the bathroom? I set the plates down on the coffee table and walk into the front entryway, intending to go upstairs to check, but I'm stopped dead in my tracks.

The front door stands wide open, wind blowing in.

"KATHERINE!" I yell up the stairs, in case I'm wrong. Maybe she opened the door to go out, saw that it was raining, and changed her mind. No answer. "KATHERINE!" I yell out the door and into the dark.

Fuck.

I run upstairs first, just to be extra sure she's not still here. I check the bathroom. I check her room, Jack's room, my room, and my mom's. All empty. I run back down the stairs and pull on a pair of running shoes left by the door. She can't have gone far.

I leap off the porch, run down the front walk and out to the sidewalk, looking frantically to my right and to my left. I don't see her. I don't see anybody.

"KATHERINE!" I yell again. No answer.

I need to decide which way to go. *Right. Go right.* I run to the intersection of Shady Avenue and Northumberland Street and look both ways. The sidewalk is empty in both directions. I run back up Shady Avenue, stopping again when I get to another cross street. A man walking a small white poodle is coming toward me.

"Excuse me!"

He's cocooned into a rain jacket with a large hood, and it's clear I've startled him. He looks at me like he's unsure of whether or not to speak to me, and I realize it's because I must look a little wild all dripping wet with no coat.

"Have you seen an older woman?" I ask. "About seventy, gray hair . . . probably carrying a purse?"

Oh my God, that is so vague. *What was she wearing?* I don't even know. My mind is a blank, blurry mess, like a TV screen that's turned to staticky snow.

The man shakes his head. "I haven't seen anyone. Sorry." He hurries along, like he's worried I'm about to mug him.

I stand frozen for a few seconds as cars sweep by on Shady Avenue, so fast. *Oh God oh God oh God.* She could walk out into traffic, she could get hit by a car, she could—*Think, Gracie, think.* What should I do? The car. I might be able to find her faster in the car. And . . . Mom. Should I try to reach my mom? I don't even know the name of Rob's restaurant. I don't have time to track her down. Jack. I should get Jack. He can stay at the house while I go out in the car, in case Katherine comes back. And maybe Mr. or Mrs. Broder can help? I run back down Shady Avenue again, this time toward the Broders' house. Their car is not in the driveway. *Shit.* That's right. It's the twins' birthday. They were going out for pizza.

Should I call the police?

I should probably call the police.

I go back inside, lungs heaving. Every second she's out there is another second she could get hit by a car, or fall, or . . . I hear scratching at the back door. I run through the house, into the kitchen, and fling the back door open as Hank runs in, soaking wet. Oh, God . . . I *left* him out there. What is *wrong* with me? I am screwing up right and left. Hank shakes himself and water flies all over the kitchen.

The police, Gracie. Call them.

I go to the alcove under the stairs, pick up the phone, and dial 911. An operator picks up: "What is your emergency?"

After I explain what's going on, I'm transferred to a police unit that's on patrol nearby. The officer I speak with tells me to stay put in case Katherine comes home on her own. He takes down her description—gray hair, purse, and *no, I don't remember what she was wearing*—and tells me that he and his partner will drive around the neighborhood to look. But honestly? They don't seem to be treating this like the emergency that it is. Katherine being out there by herself is, in some ways, the equivalent of a young child being lost in the dark. She's absolutely defenseless.

Unable to officially stay put, I go out front again and stand on the sidewalk. I call her name one more time as my voice gets carried away by the wind. Still no answer.

My eye sockets feel painful, like there's enough pressure building behind my eyeballs to pop them right out of my head. I'm useless. *Useless, useless, useless.*

Except . . . maybe I'm not.

Maybe if I'm *very*, *very* specific . . .

I run back into the house, up the stairs, and into my room. I get the hat box out from under my bed. Kneeling on the floor, I tear the lid off the box and grab the pen from my nightstand. Once I have the journal open to the next blank page, I write: *Katherine is found.*

No . . . wait. That's not specific enough. I write a new line: *Katherine Walsh is found AND she's okay.* Tonight! She needs to be found tonight . . . *Katherine Walsh is found TONIGHT, before Maggie Byrne is even home, AND she's okay. She's okay.*

Is that enough? Will it work? Up until now, I've only ever written in the journal before going to sleep. And I've had to wait until the next day for anything to happen. I feel like I'm going to scream. This is *not* going to work . . . *Please,* I say to myself. *It has to.* And for some reason, all my panicking brain can think of in this moment is Mina's favorite Smiths song: "Please, Please, Please, Let Me Get What I Want."

So I add: *Please let Gracie get what she wants. Right now. Tonight.*

I slam the journal shut, swallow back a sob and return it to its place under my bed. And then I pray to whoever might be listening.

Let Gracie get what she wants.

Just this once.

Please.

NOTHING/ EVERYTHING

FIFTEEN MINUTES LATER, THE DOORBELL RINGS.

I stop in the path that I've been pacing from the sitting room window to the study window and back again. It must be the police. My mom would use her key. I didn't see any flashing lights outside, though . . . but hopefully that's a good sign? I tell myself to stay calm and walk to the door. Hank is at my heels, but hasn't yet started to bark. I hold on to his collar so that he doesn't leap onto a police officer. "Be a good boy," I tell him as I open the door.

But it's not the police. It's Tom. Soaking wet. And Katherine.

It's Tom and Katherine. Katherine and Tom. Standing on the porch in front of me, like a mirage. Only they are real. Unlike Tom, Katherine has an umbrella. *My* umbrella, which she must have taken from the stand next to the front door.

"Oh, thank GOD!" My entire body feels like it has turned to Jell-O, I'm so relieved. She's okay. *She's okay, she's okay, she's okay.*

"Is Anna here?" she asks.

Barely able to speak, I open the door wider so they can come in. When they do, I throw my arms around Katherine and look at Tom. "How did . . . ? Where did . . . ?"

He's able to interpret my incoherence.

"We were on our way to the dance after picking up Amy and Samantha, and came up on her standing in the intersection at Aylesboro and South Negley. Marcus pulled over, and I got out and tried to get her to get in the car so we could bring her back here, but she was *not* having it . . . there was just no way I could convince her to get into the car." He turns to Katherine. "You really are a very stubborn lady."

"Thank you," she says, and then asks me, "Are you Anna?"

"I'm Gracie," I tell her, helping her take off her coat. I hang it up.

"Anyway," Tom continues, "I told the rest of them that I knew where she lived and that I'd have to try to walk her back here, or at least stay with her until I could get some help. So they went ahead without me."

Oh, no.

"Tom. I'm so sorry . . ."

"What are you apologizing for? It's no big deal, really. I can catch up with them. It's okay."

Without warning, the tension and anxiety of the last twenty minutes hits hard. I gasp in a big breath of air and try to hold back the tears, but I can't. They burst out of me like a waterfall after a storm.

"It was all my fault! I left her out here in the sitting room when I went to get dinner and I was distracted and probably taking too long . . . looking out the window and spacing out . . . and I . . . Tom, I didn't even *hear* her leave! I'm not even sure I locked the deadbolt when my mom left."

Tom puts a hand on my arm. It grounds me. "Gracie . . . it's okay. She's *okay*."

"She could have been hit by a car, she could have fallen, she could have—"

"But she didn't."

"Who didn't?" Katherine asks Tom. "What is *wrong* with her, anyway?"

He laughs and our eyes meet. Still looking at me, he says, "Nothing."

There's something about the way he says *nothing* that makes it feel like *everything*. And I can't be sure, but I sense that weird current in the air again, the one I thought I detected the night we stood in the hallway at Tom's house, in the doorway of his room. Or maybe I'm only imagining it. I imagine a lot of things, as we all know.

Katherine wanders into the living room, sits on the sofa, and starts rifling through her purse like everything hasn't been completely bonkers up until about five minutes ago. She pulls out a tube of lipstick and swipes it on. I think it's my Cherries Jubilee.

In the entryway, I'm finally calm enough to start processing sensory details again. Tom's white button-down clings to his chest. His hair is wet, and he's raked it back off his face with his fingers. A soggy maple leaf clings to his suit jacket.

"You are completely drenched," I say.

He looks at me. "So are you."

I am. Drops of water from my hair stud the floor around me. My running shoes are soaked, and they make a squishing sound when I move. Katherine is the only one of us who's relatively dry, because she not only took an umbrella, but also put on a raincoat before her Great Escape.

But she's okay.

She's okay.

"Thank you," I tell him. "Thank you *so* much."

"Sure. I'm just glad we saw her there."

The doorbell rings again, and Hank starts to bark.

This time, it probably *is* the police.

I grab Hank's collar and pull him into the kitchen to keep him out of the way. Tom is still in the entryway when I return.

"You should get going if you want to catch up to everyone at the dance," I tell him.

"Yeah," he says. "I guess I better go."

I open the door, and while I explain to the officers on the

porch that everything is fine, I watch Tom run across the street out of the corner of my eye. And then, just as they're turning to leave, I watch him run back. He jogs up the steps of the porch, passing the officers on their way out, and laughs.

"So . . . turns out I don't have a house key. And my car keys are in the house."

What a disaster.

A disaster that yet again originated with me.

That has been caused by me.

Gracie = Disaster.

But. I can help fix it. Not with magic words this time—I am *definitely* not pushing my luck with any more journal writing tonight—but with a Cadillac Seville. I fish my keys from the pocket of the jacket I wore to the game earlier today and hold them out to him.

"Take the Seville."

He stares at the keys and then glances at me. "Maybe I should just blow it off. I don't even have dry clothes."

"Don't be silly. She won't mind if you're all wet."

I mean, *I* wouldn't mind. I *don't* mind. In fact, it's 100 percent distracting at the moment.

I toss the keys at him so he has no choice but to catch them. And again, I could be imagining it, but he seems to hesitate. Like he doesn't want to go.

"Hurry up, or you'll be stuck here with me and Katherine, eating leftover tuna casserole and watching *I Love Lucy*."

"Hmmm . . . leftover tuna casserole . . . sounds so tempting."

I roll my eyes. "Tuna casserole sucks. Plus, you can't just ditch your homecoming date." *As much as I want you to.*

"Yeah, I probably shouldn't."

"So go!"

But when he's almost out the door, he turns around quickly and says, "I wanted to say yes. That day you asked. But I'd already agreed to go with Amy at that point and I wasn't expecting you to . . . I mean, I thought you and that Luke guy were, like, a *thing* . . . and we're neighbors? You know, would it be weird? *Whatever.* Anyway, I've been meaning to tell you that. And so . . . *cool.* I should . . ." He motions toward the open door and shrugs. "Bye!"

"Bye," I say, but he's already gone. And then I just stand there at the front door because my brain has turned to mashed potatoes.

Snap out of it, Gracie, I tell myself. In light of the night's events, the one thing I can't do is get lost in thought, over-analyzing everything. I need to pay attention. Because I can't lose Katherine *again*.

After a minute or so, I make sure the deadbolt is engaged, block the front door with a heavy dining room chair, let Hank out of the kitchen, and quickly reheat the tuna casserole plates I left on the coffee table. I restart the episode of *I Love Lucy* that Katherine and I were watching before everything went sideways. I'm struck by a sense of déjà vu as Katherine laughs at all the same parts. It's like nothing happened at all. Like we've been sitting here all along, eating leftover tuna casserole and watching TV as the rain poured down outside. But my still-wet hair tells me otherwise. Nothing *didn't* happen. *Lots of things* happened. Too many for me to tease apart in my head. But at least Katherine, now sitting beside me again, laughing at Lucy, is *okay*. Which is all I wanted. For once, it seems like the journal got it right.

BACK TO NORMAL

MY MOM WALKS INTO THE KITCHEN AROUND TEN A.M. SHE got home late, and I told her she should sleep in this morning. That I'd take care of breakfast. I've already decided that she doesn't need to know about Katherine's escape. *Everything is back to normal,* I say to myself. *Everything is okay.*

"How was your . . ." *Was it a date?* "How was dinner last night?" I ask as I pour her a cup of coffee.

She looks a little dreamy when she says, "It was really nice. Fun to be out. Rob's restaurant is *amazing*."

Wow, I think, *Mom has definitely got a crush.* Good for her.

I open the fridge and add some cream to her coffee before I hand it to her.

"Thanks," she says, looking at me a little suspiciously.

Maybe I should tone down the helpfulness a bit. "How was everything here last night? Quiet, I hope?"

"Yep," I say. "Katherine and I had dinner and watched TV. Jack got home around nine. He was a little amped up from all the birthday cake, but otherwise things were pretty chill."

My thoughts flash to Tom and me, both soaking wet, face-to-face in the entryway.

Katherine, who had been sitting quietly at the little table by the back door, drinking tea, suddenly asks, "But who called the *police*?"

Internally, my heart feels like it's going to pop out of my chest, but externally, I try to keep a neutral face. It figures the one time Katherine remembers what happened is also the one time I really need her to *not talk about it*.

"The police?" My mom makes a face like she's *pretty sure* it's just Katherine's normal random chatter. But I can also sense a sprinkle of *not entirely sure*.

I roll my eyes and try to laugh. "Maybe it was Hank."

Thankfully, the doorbell rings.

"I'll get it," I say, already on my way, the dog at my heels.

Before I even open the door, I know that it's Tom. I can see his tall shadow through the beveled glass in the surrounding windows. And just before he rang the doorbell, when Katherine started talking about *the police*, I was thinking that I should probably hustle over to his house to get my car keys in order to avoid the situation I'm about to find myself in right now. Tom at the door, my mom potentially walking by, stopping to chat—because *of course* that's what she'll do—and then the whole story coming out. And even if the whole story *doesn't* come out, even if he senses that I'm keeping everything about Katherine getting lost and him finding her standing in an intersection three blocks away under wraps, this moment, right now, with everyone home, is really not how I was hoping to pick up where the two of us left off last night. Which was . . . *where*, exactly? When he turned around in the doorway . . . was he trying to say he wanted to ask me to homecoming too but decided not to because we're neighbors? Or because he thinks I'm with Luke? Does he wish he had asked anyway, or is he glad he didn't? Does he still just want to be friends? These are all the things I'm wondering about. But now is not a good time to get into it. Not that I'd likely have the courage to ask any of this even if we weren't in danger of my mom barging in at any second.

"Hey," I say, only partially opening the door, as Hank pushes his way through to the porch.

"Hi," he says, scratching Hank's ears. "I . . . uh, wanted to drop off your keys." He's wearing the damn glasses again.

"Great. Thanks," I say.

He pulls the keys out of his jacket pocket, holds them out, and I take them. But his eyes search my face like they're trying to read something there.

How was the dance? I want to ask, but I can't bring myself to do it.

Maybe I don't want to know.

"Is everything . . . okay?" he asks. "I mean, after last night."

Does he mean with Katherine? With me and my mom? With us?

"Gracie?" My mom's voice rises in the kitchen. "Who's at the door?"

"It's Tom," I call back to her. "He had this math homework . . . thing . . . he needed to drop off."

Please don't come out here, I telepath to her.

Do not mention anything about me losing Katherine last night, I telepath to him.

"I gotta go," I tell him as I move to pull in Hank. "See you at school."

"Sure," he says. "Thanks for— "

I hear movement in the kitchen.

"Bye!" I shut the door.

That went well.

By late afternoon, curiosity has the better of me. I tuck myself into the phone alcove and call Mina. She seems surprised to hear my voice on the phone.

"I think this is the first time you've called me," she says after she picks up.

Is it? I guess Mina is usually the one who calls. But it's not because I don't *want* to call her. I just sometimes worry whether the person I'm calling *really* wants to hear from me. What if I'm interrupting something important? But also, I find phone conversations a little exhausting. Conversing is tough enough when you can read the expressions on someone's face.

"I promised I'd call you for the homecoming recap," I say. "Anything exciting happen?"

"Let's see," she says. "Lacey Krauss and Jamal Williams were named queen and king."

They are both seniors who are popular, which means I hardly know them.

"There was some drama with Christina Merlotti and Melissa Andre. Over Troy O'Brian, of all people."

I can *hear* her rolling her eyes.

"And then there was the thing with Marcus, Amy, and Samantha . . ."

My ears perk up like Hank's when there's a chicken in the oven.

"What thing?"

"Well, something happened with Tom—I'm not sure what—but the three of them arrived without him, which was weird. And then Samantha got sick and threw up. I think she may have had too many 'pre-dance' beverages? Anyway . . . Marcus and Amy had to practically carry her out."

"And then what?" I ask.

"And then Tom showed up all soaking wet, but they were already gone, so then I think he left too? I didn't see him the rest of the night."

"Oh . . ." Did Tom come home early? I didn't hear him arrive, but I went up to put Katherine to bed when Jack got home, and her bedroom faces the backyard. "So how was the rest of the dance?"

"It was fine. Daniel and I left on the early side to get food and then went to the midnight *Rocky Horror* at Kings Court, which honestly was more fun than homecoming. You didn't miss much. And, on the bright side, now everyone will be talking about Samantha Reed barfing instead of you!"

"Cool."

"But . . . I wonder what happened with Tom. Why he showed up late and soaking wet, I mean." I can hear the curiosity in her voice.

There's a built-in bench inside the alcove, where I sit cross-legged. The space is closed in and dark and the wood paneling smells like Murphy Oil Soap. It kind of makes me feel like I'm in a confessional at church. I could tell Mina the whole thing, but for some reason I don't want to, not yet. I just want it to be my story and mine alone. For now. So I say,

"I wonder too." Which is technically still sort of true.

For the next few weeks, school gets back to mostly normal. The homecoming buzz dies down, aside from the one bit of gossip that came out of it all: Apparently, Amy Taylor and Marcus Hall are now a couple. It turns out that everything that happened that night—with Tom being late and Samantha getting sick—threw them together in a way they weren't expecting. If it bothers Tom, he's really good at hiding it, because he's as friendly as ever with both Marcus and Amy at lunch, even when they're all over each other. From time to time, we make eye contact across the cafeteria and he always nods or waves, which Mina, of course, always notices.

"Have you talked to him?" she asks one Wednesday afternoon.

"About what?"

"I don't know, anything?"

Immediately, this makes me think of him standing on my porch that night, after I'd given him the keys to the Seville.

I wanted to say yes. That day you asked.

"No," I say. "We don't carpool anymore."

"Still," she says. "I think you should talk to him."

But I never seem to find the right moment.

I was so caught up in the post-homecoming, post-Katherine fallout that it took me a few days to realize that Luke had finally stopped asking me to skip seventh period with him. Which was a huge relief, because I was starting to feel stuck inside a story I couldn't get out of.

But now that I've noticed it, I can't stop thinking: even the most straightforward entries in the journal can have weird, unintended consequences. I got lucky that night with Katherine.

Next time, I might not be so lucky.

THREE RIVERS

TOM'S MOUTH IS MOVING BUT I CAN'T HEAR A WORD HE'S saying, so I pull my Walkman headphones off as I try to catch my breath.

"I'm sorry!" He raises his hands like a person trying to show they don't have a weapon. "I didn't mean to startle you." I'd been listening to R.E.M. while raking up the enormous pile of leaves we've neglected in the front yard, when I glanced up to find him standing on the sidewalk, in almost the same spot where he appeared on the day we met.

"It's okay. I just . . . How long have you been standing there?"

He takes a step closer.

"Like, two seconds, tops. I just got back from a run. Do you . . . want some help?"

"Oh," I say, willing my sympathetic nervous system not to go further into overdrive. The surprise of seeing him standing there has already hit me with enough of an adrenaline rush. "Sure. Thanks."

He walks into the yard and picks up one of the black trash bags I left on the grass and holds it open so I can push leaves into it with the rake. We work in silence for a few minutes until he breaks it.

"Soooo," he says. "Want to give me your take on the key themes of *Macbeth* while we work? Class discussion is tomorrow."

I relax a bit. *Macbeth* is a topic about which I can competently converse.

"Did you *read* it this time?" I ask.

"Sort of?" he says. "I mean, I got the gist—don't, like, *murder* your friend to get ahead—but I gotta admit, all the thees, thys, thous, tises, and 'tweres make me zone out a bit. But for *you*, I mean, Shakespeare must be a weird-word gold mine. Right there in Act I, you've already got *hurly-burly*, which I, for one, think we should bring back into regular use, even though I have *no* idea what it means."

"Boisterous," I say, while thinking about how adorable he looks when his cheeks are all flushed from running in the cold.

After we fill three bags, and I cover *Macbeth*'s main themes of ambition, loyalty, guilt, and fate versus free will, Tom points to the Halloween pumpkins still on the steps of our front porch, their mouths caved in so that they look like toothless old men.

"Are you . . . going to get rid of these?"

"Nope," I say. "Just going to wait until they disintegrate."

"Ha. Let me get them. That is really bothering me."

I remember his surprisingly tidy room.

He collects them in another plastic bag and then we pull everything to the curb.

"So," he says, as I'm brushing leaves off my pants, "Want to go for a drive in the Beetle? I can take you somewhere for a change. And maybe you can show me how to better navigate around here. Nothing about the layout of this city makes sense to me."

My stomach flip-flops. He wants to go somewhere? Together?

"Sure," I say. "Let me just put this stuff away in the shed."

"And maybe give me ten minutes?" he asks. "I'm going to change out of my running clothes. I think I probably stink."

Should I change? I wonder after he leaves. I'm wearing a pair of jeans with holes in the knees, an old work shirt that was my grandfather's, and hiking boots. After overthinking it for almost ten minutes, I settle for ripping off the work shirt and pulling a somewhat nice sweater over my head.

Tom's green Beetle is much *smaller* on the inside than the Seville. Once we are in our seats, it feels like we are just inches apart. His hair is wet, which means that he must have showered in the last ten minutes. I should have put on different jeans.

"So . . ." he says. "Where should we go?"

"Well," I say, "where do you want to go?"

He shrugs and laughs a little. "I hadn't thought that far ahead yet. How about you show me your favorite Pittsburgh spot?"

I consider it for a minute, unsure. I mean, this is Pittsburgh, not Paris. But then a very good idea comes to me.

"I know *just* the place for you."

"The Monongahela Incline?" he says, grinning, after we've parked on West Carson Street and walked to the redbrick base station at the foot of Mount Washington.

"Named after your favorite of the three rivers," I say.

"Awww, you remembered."

We both gaze at the set of tracks extending vertically up the side of a steep hill that rises above the west bank of the Monongahela River. Two yellow passenger cars pass each other on the tracks, one going up, and one going down.

"You're not afraid of heights, are you?" I ask.

"Don't think so," he says. "But keep in mind that I am from Chicago, where everything is flat."

We go inside the base station. Tom gets the tickets while I look around. I haven't been on the incline since I was a kid. I remember my dad taking me and Jack once when we were little. We also went to see the dinosaur exhibit at the Carnegie Museum that day.

I point out city landmarks while the car clicks up the steep track. The Smithfield Street Bridge. Station Square. The US Steel building.

"Want to know the technical name for one of these?" I ask, gesturing to the car we're in.

"Of course," he says. "Tell me."

"A funicular. Cable railway system connecting two points on a steep slope."

He shakes his head.

"You just knew that off the top of your head?"

"No," I admit. "I read that on the display down below while you were buying the tickets."

We reach the top and exit into the neighborhood on the hill above. There's a concrete viewing platform nearby that extends out from the top of the slope. We walk out to the edge of the platform and lean against the railing, looking down at the city and the spot where the Monongahela, Allegheny, and Ohio Rivers converge. It's a clear, sunny day, but cold, with a chilly wind shaking the almost bare tree branches. Tom's cheeks are still rosy red.

"For your viewing pleasure," I say, sweeping my arm out like the ringleader of a circus. "Pittsburgh's Three Rivers." The downtown area of the city comes to a triangular point—in the shape of a pizza slice—right where the three rivers meet.

"From up here, Pittsburgh kind of looks like a slice of pizza," Tom says.

I laugh. "That's what I was thinking."

"Maybe we're just hungry." He turns to me. "This is cool. Thanks." And then he's quiet for a few seconds before continuing, "I kind of thought you were mad at me that day I brought back your keys."

"Oh . . . no," I say. "I just hadn't told my mom about Katherine the night before and I was worried you might say something. Not on purpose . . . it's just . . . my mom is super nosy and would have asked why you had my keys and everything could have snowballed from there. I didn't want her to freak out about it. She's kind of stressed . . . like, *all* the time lately. And she was in a good mood that morning and I didn't want to ruin it."

What I *don't* say is that I still have multiple questions about everything he said at the front door before he left that night. But now that a few weeks have gone by, I think I've waited too long and it would be weird to bring it up now.

He nods. And then his face turns serious. "Can I ask you something?"

"Sure," I say.

"Katherine. How long has she been like she is?"

"She was officially diagnosed five years ago, but it's progressive, so the last few years everything has accelerated a lot."

"I'm sorry," he says. "That must be really hard for your mom. And for you."

"It is," I say. Which is true. I don't talk about it much with people outside my family, but somehow it feels okay to talk about it with him. He knows the score with Katherine at this point.

"And you don't have any aunts or uncles who can help?"

"No," I say. "My mom's an only child. I only have uncles and aunts on my dad's side."

"You don't talk about your dad much," he says.

I shrug. "He's remarried and lives in Maryland. He and his wife, Kirsten, just had a baby . . . so we have a new sister. Ashley. We're going to meet her over Thanksgiving."

I eventually caved because Jack really wanted to go. Plus, we haven't met Ashley yet and she *is* our sister, even if it feels strange to say it.

"That's . . . cool," says Tom. "But maybe a little weird for you guys, huh?"

"A little," I say. "I mean, things are much better now between him and my mom, but at first it was kind of rough. She wasn't too psyched about him moving, but he changed jobs and kind of needed to."

He nods and a cold gust of wind blows across the platform, scattering dry leaves.

I *don't* tell him my parents split up because Kirsten and my dad had an affair. And it all came out because *I* saw them holding hands outside a restaurant in downtown Pittsburgh when my eighth grade class was on a field trip to the symphony. It was just random bad luck that we were both in the same place at the same time, two hours from home. "You can't lie to Mom," I told him later. "I know," he said. He told her the next day. And that was the end of my family—*poof!*—all because I decided to speak up.

"Maybe we should head back down," I say. "It's chilly up here."

He pushes off from the railing. "To the funicular!"

We start walking.

"Is that one going in your word notebook?" he asks.

"Maybe," I say.

"What about hurly-burly?"

"Definitely."

On the way back down, a thought occurs to me. All this time, I thought I wanted to be noticed. But maybe being *noticed* isn't the same as being *seen*.

We stop for pizza on the way home.

For the next few weeks, Tom and I bump into each other more often than we usually do. At Frick Park, walking our dogs. In the morning, getting into our cars before school. One day he even comes by my table at lunch to ask for help with an English assignment.

After he leaves, Mina squints at me and says, "I don't think he *really* needed help with that."

And Daniel says, "Just an observation. He's not as *hot* as Luke Carr, but he's more *attractive* somehow, don't you think?"

I don't say it out loud, but inside I say, *YES.*

And then there's the observation I make to myself: ever since homecoming night, I haven't touched the journal under my bed. Maybe it's because my life, my *real* life, actually seems kind of okay again. And I don't want to screw it up.

BASOREXIA, PART *DEUX*

I PICK KATHERINE UP IN THE CAR TODAY AT PARK MANOR. It's chilly out, and there's a lot to do this evening: Walk Hank. Get dinner started. Pack for Thanksgiving in Maryland. Jack and I leave first thing tomorrow, but we're flying instead of driving with Grandma and Grandpa Byrne. They decided to leave earlier and stay longer, to help with the baby.

Katherine and I walk into an unexpectedly noisy house. Hank and Hypatia greet us at the door, their tails whipping at my legs. Jack, Isaac, Leo, and *Tom* are all in the sitting room watching TV. Correction—the TV is on, but the primary activity looks to be a game of indoor Nerf football. The ball bounces off the mantel when we come in.

"Your mom told my mom the boys could hang here after

school," Tom says by way of explanation, as he catches the ball and Jack runs by to grab it. "I guess my mom thought the day before my grandparents arrive from Chicago for Thanksgiving would be a good day to paint the dining room." He shrugs. "She's kind of chaotic like that sometimes. Anyhow, I guess I'm here to make sure they don't wreck your house. Hope that's okay."

I nod. "Sure . . ."

Jack chucks the ball at Leo, who misses the catch. It bounces off the windowsill. "I'm sorry," Tom says sheepishly as he picks up a couch cushion from the floor. "I may not be doing the best job intercepting all the house-wrecking."

"We'll be right back," I say.

I take Katherine upstairs to the bathroom, because that is what we always do when we first get home, but also, I need a second to collect myself. When she's done, I go in to turn off the water she left running in the sink and quickly check the mirror. *Maybe I should put on some lipstick?* No. Too obvious. Plus, I'm pretty sure Katherine still has my magic tube of Cherries Jubilee in her purse. *Lip gloss?* She's already heading down the hall toward the stairs, so I swipe on some gloss and hurry after her.

The boys are still wrecking the house when we return.

"Maybe you guys should play a *board* game," I suggest as I lead Katherine to her favorite chair. I hand her her knitting project. I'm not sure exactly *what* she's knitting, but it keeps her hands busy.

"Yeah, guys," Tom adds. "Quit wrecking the house."

I give him a *gooood job* thumbs-up and open the cabinet where we keep the games. "How about Scrabble?"

"Ugggggh, *NO*." Jack doubles over like he's in physical pain. "You know I hate Scrabble, Gracie!"

Tom backs him up. "Seems like you'd have an unfair advantage with that one."

"True," I say. "Monopoly?"

Jack is still not sold. "Maybe."

"Clue?"

"I love Clue!" says Leo.

"Clue it is." I pull out the game and hand it to Jack. "No cheating," I tell him.

"Aren't you going to play with us?" Leo asks.

"Ahhh . . . I have a few things to do," I say.

"One game?" Jack asks.

"Oh, all right." I join them around the coffee table.

For the next thirty minutes, we play Clue. Leo correctly guesses that it's Professor Plum in the conservatory with the revolver. The clock on the mantel strikes the half hour.

"Okay, guys," I say. "I need to get dinner started."

Tom looks at me over the game board. "Want some help?"

"Sure," I say, stomach bees buzzing. "Unless you want to keep playing."

He shakes his head, "Nope!"

I motion to Jack. "Can you put on *I Love Lucy* for Grandma?" She's already set her knitting aside.

Tom follows me into the kitchen and the door swings shut behind us. Now that we are alone—I hear a loud clunk in the sitting room, so alone-*ish*—I'm feeling a weird mix of anticipation and anxiety, sensing that over the last few weeks something has shifted between us, but then doubting my senses. Maybe, as usual, it's all in my head. *You need something to focus on,* I tell myself, so I start by filling a large pot with water.

Tom drums his hands on the butcher block and asks, "Soooooo . . . what are we making?"

"Well," I say setting the pot of water on the stove and turning on the gas underneath, "Just pasta. Maybe some garlic bread?" I go into the pantry, find a box of spaghetti and a jar of Prego, and set them on the counter.

Tom picks up a small ceramic black bird from the butcher block. Its beak is wide open and the inside is hollow. "What *is* this?" he asks.

"I think it's a pie bird? My grandma used to use it when she baked pies, but I honestly don't know exactly what it's for." I shrug. "There's a lot of weird grandparent-y stuff around here."

Tom shakes his head. "What *is* it with the weird grandparent-y stuff? Do they all have a checklist of required items they need to keep around to be official or something?" He nods toward the fridge. "I see yours has the standard issue set of refrigerator fruit magnets."

I grin. "What about a knitted zigzag blanket? Your grandparents have one of those?"

"Hell *yes*," he says. "And a tin that looks like it should have cookies in it but is disappointingly full of buttons."

"Oooooh, with the pincushion that looks like a tomato?"

He nods and laughs. "The plastic bag with a bunch of other plastic bags inside it goes without saying."

"Of course. What about the ceramic Christmas tree with the little lights?"

"Nope! We're partially Jewish, so you got me on that one."

"What do you mean by 'partially'?"

"My dad is Jewish, my mom was raised Lutheran but is basically agnostic so no Christmas tree. We celebrate Hanukkah." He shrugs. "That's about the extent of our religious activity."

"Got it," I say. "The *Byrne* family is full Irish Catholic over here, so my mom makes us go to church. At least on Christmas. She's been a little lax about regular Sundays lately."

Tom nods.

"Okay." I clap my hands together, getting back to our game. "So what about . . . a decorative spoon collection?"

He crosses his arms and squints, faking seriousness. "I'll see you one decorative spoon display and raise you a collection of porcelain thimbles. My nana has one from every state in the union, including Alaska and Hawaii."

"Wow," I say. "I fold. Your nana's got it all."

"That she does."

Our eyes meet, and an electric current travels across the room. This time, I'm certain I'm not imagining it.

"Okay, what can I do?" Tom asks. "You need to give me some dinner-related task to complete."

"A task . . ." I say.

"Yeah. A chore. An order. A command. Just tell me what you want me to do . . . and I'll do it."

Somehow, it feels like we're no longer *just* talking about him being helpful in the kitchen. My pulse picks up speed. I nod to the cabinet behind me.

"You . . . could get the pasta bowl down. I can't quite reach the top shelf."

Tom pushes back from the butcher block and walks over to where I'm standing below the cabinet. He slows to a stop in front of me. The room suddenly seems much warmer, like the temperature has increased by ten degrees.

"Up here?"

"Uh-huh."

He reaches over my head to open the cabinet, takes out the bowl, and sets it next to me on the counter. "Is that the one you wanted?"

"Yes."

He's so close that I can feel the heat of him. I swear I can hear his heart thumping in his chest.

"Gracie . . ."

I have to look up now to see his face. His cheeks are flushed.

"Are you . . . blushing?" I ask.

"You make me nervous," he says.

"*I* make *you* nervous?"

He nods. My breath catches.

I stare at his lips and it's basorexia all over again. Times one hundred. Times one thousand.

Do it, Gracie. Just do it.

I rise up on my toes and kiss him. Tom immediately moves closer, leaning in to cup both sides of my face in his hands, and kisses me back. His mouth is soft, warm, and minty fresh. I loop my arms around his neck and pull him closer. Closer. Closer.

This kiss.

This kiss feels like chemistry. Everywhere. All the way from the top of my head to the tips of my toes. I don't want to day-dream myself somewhere else or leave my body and watch from a distance. I don't want to be anywhere else but here.

One of his hands drifts down to my hip. I weave my fingers into his hair. We press against each other, all heat and breath and heartbeats.

The kitchen door bangs open, startling us both.

Tom and I jump apart.

It's Isaac. He just stands there frozen for a few seconds, like someone put him on pause.

Then he says, "Uhhhh . . . do you have any . . . snacks?"

The pasta water is boiling furiously, steaming up the kitchen.

Tom runs a hand through his hair, but in a way that's not practiced or self-aware, just . . . maybe a little frustrated, I think, at the interruption.

"We should probably head home soon, bud. Mom will want us for dinner."

"Okay," Isaac says. And then he turns and flees.

I hear a voice calling from the front hallway. "I'm hooooome . . ." My mom.

Tom and I look at each other. He laughs.

"Your mom has *great* timing," he says.

"Isaac too," I say.

He nods.

"Will he . . . ?" I ask. It would just be so awkward if he told everybody out there that Tom and I were kissing in here.

Tom shakes his head. "Isaac? He's terrified of anything kissing-related so I'm pretty sure he won't mention it." He lets out a breath. "So I guess . . . I'll see you after Thanksgiving?"

Five days from now. What I thought was going to feel like an extra-long long weekend is now going to feel like . . . *forever.*

"Yeah. See you next week."

But I wonder if things will be different once we're back in school.

He follows me into the sitting room.

It looks like every game we own has been opened and scattered across the floor. Jack and Leo are trying to get Mousetrap to work. (It never does.) Hank is allowing Isaac, who appears to have recovered from catching us kissing, to scratch his belly. Katherine is sitting in front of the coffee table, sorting Monopoly money into stacks according to color. Mom is hanging her coat in the entryway.

The windows are getting all steamed up from the pasta water that continues to boil without any pasta. But in my head, they are steamed up for a completely different reason.

"Oh, hi, Tom!" my mom says as she walks into the sitting room. "I didn't know you were here too. It was lovely of your mom to invite Katherine and me over for Thanksgiving. Is she sure it's not too much trouble?"

"I don't think she would ask if it was," Tom says.

"Well, okay. Tell her to let me know what we can bring."

"Sure," he says.

Katherine and my mom are spending Thanksgiving with the Broders?

Mom looks at the boys rolling around in the living room like a pile of puppies.

"They are so sweet together," she says. "I'm so glad they've become such good friends."

The smoke detector starts chirping in the kitchen, probably because of all the steam.

My mom looks at me. "Is something burning, Gracie?"

"No, no," I say. "It's just the pasta water. I'll get it." I glance at Tom. "I gotta go. Happy Thanksgiving!"

"Happy Thanksgiving," he says.

The smoke detector chirping gets more high-pitched and intense. I duck into the kitchen, turn down the flame under the boiling water, and throw in the spaghetti. I pull the chain on the exhaust fan above the back door and wave a magazine back and forth in front of the smoke detector, dissipating the steam. It stops chirping. I can hear Tom and his brothers saying their goodbyes and walking out the front door.

I find the colander and set it in the sink. I pour sauce into the saucepan and set it to simmer. I consider making a salad.

My lips are still buzzing from that kiss.

I can't decide if I hope it doesn't change anything or I hope it changes everything.

GIVING THANKS

BETHESDA IS LIKE AN ALTERNATE UNIVERSE. MY DAD AND Kirsten's new house is big and modern and everything works. I think my dad's current job was a big step up for him. Also, Kirsten has a great job too, and her family is pretty well off. They have a huge backyard, with a pool, which dad promises will be all ours to enjoy when we come visit in the summer. (I can tell Jack wishes we could try it now, but I remind him that it's forty-five degrees.)

We've now officially met Ashley. She's too young to really have much of a personality yet—mainly all she does is cry, eat, drool, and poop—but she's got cute chubby cheeks and tiny fingers that Grandma Byrne just can't get enough of.

Kirsten has been up with the baby and looks tired, but still has gone out of her way to make me and Jack feel comfortable.

We each have our own room, with stacks of big, fluffy towels, and she made sure that my dad picked up all our favorite foods. They even got early Christmas presents for us since we're going to be with my mom for the December holiday break. Spending time with Kirsten is still weird, though. While she's basically a nice person, and, in any other context, I'd probably like her, it's hard to let go of the fact that she broke up my parents' marriage. Well, not just *she*. It was my dad too, obviously, but I guess it's easier to hold someone at arm's length who wasn't part of your family in the first place.

My dad is happy we are here. It's our first visit since they moved. But I can tell it pains him that we don't talk like we used to. It makes me feel bad too. But it's hard to see how we can ever get back to where we were before. The distance just makes it harder. We only see each other in these spaced-out increments—holidays and summer vacations, the occasional long weekend here and there—which is different from seeing someone every day. On top of that, it's painfully clear that the divorce very much left my mom with the short end of the stick, and I feel I owe it to her to still be a little mad. It almost feels like a betrayal if I enjoy the time with my dad too much.

Jack and I call my mom on Thanksgiving morning.

"I *miss* you guys," she says, after Jack says his hellos and heads back downstairs.

"We miss you too," I say.

"Also," she says, "do you know where Hank's leash is at?

He's super wound up and I need to try and get him out for a walk. *If* I can get Grandma to go with me. It's a little hard to manage them both at once."

Don't I know it.

"It might be on the shelf by the back door," I say. "But you could just take him over to the Broders' tonight. He'll play with their dog."

"Maybe," she says, sounding a little stressed. "I don't want him to knock one of Alan's parents down. That's all I need."

"Have fun tonight," I say. "Tell everyone we say hello."

Of course, all my brain can focus on when I say *everyone* is *Tom*.

"I will," she says. "You too. Wish Grandma and Grandpa Byrne, and your dad and Kirsten, a happy Thanksgiving." And I can tell by her voice that it took a *lot* for her to say that.

The rest of the day is pretty uneventful. Grandma Byrne makes the turkey, sweet potato casserole, and a bunch of pies, my dad does the mashed potatoes and stuffing, and I do cranberries and green beans. After helping Grandma Byrne with the pies, Jack plays about a million games of chess with Grandpa Byrne, who doesn't help with anything because . . . *patriarchy*. We eat until we're about to burst. Afterward, I stay in the kitchen to help my grandmother clean up, but my dad comes in and tells her she should relax and that he and I can get it. He plucks the dish towel from where she has thrown it over her shoulder. "Take it easy, Mom. You did all the cooking. Plus, Kirsten would love it if you could hold the baby for a bit."

That's all anyone has to do to get Grandma Byrne to switch gears—mention *the baby*.

"So," he says after we've finished loading the dishwasher and have started in on all the greasy pots and pans and serving plates. "How's everything back in the 'Burgh? Getting used to the new school?"

"It's good," I say. "For the most part."

There's a long silence. He washes a pot and hands it to me to dry.

"I miss you and Jack," he says. "I'm really glad you came. I hope we can do this more often, now that we're settled in here. I know things were a little busy with you and Jack and Mom moving and then us moving this year."

I nod.

"Is your mom okay?" he asks. "How are things with Katherine?"

I shrug. "You know, it's hard. Katherine doesn't remember Jack and me anymore. Or Mom. She's going to this day care place, but Mom says it's expensive."

He frowns. "I'm sorry. That sounds . . . worse than I'd thought."

I shrug again. "We don't have to talk about it. It's not your problem anyway."

My dad stops what he's doing at the sink and faces me. "Gracie," he says. "Don't say that. It is my problem too. She's your and Jack's grandmother. You live with her. Just because your mom and I aren't married anymore doesn't mean I don't care about what's going on." He sighs. "I know you're still angry with me. I get that. And I know I've made mistakes, but I hope you know you can still talk to me."

"I do . . ." I say.

"Hmmm . . . that doesn't sound entirely convincing."

"It's just that the last time we *really* talked . . . everything fell apart."

And just admitting it makes me realize how heavy it's been. To carry the weight of it. Because if I hadn't seen him and Kirsten that day, maybe things would have turned out different.

He's silent for a long minute, his face grave. "Gracie, no," he says. "Your mom and I . . . Things were not okay long before then. But if it hadn't been for you . . . for you having the courage to speak up, to *talk* to me, we might have just continued to *not* be okay, which wouldn't have been good for any of us. I'm so sorry about how everything happened, and I'm unbelievably sorry you feel like you ended up in the middle of it. But I hope you can forgive me. And I hope you know that no matter what happened with your mom and me, it's done nothing to change how I feel about *you* . . . even if it's changed how you feel about *me*. I want to earn back your trust."

"Okay," I say, feeling some of the anger and sadness I've been holding in my heart beginning to lift. The rest will take time, but it's a start.

"Okay, good. And talk to your mom. Let me know what I can do to help."

I don't know if my mom would even accept his help, but

I'm glad he's offered. I know for sure she would never ask. But she *might* say yes to an offer.

"I will."

He steps forward and we share an awkward hug. When we pull apart, he surveys the remaining dishes. "Let's finish up so we can do this Star Wars marathon with Jack—I rented the entire trilogy at Blockbuster."

"Are you going to make popcorn?" I ask.

He laughs and shakes his head. "How can you even think about eating anything else right now?"

"I'm a teenager. We have high metabolisms. Plus, we've missed your popcorn. Somehow you always nail the correct butter-salt ratio . . ."

For a second, he looks like he's going to burst into tears. But then he says, "Popcorn it is."

The room I'm staying in at my dad's house is quiet and dark. There are no clanging radiators here that boil and hiss, only the soft hum of the forced-air heat when it kicks on. Still, I can't sleep. I stare up at the ceiling in the dark, but there's no crack in the plaster to center my focus, and no journal under the bed to dominate my thoughts.

I wonder if my mom and Katherine had a nice dinner at the Broders' house.

I also wonder about me and Tom. This trip has given me too much time to think about where we go from here and what might happen after I get back. Are we still friends? Friends who sometimes kiss? More than friends? What will it be like at school? Will everyone start talking about the two of us? That sounds kind of stressful. And what if whatever this is quickly flames out, and then everything is weird and awkward after? That also sounds stressful. I think about what Daniel said that one time, about high school being too early to meet "your person." Maybe he's right about that, because look what happened with my mom and dad. What if Tom could potentially be my person and I met him too soon?

All these thoughts are ping-ponging around in my head in sort of an abstract way, but they are also simultaneously overshadowed by the other thought that is taking up the bulk of my consciousness: I just want to kiss him again.

And again, and again and again and again.

BREAD CRUMBS

OUR FLIGHT HOME IS DELAYED OUT OF WASHINGTON DULLES and we don't get to Pittsburgh until late. Mom looks exhausted when she picks us up at the airport, which is not surprising. It's just been her and Katherine for five days straight. When we finally pull into the driveway at the house, it's after midnight. Jack is snoring in the back seat next to me and I have to gently shake him awake. Katherine, on the other hand, is *wide* awake. "She fell asleep in her chair at home before we left for the airport, and I had to wake her up to come get you guys," Mom explains. She sighs. "She's probably going be up half the night now."

Outside, the weather is clear and cold. We all file into the house as Katherine asks me, "Who are you?"

"I'm Gracie," I tell her.

"Do you know where they put the letters?" she asks.

"I took them to the mailbox earlier," I tell her.

"Oh, good," she says.

After greeting an ecstatic Hank in the entryway, I carry my bag upstairs and drop it next to my closet. It's freezing in the house, so I pull on some flannel pjs. And then I peek around the window blind to look across the street.

Tom's room is dark.

Out in the hallway, I hear Katherine arguing with my mom.

I go out and see them in the bathroom doorway, my mom holding Katherine's nightgown.

"That is *not* mine!" she yells.

My mom looks like she's about to start crying. She turns to me. "*This* has been going on the last three nights. She just won't go to bed."

I take the nightgown from my mom. "Hey, Mom, why don't *you* go to bed? I'll watch some TV with her until she's ready to sleep."

"Thank you," she says.

I can tell she's too tired to argue. And I'm too amped up to sleep. I take Katherine downstairs and periodically glance out the front window, just in case his light goes on.

Even though I'm going on less than five hours' sleep at school on Monday, I'm a ball of nervous energy by lunchtime.

As I make my way to the cafeteria, all I can think about is the fact that I haven't seen or talked to Tom since our kitchen kiss.

How am I supposed to act when he walks in? I have no idea.

I set my lunch down at our table.

Today Mina and Daniel look like they should be in a music video together. She's wearing a tight black minidress and her dark hair is in a sleek bun. Daniel is in pleated black pants and a colorful graphic button-down. All he needs is a sax.

The three of us catch up on any happenings over Thanksgiving break, but all my sensors are pointed to the entrance to the cafeteria. And about fifteen minutes into lunch, I see Tom walk in with his tray. Right before he sits, he looks our way and raises a hand.

Is it a *just friends* wave?

A *Hey, I'd like to kiss you again* wave?

I'm not entirely sure, and it's driving me crazy.

I wave back, and my brain replays the kiss. In detail. I can feel my face getting hot.

Lunch, Gracie. Just focus on your French bread pizza.

But Mina is staring me down like a hawk about to swoop in on its prey.

"Wait a minute . . . what was that all about?"

"What was what all about?"

"That cute little wave you both did," Daniel chimes in.

"Is there something going on with you two?" Mina asks, grinning. "Did you see each other over Thanksgiving break?"

"Mina, I went to my dad's, remember?"

"What's up with your face?" asks Daniel. "You look like a tomato."

"Nothing!" I snap.

They look at each other and seem to come to some sort of silent agreement on something.

"They totally kissed," Mina says. "I don't know how or when, but it happened."

"*Totally,*" says Daniel.

"You guys . . . Stop. Please."

But they don't stop. Immediately, they start bombarding me with questions.

"How did it happen?" *I asked him to get me a bowl.*

"Was it good?" *Yes.*

"Like, *how* good?" *Very.*

"What *else* happened?" *Nothing. Yet.*

"Are you two a couple now, or what?" *I don't know.*

Except I don't actually answer any of their questions. I just keep saying, "Stop. Stop. Stop."

I haven't even talked about it with *him* yet, so I'm not about to talk about it with anyone else.

The rest of the day drags. In art, Luke has switched to wearing a vintage leather motorcycle jacket, which looks just as good on him as the vintage army jacket. Even better—I'm fairly certain that I did not have a thing to do with it. Occasionally, we chat about the project we're working on, but there's no more talk of strange dreams or possible outings to Frick Park. Which leads me to wonder: Have the effects the journal had on Luke worn off? If so, I'm relieved.

As soon as I get home, I walk to pick up Katherine, even

though it's windy and cold. My hope is that if she gets some exercise, she might be tired out when it's time for bed tonight. Tom's Beetle is not in the Broders' driveway when we return to the house. I remember him mentioning something about basketball practice starting after Thanksgiving. Later, I take Hank out for a long walk, returning after it's dark. His car is still gone.

Jack is playing cards with Katherine in the sitting room when I return. I think they're playing War, which is usually simple enough for her to follow. If she gets lost, he just lets her make up her own rules.

I walk into the kitchen and find my mom standing at the butcher block, chopping an onion.

"You're cooking," I say.

She rolls her eyes. "Don't sound so surprised. I got off early tonight."

"What are we having?"

"Meat loaf," she says. "It's Grandma's recipe. I haven't made it in a while."

"Oh, nice," I say.

She looks up from her chopping and her eyes are all watery. I hope it's just from the onions, but I'm not so sure. "I'm sorry we've had so much takeout lately. Between work and Grandma, it's hard to find time to cook. Want to help me out?"

"Sure."

"The celery needs to be diced."

I grab an extra knife from the drawer and join her at the butcher block.

"Is everything okay?" I ask her.

"Oh." She shrugs. "It was a long weekend." She nods in the direction of the sitting room. "She's been a lot to handle lately. I feel like she's losing more words, and getting more unsteady on her feet . . . I'm going to have to get a new gate for the top of the stairs. The one we have isn't as sturdy as I'd hoped, and I've been worrying about her getting it open and falling at night, she's been up so much."

I nod. I don't know what else to say. It sucks.

"But it seems like she's doing really well at Park Manor, right?"

"Oh, yeah. That place has been a godsend. Sometimes I think she'd be better off there full-time, if a space opened up. But I'd have to figure out the finances."

I think about the conversation I had with my dad over Thanksgiving and almost mention his offer, but decide to wait. I need to consider the best approach.

My mom nudges my shoulder. "Anyway. I missed you guys. Did you have fun at Dad's?"

"It was fine," I say, being careful about what details I share. "We went into DC and visited the Lincoln Memorial and the Air and Space Museum."

"Oh, Jack mentioned that was cool," she says. "And how're Grandma and Grandpa Byrne?"

"They're good."

"And the baby?"

"Up a *lot* at night." At least mom can know that she's not

the only one not getting any sleep. "What about you? Did you . . . see Rob?"

She shakes her head. "Ahh . . . no. We had plans to get together for lunch one day but Grandma had a bit of a meltdown, so I canceled. And he's really busy at the restaurant now that it's holiday season, so, you know . . . I don't know."

I wish I had some advice about dating while being a single parent of two kids *and* a caregiver of a mom with Alzheimer's, but I don't. But I hope that's not the end of things with my mom and Rob. He seems really cool. And, he *cooks.*

"Okay, celery is chopped," I say. "What can I do next?"

"Want to get the silver mixing bowl for me? And the ground beef and two eggs out of the fridge?"

It's a different bowl.

Easy to reach.

But of course now all I can think about is Tom standing in front of me, barely a few centimeters between us.

I gather the remaining ingredients from the fridge while my mom minces garlic.

The way he said, *Just tell me what you want me to do . . . and I'll do it.*

I unwrap the ground beef and put it in the bowl.

My mom scrapes up the chopped onion and celery with her hand and the side of the knife and adds it to the beef.

"Shit," she says. "Bread crumbs. We need bread crumbs."

I wipe off my hands. "I'll look in the pantry." I rummage through the disorganized mess of cereal boxes and bags of chips and canned soup that probably expired six years ago and can't find anything resembling bread crumbs. I come back out.

"I don't think we have any."

"Hmmm," she says. "Let me give Trish a call. I'll bet they have some we can borrow."

She disappears into the alcove under the stairs.

Should I offer to go over there? Will it be super awkward if he answers the door? He's probably not even home . . .

I snap out of it just in time to hear the tail end of the conversation: ". . . Thank you! I'll send Gracie over."

My mom comes back into the kitchen.

"They have some. Will you run over there for me?"

On the outside, I hope I still look normal. On the inside, I'm full of butterflies, bats, and birds and bees.

"Sure."

It's cold, so after pulling on my shoes, I throw on a coat and a hat. As I jog across the street, I see that Tom's car is back.

There are four other people who could open that front door.

But before I even make it to the Broders' front walk, he steps out onto the porch in a sweatshirt and basketball shorts. No coat.

He looks like he's freezing, but he smiles, holding up a ziplock bag.

I climb the porch stairs, taking two at a time, and stop in front of him, heart thumping.

"Hi," I say. "Aren't you—" but he stops me with a kiss.

A hungry, steamy, all-consuming kiss.

I don't even remember what I was about to ask.

As we break apart, he says, "That's all I've been thinking about for five days."

Me too, I think.

But I say, "Really? That can't be all you've been thinking about. Five days is a long time."

He flashes his slightly crooked smile. "Okay, maybe I was also thinking about whether the Bears were going to beat the Packers on Sunday, but mostly I was thinking about kissing you again."

Hearing him say this makes me feel happy. Relieved. But further confirmation would be even better. "So if we graphed 'Tom's thoughts' on a curve, 'kissing Gracie' would be . . . ?"

He laughs. "Definitely at the top of the curve. It's been really boring around here without you. How was your dad's?"

"It was okay," I say. "We ate a lot of turkey. Went to the Lincoln Memorial."

"Same," he says. "Well, except for Lincoln."

This time, I kiss him.

He slides his hands inside my coat and around my waist, pulling me closer. And all I can think about, aside from the kiss, is this:

I really like this boy.

"You know," he says, his lips on my ear, "You can borrow whatever you need from us anytime. Sugar, flour, bread crumbs, you name it. Our pantry is your pantry."

"Anytime, huh? Your mom might come to regret that. We are always out of something."

"That's lucky for me, though."

It's so cold that our breaths come out like smoke.

"You are freezing," I say. "I should go. My mom is waiting for your bread crumbs."

"See you tomorrow," he says. "Maybe I can come over after practice one night this week to help you with that math assignment . . ."

"What math assignment?"

He rolls his eyes.

Ohhh.

"Okay . . ." I say, walking away backward.

"Leave me a trail of bread crumbs," he says.

"Ha."

I run back across the street.

"Were they making them from scratch?" My mom is rinsing broccoli in a colander when I return. My face goes warm.

"No. I was just talking with Tom for a second . . . about this math assignment."

"Ah. The math chops must run in the family." She pauses and studies my face. "He's also kind of adorable, don't you think?"

Yes, I think. But I'm afraid to talk about it. This . . . *whatever* that is going on with us feels so new and fragile. I'm afraid if I talk about it, it might break. So I just give a noncommittal shrug.

"I'm going to go hang up my coat."

I go out into the entryway and kick off my shoes, still thinking of Tom.

I like him so much, sometimes this thing between us doesn't seem real.

And then, just like that, a heavy, unwanted thought crashes onto my head like a bowling ball.

How could I not have considered this sooner?

What if . . . it isn't?

What if me, him, the kissing—all of it—isn't *real*?

That night when I lost Katherine. I wrote in the journal for her to be okay and she was. But I also wrote: *Please let Gracie get what she wants.* I meant that I wanted to find her. *That night.* That's all I was thinking about in that frantic, panicked moment. But it was *Tom* who showed up with her, and wasn't that the moment when everything changed?

My stomach clenches as I rewind and replay everything that's happened since.

Tom at my door with Katherine.

The way he said "Nothing" when she asked what was wrong with me . . .

How he acted like he wanted to stay.

Amy conveniently passing Tom over for Marcus.

Him coming over to help me with the leaves.

Our kitchen kiss.

And tonight, when I was hoping for him to step out onto the porch. And he did.

Did I *make* all that happen, even if that's not exactly what I meant when I wrote it?

I *just* wanted Katherine to be okay.

But . . . maybe I'm kidding myself right now. Because when I wrote *Please let Gracie get what she wants,* maybe there was a piece of me, somewhere deep inside, that meant I wanted *everything*? Because I did want him. I do want him. And if I did mean *everything* then—even just a little, even subconsciously—what does that mean about *now*?

Is it all a lie?

What about my dad offering to help? Is that a lie too?

Can I trust *anything* good?

What if I'm like a tax cheater—a *fraud*—because I've manipulated the natural order of things?

No.

No, no, *NO*.

I'm doing what I always do: sabotaging myself. Afraid that if something good happens, there has to be a catch. Because if I *truly* had everything I wanted, Katherine wouldn't have Alzheimer's disease and my mom wouldn't be on the verge of a nervous breakdown and Hannah and I would still talk regularly and my dad wouldn't live hundreds of miles away. And I'd never overthink a single thing ever again. Which is *clearly* not happening.

I need to push this train of thought right out of my mind,

because otherwise, from now on, for the rest of my life, I'm going to question everything.

Later, right before I go to bed, I look out my window just as Tom's light goes on. He walks to his window and raises a hand. I raise mine too and whisper, "Good night."

I turn out my light and climb into bed, but I can't sleep. I toss and turn, unable to get comfortable, first too cold and then too hot.

I can't stop fixating on the journal under my bed.

It almost feels like a malevolent presence now, agitating my conscience like some chain-dragging Dickensian ghost.

FOR THE NEXT THREE DAYS, I COMMIT TO IGNORING MY doubts.

I ignore my doubts when Tom and I take the dogs out late on Tuesday, and kiss at the corner of Aylesboro and Barnsdale.

I ignore my doubts when he ducks into the library with me at lunch and we kiss in the stacks farthest from the front desk, right next to all the biographies.

And I ignore them when he comes over on Thursday night to help me with my "math assignment."

Both Jack and Katherine are asleep upstairs. My mom is working late. Tom and I are on the sofa, definitely *not* working on any math assignment. This is the first time we've had more than a few minutes together, in a place where we're not in immediate danger of being walked in on at any second, and it's making us both a little eager for *more*.

This time, the kissing is more horizontal than vertical. Tom's sweatshirt is on the floor. I slide a hand under his white tee, running my fingers up the side of his rib cage. His skin is warm. We're so close, I can feel his heart hammering against mine.

And then the thing that I've been trying so very hard *not* to think about works its way into my consciousness like a parasitic brain worm.

What if . . . this is not real? What if you made this happen? What if all of this is not really his choice?

I push on his shoulder to get him to move back, and then I sit up against the sofa cushions.

"Is everything okay?" he asks. "You look a little . . . I don't know."

I need to tell him. I have to tell him.

But how?

It's not like anything I have to say is even remotely believable.

But I like him too much. I like him too much to do anything less than tell him the truth.

I try to think of a way to start. "I really like you, Tom . . ."

And almost immediately, his face gets this kind of "lost puppy" look. "There's a 'but,' isn't there?"

"I'm just worried . . ."

He nods, like he really wants to understand what I'm trying to say. "Okay. About what? That things are moving too fast? We can totally slow it down. Whatever you want."

My heart freezes. *Please let Gracie get what she wants.*

"No." I shake my head. "It's not that." I take a deep breath. "I'm worried . . . that all of this is not real. That I wished it."

"That you wished what? Us?" He shakes his head and takes my hand in both of his for emphasis. "No. We are on the same page. I wished for this too."

"That's not what I mean," I say.

The anxiety starts to course through my veins, making my temples throb. I haven't mentioned a *word* about the journal. To anyone. Well, except Katherine, but she not only doesn't remember the journal, she also doesn't remember me asking her about it.

He waits for my explanation.

I feel like I'm on that broken roller coaster again, about to plunge down, down, down into the abyss.

"I know this is going to sound totally unbelievable, but I have this way of . . . manifesting things?" That sounds okay, right? *Manifesting*, not *manipulating*. I continue, "I found this old . . . book . . . this writing journal. I think it was Katherine's, and it enables me to, kind of, I guess, alter reality?"

Tom sits up straighter and he looks like he's either about to flee or burst out laughing. "Uhhhh, *okaaaay*, what do you mean?"

I plow ahead. "Do you remember that day I got really high at school with Luke Carr?"

Tom smiles. "Uh, yes. You mean the day you asked me why I always smelled so good?"

Oh, God.

"Yes. Well . . ." And I tell him everything that led up to it.

Finding the journal. The nightclub story I wrote about Luke, which is a little bit awkward to admit to, but I assure Tom it was *well* before everything that happened with the two of us. How every detail of my story somehow made it into *Luke's* dream.

How I experimented with the story to test that I wasn't imagining it and how, in real-life PE, Christina handed me a fictional lipstick.

How the skipping-seventh-period entry resulted in Luke and me getting high in Frick Park. (I leave out the kissing Luke part. It is not necessary information.)

How on the night I lost Katherine I wrote that I wanted her to be okay. And then I wrote, *Please let Gracie get what she wants,* and minutes later, *he* showed up at my front door.

When I'm done, Tom is quiet for a long minute. And *this* uncomfortable silence is a million times worse than that day in the car, which also feels like a million years ago, when I asked him to homecoming.

But then he breaks into a grin. "You're totally messing with me right now, aren't you?"

I wasn't expecting this response, but I should have been. This all probably sounds like a ridiculous practical joke.

"Look," I say. "I get it. There's no reason you would believe this. I know I must sound like I've lost it. But it's true."

His grin fades and now he just looks confused. Or maybe

worried. About my state of mind. I know I promised myself I was going to lay off the journal, but . . .

"I can prove it," I tell him.

He squints at me and then half smiles, his expression hinting that he's returned to thinking I'm just goofing around.

"Okay," he says, making a *yeah, sure* face. "How?"

I think for a minute. It has to be something impressive enough to be undeniably magical, but not something that's going to cause too much chaos.

"We'll do an experiment."

He nods like he's playing along. "An experiment."

A demonstration of my power.

"Wait here."

I go upstairs as quietly as possible and get the journal out from underneath my bed. I haven't touched it since the night Katherine went missing.

"Looks like a regular old notebook to me," he says when I sit back down on the sofa next to him.

I ignore this and open the journal to the first blank page. "Tell me something you've always wanted to do or a place you've always wanted to go."

"Time travel!" he says.

I haven't considered time travel as a possibility. And even if it were possible, it seems a little . . . dangerous? What if we ended up stuck somewhere, in the middle of a war or a plague or something?

"I don't know if that will work—or if we want it to. Give me something else."

He rolls his eyes. "Okay . . . okay." He thinks for a few more seconds. "I've always wanted to see the northern lights."

I nod my head. "That might be doable."

At the top of the page, I write: *Aurora Borealis.*

"Now what?" he says.

"So I'm going to write a . . . *scene*. Here in this journal, about you and me seeing the northern lights."

He narrows his eyes. "And then what?"

"And then something should happen."

"Like, I'll dream about the northern lights, or what?"

"Maybe. I don't know exactly what will happen, but something will."

"And when is this *something* supposed to occur?"

I think for a minute. I really don't know, do I? Originally, I thought I had to sleep on it, but that night with Katherine, it seemed to work almost immediately. But maybe that's because I specifically asked for that . . . ? "Maybe tomorrow? Maybe sooner?"

"This is an elaborate practical joke, isn't it?" He leans back and gets a worried look on his face. "Wait, are you *sure* there's not something else going on? It's not because of that guy, Luke? I mean, this isn't some backhanded way of breaking things off, is it?"

"*Tom*. No. I promise."

It kind of kills me that he thinks *I'm* the one who's going to break up with *him*.

"So, what do I need to do?"

"Nothing. Maybe you should even go home."

"But I want to stay here," he says, moving toward me on the sofa.

I flash back to fifteen minutes ago, and wish we could rewind. But there's no going back now. "My mom is going to be home any minute anyway."

Tom sighs. "Okay." He stands, picks up his sweatshirt, and pulls it over his head. I walk him to the door. But before he leaves, he leans in to kiss me one last time, and I remind myself to burn it into my memory. Because I think once he sees that I am able to totally manipulate reality, and possibly him included, he might not want me to kiss him again.

"You are a strange girl, Gracie Byrne," he says after we break the kiss.

"I'm sorry," I say.

He leans his forehead against mine. "I think your strangeness is a pro, not a con."

I watch him cross the street, maybe for the last time, and then I shut the front door.

I know Tom thinks I'm joking or trying to break up with him or that I've possibly lost my mind, and maybe I have, but I'm curious about what's going to happen now too. And not just curious. I'm excited, fueled by a wild energy. I realize now that I want, I *need*, someone else's confirmation that this all isn't just in my head.

Just as I'm about to go upstairs to finish writing an aurora borealis journal entry, headlights turn into the driveway. It's my mom.

I open the front door for her as she comes up the porch stairs.

"Hey, sweetie," she says with a yawn. "What are you still doing up?"

"I'm a teenager. We're supposed to be nocturnal."

"Oh, yeah, I forgot. Been awhile for me. Everything okay here tonight?"

"Yeah," I say. "Not a creature is stirring, except me."

"Well, that's good. I'm going to go up to bed," she says.

"I was just about to head up too."

In the hallway upstairs, I give her a hug. "Love you, Mom."

"Love you too, Gracie-girl." She looks at the journal in my hands. "What's that book you've got?"

For a minute I almost panic. What if she knows that Katherine had this locked in her vanity drawer? What if she knows all about it?

"Oh, it's just an old notebook I found. It was blank, so I thought it would be okay if I used it."

She shrugs. "Oh, sure, take it. Good night."

"Good night."

Two minutes later, I'm in my bed, pen poised over the journal.

Okay.

So. Me. Tom. The aurora borealis. I try to think. Where do they normally appear? Somewhere very far in the Northern Hemisphere, right? Canada. Alaska. Scotland. Iceland. Norway? But maybe the actual location doesn't matter. I click my pen. The clock downstairs on the mantel chimes. It's midnight.

> *We stand side by side as green, purple, and pink lights ripple across the sky, blending into each other like some kind of magical psychedelic dream. I've never seen anything more beautiful. I reach for Tom's hand and—*

A roar rises in my ears and I feel like I've been tossed over the edge of a cliff. I break out in a cold sweat as a tidal wave of nausea washes over me—so strong I'm certain I'm about to vomit. My vision goes all spotty. I squeeze my eyes closed.

WHAT IS HAPPENING?

SOMETHING IS *VERY* WRONG.

AM I HAVING A STROKE?

But before I can wig out too much, the sensation subsides, as quickly as it came.

I open my eyes.

What the—

Tom's voice, to my left, completes the sentence: "*—fuck?*"

It is ridiculously cold. So, so cold.

Somehow, I'm wearing a huge hooded parka, snow pants,

boots, and the kind of gloves you would maybe ski with? I don't know for sure; I've never actually gone skiing. A dark, flattened expanse of snowy ground crunches and squeaks beneath my feet.

"What. THE. FUCK."

Tom's face, barely visible because of the hood on his jacket, is turned to me. He looks like *he* might be about to have a stroke.

"Where *are* we?" he asks.

It's a very good question. I'm still trying to wrap my head around what's just happened. I was expecting something—a shared dream, maybe. Or an aurora appearing in the sky above Pittsburgh, like that owl showing up at school. But this feels like we've actually *gone somewhere else*.

"I'm not sure," I say, looking around. We appear to be somewhere very cold, in the middle of nowhere. "Maybe Iceland? Or Norway?"

"NORWAY?"

The snow all around us is pristine. There are no footprints. Up ahead, there is an ice-capped rock formation. In the distance, I see the jagged black silhouette of the edge of a forest.

"I wasn't quite expecting . . . all of this," I say.

"What *were* you expecting?" Tom stares at me.

I try my best to explain. "Well, so far the journal has only changed things in my regular life. You know, at school and at home and stuff. In sort of, like, subtle ways," I say, although I don't know if that's entirely true. The owl wasn't very subtle.

"It's never transported me elsewhere. I didn't think this was even possible."

Tom starts to pace, looking around. "How is ANY of this possible?"

He is obviously freaking out, which means that *I* can't. One of us has to stay calm.

"I don't know," I say. "But look." I point at the sky. Columns of neon green light are waving and dancing in front of the stars. We stare, transfixed, as beams of pink and violet weave into the green and back out again. It's like magic. Or maybe it *is* magic? But the cold feels pretty damn real. The air is so frigid it burns my lungs. I try to keep him focused on the aurora.

"Why does it happen, do you think?"

"It's caused by electrically charged particles from solar storms colliding with Earth's atmosphere," he says.

"Wow." I pause, searching for something else to say. "Did you know that the name aurora borealis is derived from Greek? *Aurora* means sunrise and *boreas* means wind."

He glances at me. "Why am I not surprised you would know this?"

I shrug. "Well, *you* knew about the electric particles."

He continues, "The color of the aurora depends on the type of particle—or *ion*, as they're technically called, word-nerd—and the type of gas colliding together, as well as the altitude. So when charged ions hit nitrogen at a high altitude, you get blue, and when they crash into oxygen at lower altitudes, you get green, which is the most common color that's typically visible."

I sense that he is calming down a bit. At least for the moment.

"The Southern Hemisphere has auroras too," I add. "Aurora australis."

. . . green, purple, and pink lights ripple across the sky, blending into each other like some kind of magical psychedelic dream. I've never seen anything more beautiful.

"It really is beautiful," I whisper.

"It is. It's the most amazing thing I've ever seen," he says. We are quiet for a minute. The frigid wind stings. "But Gracie?"

"Yeah?"

"How do we get back?"

Despite the cold, I start to sweat inside my parka. *I don't know*. I had no idea the journal was capable of transporting me—and Tom!—to a different physical location. Or . . . what if this a different reality altogether?

What if we can't get back?

What if I've trapped us somewhere in Norway, or Iceland, or some weird alternate northern lights universe?

I haven't seen signs of another person, or a car, or a road, or a house, or anything.

And I don't have the journal *with* me, so it's not like I can try to write us home . . .

We could freeze.

We could freeze to *death*.

And if we die here, do we die for real?

"I don't know how to get back," I admit.

Tom exhales and his breath looks like dragon smoke. "You don't know?"

I didn't think I'd have to get us back from *somewhere else.* I *didn't think*. I didn't even have a chance to finish the story.

I try to push back the panic rising in my own chest.

"Maybe we—"

But I don't get to finish my sentence. A roar rises again in my ears. The nausea returns, along with the feeling of being hurled off a cliff. And then I am back in my own bed. Katherine's journal is on my lap. My head is spinning. I look around my room. My desk, in shadow, is right where it always is, pushed up against the window. The standing mirror in the corner catches a glint of light from the streetlight outside. The house is quiet.

Okay. *Okay*. I exhale slowly. *Okay, okay, okay, okay.* What *was* that? It was a dream, right? An exceptionally vivid dream. Even though I don't recall falling asleep. Or waking up. But it had to be. The question is, did Tom have the same dream too? And will he remember it in the morning? Or not remember it at all and think I need to have my head examined? Everything *felt* so real, though. The cold. The snow squeaking beneath my feet. And—I raise my hands. I'm still wearing one of those gloves. I pull it off my hand and stare at it.

Something taps my window. *Oh, God. Is the owl back?* It can't be—that was an entirely different story. And I ripped that one out.

There it is again. Like a pebble hitting the glass.

I get up and run to the window, conscious of Hank sleeping in Jack's room across the hall. If it wakes him up, he'll bark, and then the whole house will be up.

Tom is standing in the yard below, looking wild-eyed in sweats and boots and a parka. He's motioning for me to come down.

Putting a finger to my lips, I signal that I'll be right there.

I guess it wasn't just me. He's part of this now, whether he wants to be or not.

BREAKING BENFORD'S LAW

AS QUIETLY AS POSSIBLE, I STEP OUT ONTO THE FRONT PORCH and close the door behind me.

"Let's walk," I whisper when I join Tom on the sidewalk. "So we don't wake everybody up."

He nods and follows me as I start moving in the direction of the park. It's quite cold outside, but it almost feels balmy in comparison to wherever the hell we just were.

"What the fuck just happened?" Tom doesn't really swear that much, but he's been swearing a *lot* tonight.

"Now do you believe me?" I ask.

He's silent for a few paces and then says, "Just . . . okay, I need to confirm this. Where *were* we about ten minutes ago?"

"Well," I say, "I don't know *exactly*. Maybe Norway? Or

Iceland? It looked like there was a forest in the distance . . . ?" Not that that narrows it down at all.

He stops on the sidewalk to face me, pulling on the front of the parka he's wearing. "*This* is not *my* coat."

"I came back with a glove . . ."

"Holy shit, holy shit, holy *shit*," he whispers.

"I know," I say. "I think I broke Benford's law or something."

"More like *all* the laws of physics." He starts walking again. "Can you explain this from the beginning again?"

So I do. I tell him about finding the journal. And about the story with Luke. I tell him about my experiment with the Blakiston's fish owl.

"Wait," says Tom, stopping me there. "The owl you wrote about appeared at school? *Our* school? That definitely sounds like something I would remember."

I glance at him, and my face starts to heat.

"Well . . . I erased that one."

"What do you mean you erased it?"

"Things got a little out of hand with the owl, and I was kind of freaked out about it. So that night, I ripped out that page from the journal. And then, the next day, nobody remembered it even happened."

"So you made everyone forget about an owl that you . . . manifested . . . at school?"

"Well," I say. "Yeah. But not intentionally. I didn't have any idea that that's what would happen; I was just . . . I don't even know. I was just overwhelmed by the entire day. Anyway, I put the journal away after that and didn't really use it until that night I lost Katherine."

"And the day at the park. With Luke."

"Yeah, and that." This is starting to sound worse than I had hoped.

"Remind me again why you did that?"

I feel like Lucy in that *I Love Lucy* chocolate factory episode that Katherine and I watched. Trying to keep up with the unwrapped chocolates whizzing by on that conveyer belt that just gets faster and faster and faster. Only, in my case, the chocolates are all of my mistakes. I could make up some explanation that is slightly less embarrassing than the truth, but that would only add to my mistake tally.

"I think it was my screwed up way of getting a homecoming date after you'd turned me down." This is absolutely humiliating to admit.

Tom stops and studies me. "Gracie," he says. "This is a lot for me to try to make sense of."

"I know," I say. I can feel my eyes starting to sting.

"I mean, I don't know. I guess I would have been curious about what that book could do too. And what just happened tonight? That was *amazing.* Magical. But also, *terrifying*. You can't just make other people your puppets."

"I know. I'm *so* sorry. That's *not* what I intended. That night I lost Katherine, I was just *so* scared. I didn't even mean for it to impact you."

"I'm not even really talking about me," he says. "I'm glad

I found her, even if you kind of, sort of, made it happen. But what about everyone else? What about Luke?"

"Why are you worried about Luke?" I ask. "That is so *completely* over with, I promise."

"I get that," he says. "But I meant what you did with the journal. Because he's, like, a *person*? Who's supposed to have free will?"

A wave of guilt washes over me. I had no business using the journal to manipulate Luke. Or Christina, or Becky, or a Blakiston's fish owl, or *anyone*. The first time with Luke was basically an accident, but the Frick Park day was most definitely not. The tears start to flow, which only makes me feel more terrible. I don't deserve to cry.

"I know," I keep saying. "I *know*. I do think it wore off, though. With Luke. And Christina." I haven't thought much about her lately, but now realize that she hasn't complimented me on my outfit for weeks. "For a while, it was like whatever I wrote in the journal lingered in their consciousness or something? But now it's like it never happened at all."

"Still," he says.

"I know."

He takes a long breath. I can see that he's still really freaked out. And how can I blame him? Not only do I suck, but I also just ripped the rug of reality right out from under his feet.

He looks at the ground. "I think I need a little time to wrap my head around all this, okay?"

All I can do is nod. Because I know that there's really nothing that I can say to make this right.

We walk back toward Shady Avenue in silence.

And when we turn the corner onto our street, I see the lights of the ambulance out front.

I TAKE OFF RUNNING DOWN THE STREET. MY MOM IS STANDING on the sidewalk in her robe as two paramedics load Katherine into the back of the ambulance.

"Mom!"

She looks up at me and I can tell immediately that she's *really* upset.

"*Where the hell were you?*" The look on her face is *angry*. Scared too, but mostly angry.

"I went for—"

Tom catches up behind me. My mom looks from me to him and narrows her eyes, obviously wondering why the both of us were out here in the middle of the night.

"—a walk," I finish. "What happened?"

"She fell. I found her on the landing of the stairs—she got

the gate open. I didn't even hear her get up! I think she probably broke her hip."

One of the paramedics approaches my mom. "If you want to ride along, we're ready, ma'am."

"You go," I say to my mom. "I'll meet you with the car."

"Yeah, okay." She gets into the ambulance. The paramedic shuts the door, tells me which hospital they're going to, and they drive away.

"Gracie." Tom touches my arm, trying, I think, to jolt me out of my frozen state.

"I have to go," I say. I turn and see that Jack is sitting on the porch steps in his pajamas, looking like he's about to cry.

"Hey, buddy," I say as I join him on the stairs and put my arm around him. "It's going to be okay."

"Mom was yelling for you," he says. "She got really worried when I told her your room was empty."

I feel sick.

"You know what, Jack?" says Tom, who is somehow still here, despite the fact that I'm the worst. "Why don't you come over to our house for the rest of the night?"

"That's not a bad idea," I say. "So you're not here all alone. How about you go inside and grab your coat and a pillow? I'll come over and get you in the morning, okay? Grandma's in good hands now."

"I'll help him get his stuff," Tom says. "You go meet your mom."

I run inside and grab my car keys.

As I drive to the hospital, I can't shake the feeling that this is somehow, yet again, all my fault.

Katherine's hip is broken. And her left arm.

"She's going to have surgery," my mom says when I join her in the waiting room on the third floor. "They're prepping her now. And then rehab, and then . . . I don't know."

"What do you mean?"

My mom rubs her eyes. "Rehab is not always successful with dementia patients. And if she can't get back to being relatively mobile, we'll have to find her more advanced care."

"You mean, like, a nursing home?"

My mom sighs. "Yeah. I mean, at a place like Park Manor, the residents can be in a wheelchair, but they can't be in need of really advanced services. They're just not set up for that. Goddamn it!" She kicks one of the mauve waiting room chairs in frustration. "I should have dealt with that gate right away . . ."

I start to cry. For the second time tonight. But I can't help it. "Mom. I'm *so* sorry. I'm so, so sorry. I shouldn't have left the house in the middle of the night like that and I wasn't there when you needed help and I feel like this is all my fault . . ."

"Gracie," my mom says, sinking into a chair. "This is not your fault. None of this is your fault, okay? I'm sorry I yelled when you came running down the sidewalk. I was just really, really stressed. I *am* really stressed. I know I should be used to it by now, but it is really hard to see Grandma—to see my *mom*—like this. And to see that she probably needs more care than we're able to give her."

I think about how it would feel for my mom not to recognize me, for her to feel like my child instead of my parent. It would be devastating.

"She got lost about a month ago," I confess. "When I was watching her. She walked right out the front door and I didn't even hear her. It was raining . . . and I called the police . . . and Tom found her in the crosswalk a couple of blocks away and brought her home. She was okay, but Mom, she could have been hit by a car, she could have—"

My mom puts her hand on my back. "It's okay. It's *okay*."

"I'm so sorry, Mom."

"I know you are. But it's not your fault."

"It *was* my fault!"

"*No*. It's not your fault. It's not anyone's fault. You are so helpful, Gracie, but I've put too much on you. This isn't sustainable. Grandma just got dealt a shitty hand, that's all. You don't know how much I wish there were some magical cure to release her from all this . . . or to give her back herself, but there's not."

And her saying this makes my stomach lurch.

Some magical cure.

I *know* that journal has ultimately given me nothing but trouble, and that I have basically abused its power, but maybe it wasn't meant for *me*? If I was able to use it to erase memories with the owl, couldn't it, in theory, be used to give memories back?

No.

No, no, no, no, no.

That journal has already caused me to make a huge mess of everything. And I clearly don't have a handle on how it's supposed to work—certainly not enough of one to be mucking around with someone's brain. What if I made everything worse for her? But why does it exist, then? *What is it fucking for?*

"I hate Alzheimer's," I say to my mom.

Her eyes fill with tears. "Me too, Gracie. Me too."

There's nothing we can do at the hospital for the next few hours, so we go home. My mom wants to change into regular clothes and pack a bag for Katherine. After the surgery, she'll need to stay at the hospital for at least a few days or more before being moved to a rehabilitation facility.

"So what's going on with you and Tom?" my mom asks on the drive home.

"Nothing," I say. "Not anymore, anyway."

"Didn't seem like nothing."

"I don't really want to talk about it."

She sighs. "You never want to talk about anything, Gracie. I really wish you'd let me in."

But I don't even know where to begin with the whole Tom situation. Like, what am I supposed to tell her? Things were going great until I almost got the two of us stuck in Norway or Iceland or wherever, and now he's sort of terrified of me? And that I don't even know if the "great" part was even *real* or something I just manifested with the help of this reality-altering journal that I found in Katherine's vanity drawer?

I know I should say *something* to make her feel like I'm not shutting her out, but I just don't have the words.

We get home and sleep for a few hours. Around five a.m., my mom is showered and dressed and standing in my bedroom doorway. "I'm going back to the hospital," she says. "Can you run some clean clothes across the street for your brother in a few hours? Trish can drive him to school. It's fine if you stay home, but I already had to have a meeting with Jack's teacher last week about his grades, so he probably should go."

I didn't know Jack was having issues with his grades. What else has Mom been shielding me from?

"Sure."

The dark circles under Mom's eyes make her look spooky in the dim light. She really needs a good night's sleep. Multiple good nights' sleep. While on an all-expenses-paid vacation with tropical drinks.

"I'll let you know the update after I talk to her doctor."

"Okay."

She disappears into the hallway, and a minute later, I hear the front door close.

I don't have to get clothes to Jack until around seven, but I can't fall back asleep. I can't stop thinking about the whole situation with Katherine. This is bad. She might not recover enough to come home, and then she'll have to go to a full-time senior care facility.

Facility. There's a dismal word. One that immediately conjures up linoleum hallways and too-bright lights and beige walls. We all visited one earlier this year, after my grandfather died, and before my mom made the decision for us to move in at Katherine's. That visit was a big reason *why* we moved in with her. I remember that day well, because it was one of those times when the three of us—my mom, Jack, and me—were united. All of us on the same page. Even me, who, up until then, did *not* want to move.

Mom had been given a list of places for us to check out from Katherine's primary care doctor, but many of them were astronomically expensive. And those that weren't had long waiting lists, leaving us with only a few options. When we drove up to Evergreen Living, there was not a single evergreen in sight. Just a big paved parking lot and a long, low building with sliding hospital doors in the front. The inside wasn't much more welcoming. We checked in for our tour, and while we waited in the front lobby, which honestly was the nicest part, Katherine was already agitated. The aide who appeared to show us around seemed frazzled, like someone had forgotten we were visiting, and while she led us through the various highlights—dining room, TV room, game room, typical resident's room—as quickly as she could, Katherine slow-walked it the entire time. So it felt like we were there for an eternity.

The thing I remember the most is the feeling that the people there were *parked*. Parked in front of TVs that droned, even though it seemed that nobody was really watching. Parked around tables in the dining room, staring at mushy-looking meals. Parked in the hallways, waiting for someone to come and get them and park them somewhere else.

Occasionally, we'd hear a voice calling from one of the open rooms. The place had a strong disinfectant smell. Jack finally said, "Can we *go* now?"

"Yes, let's," said my mom, and as we walked quickly through the parking lot back to the car, almost as if we were trying to flee, she said, "Don't worry, we are *not* going to let Grandma live in a place like this."

"Good," said Jack, who looked like he was about to burst into tears.

"There's *no* way," I agreed.

Park Manor is nothing like Evergreen Living. It's cozy and comfortable and well-staffed. It's walking distance from our house. But all I can think about is what my mom said at the hospital. *If she can't get back to being relatively mobile, we'll have to find her more advanced care.*

How did everything get to be such a mess? Katherine is hurt. My mom is beyond burned out. I think I've totally screwed up everything with Tom, and even Jack, who always seems like nothing bothers him, is apparently struggling. I can't remember the last time I wasn't overthinking absolutely everything. When I wasn't feeling anxious or awkward or unsure.

Hiraeth: longing for a home you can't return to, or that never was.

That word is exactly how I feel. Homesick. But I don't

know if I can articulate what, specifically, I'm so homesick for. Is it for my old house, my old school, my old life? Or is it for a feeling? Maybe it's for that feeling I used to have when I was younger, when my parents were still together, and I was perhaps more secure about my place in the world. That feeling of safety, of comfort. Of not having to make difficult decisions or recover from big mistakes. If I had to describe it, I'd say the feeling would be like eating pancakes in the kitchen on a cold day, snow falling softly outside. Like warming your hands at a cozy fire.

Sometimes I wish I could just rewind the last few months. Just go back and start over. And having the ability to—perhaps—do just that? It's tempting me like a drug tempts an addict. The journal is not under my bed. It's in the bed, right next to me. Right where I left it last night when I ran outside to meet Tom on the sidewalk. And I wonder. What if . . . I just ripped it all out?

The nightclub story.

Skipping seventh period with Luke Carr.

Please let Gracie get what she wants.

The aurora borealis with Tom.

Is this journal capable of time travel? Would I end up back in early September, ready to begin again with a clean slate? Would everyone forget all of this? Would *I* forget all of this?

No. Trying to undo it all would be galactically foolish. There are too many layers now. I don't really know what ripping it all out would actually do. Maybe it would be like pulling a loose thread from a sweater, only, in this case, the entire fabric of reality would fall apart.

Hiraeth. I write the word on the next blank page. I scribble it over and over and over: *Hiraeth. Hiraeth.*

I cover all the available white space until the entire page is a sea of the same word. *Hiraeth.* The word, repeating and repeating and repeating on the page, blurs in front of me as my eyes fill with tears. My tears fall on the page, making the black ink bleed.

And then I get a hold of myself.

No more.

I need to stop messing around with this journal. Stop thinking it has anything to offer me aside from chaos. I rip out the hiraeth page, toss it in the trash, drop the journal on the floor, and finally, finally fall asleep.

WHEN I WAKE UP, IT'S SNOWING. BIG FLUFFY FLAKES ARE falling outside my window, and the backyard is a winter wonderland of white. Even the swing set, which normally is a little worse for wear, looks bright and magical.

Wait.

What am I looking at? This is the backyard of our old house. I sit up in bed and look around. I'm in my old room. My old room, but not quite. The *Joshua Tree* poster that I put up only a few weeks ago—in my bedroom at Katherine's—is on the wall. The black oxfords that I bought for my first week at Morewood High are on the floor next to my old closet. Something isn't right.

I go to the window and stare at the snow. The glass is cold to the touch, with tiny crystals of frost building up around the corners. I hear noises in another part of the house. Plates clinking, and the gurgling sound of the coffee maker. I smell bacon.

And pancakes.

Hiraeth.

But how?

I ripped it out.

"SNOW DAY!"

Jack's voice rings in the hallway. He's banging on my door. "They just announced school's canceled!"

"Getting dressed," I warn, before he barges in. I'm still trying to get my bearings.

"High school too," he adds from the hallway. "Going to go sledding with Kevin after breakfast." Kevin is Jack's best friend from our old neighborhood.

"Cool."

"And Dad's making pancakes, so hurry up!"

My *dad* is here.

"I'll be down in a little bit."

I open the closet and look at myself in the full-length mirror on the back of the door. It is present-day me, isn't it? I haven't gone back in time?

Hiraeth. Longing for a home you can't return to, or that never was.

What the . . . ? I'm not sure why my ripping that page out didn't prevent this from happening. Unless I'm dreaming, but it really feels like I am not. I stare at my face in the mirror. I got sucked somewhere else again. Like last night with Tom. But this is definitely, for sure, a *different* version of reality, isn't it? I mean, it *has* to be. Because in real reality, I no longer live in this house. And my dad hasn't lived with us since he and my mom split.

I look around the room, and out the window again. I have no idea how long I'm going to be stuck here—if it's going to be minutes or hours—so I guess I may as well go downstairs and check the situation out. Plus: bacon.

When I walk into the kitchen, my dad is in front of the stove, making pancakes.

"Hey, kiddo," he says. "Bacon's almost ready. How many pancakes do you want?"

I pause for a few seconds. It's definitely present-day him. His beard has those gray patches that weren't there a few years ago. When he was still part of *our* family. But he's wearing his old clothes. Jeans and a flannel shirt. He started dressing differently when he got together with Kirsten. It was weird.

I walk over to him and he gives me a hug, the stubble from his beard scratching my face. I hug him back and don't understand the ache in my chest that this seems to trigger. I just saw him at Thanksgiving. But seeing him here, in this house, in his old flannel shirt, is different. Hiraeth.

"Maggie!" he calls. "There's coffee!"

My mom wanders into the kitchen and pulls a mug down from the shelf. This is still the same; *nobody* talks to my mom before she's had her coffee. She fills her mug, opens the fridge, and adds a little half-and-half.

I take in both of my parents. Still married. In the same room. My mom leans against the counter and sips her coffee. My dad flips a pancake on the stove. Nobody is talking, so I study their body language, trying to get a read on the current status of their relationship. Are they happy? Are they not happy? Is he still seeing Kirsten and we just don't know it yet? It's hard to tell.

Jack is thumping around above us. "Has anyone seen my snow boots?" he yells.

"On the basement stairs!" Mom yells back.

As I take everything in, I become aware of a very specific absence. Hank. There is no Hank. We got him after my parents split up, when my mom caved to Jack's pleas about us getting a dog.

My dad puts a platter of bacon and a plate stacked with pancakes on the table. "Breakfast is served!" he says.

Jack comes in, half-dressed in snow pants.

My mom passes around plates and utensils. She fills glasses with juice.

We all sit. For the first time in three years, my entire family is seated at the breakfast table. Together.

The radio is on and the traffic report is all about the many backups caused by the snow. I hear the announcer say, *"The phrase of the day is 'take it slow'!"*

My mom sighs. "I'm going to have to leave an extra hour to get to work."

Katherine, I think. I need to see Katherine.

"Can we go to Katherine's?" I ask my mom. I turn to Jack. "We can sled on that big hill in Frick Park."

My mom looks confused. "Katherine's? You mean Grandma's house?"

"Yeah," I say quickly. "I was just . . . wondering how she's doing? Could I . . ." I don't know the car situation in this reality, so I just guess. "Take the car?"

My mom quickly shakes her head.

"No. Your dad and I both need to get to work. No snow day for either of us, unfortunately."

"I can drop you off on my way," my dad says to my mom.

"And then I can take the other car?" I ask. This might work.

But Mom is not having it. "No, Gracie, Grandma's is two hours away! Not in this weather."

"The Ford has all-wheel drive," my dad offers.

My mom sets down her fork and glares at him. "She *just* got her license."

My dad shrugs at me. "Maybe tomorrow."

"*If* the roads are clear," my mom adds.

I can feel the tension between them and try to figure out if it's just normal "married for years" tension or something more.

Jack bangs out the door not long after my dad leaves for work. I watch through the window as he drags his sled up the road toward Kevin's. So now it's just me here in this house—*my* house but *not* my house—alone. I look at the clock. More than an hour has gone by. This experience is definitely lasting longer than the aurora borealis, and I wonder when it will wear off. I feel like it has to be soon, so I skip cleaning up the kitchen even though I told my mom-not-my-mom that I would do it.

Around eleven, I'm a little weirded out and tired of being all alone. *I should call Hannah,* I realize. That might be interesting. See what's happening with me and Hannah in this alternate reality where I never moved away and she's still my best friend. I go to the phone that's attached to the wall in the kitchen and dial her number. She picks up on the fourth ring. "Hello?"

"Hey! It's Gracie."

"Gracie. Hi." I can't be sure, but she *almost* seems surprised to hear from me.

"How's it going?" I ask.

"Well, I can't be the only one jumping for joy that we got a snow day, on a Friday, on the day of the trig final, right?"

I laugh. "Right." Maybe I should get out of the house. Get some fresh air. Maybe that will help me clear out the fog that seems to have gathered, thick and heavy, in my head. "What are you up to today?" I ask her. "Want to hang out? Go for a walk in the snow or something?"

There's a pause. "I can't. Jason and I are heading out in about a half hour with Kerry and Dave and those guys to go sledding up at Hamilton Hill. Maybe we could do something later this weekend? I have plans with Jason tomorrow, but maybe Sunday afternoon?"

"Uh . . . sure." I mean, *I* most likely won't be here, but she doesn't know that. "I'll check in with you then."

"Cool," says Hannah. "It's nice to hear from you, Gracie."

"Have fun sledding," I say.

After I hang up, I note a few things about the call that seemed weird: Hannah's *it's nice to hear from you* definitely made it seem like we don't talk much. She also didn't ask if I wanted to come sledding. And since when does she hang out with "Kerry and Dave and those guys"?

Maybe we're no longer best friends in *this* universe too? What's up with that?

At noon, I go ahead and clean up the kitchen, just to have something to do.

Jack comes home for lunch shortly thereafter, and I make us both a grilled cheese sandwich with sliced apples. Afterward, we build a snow fort in the backyard.

My mom brings home pizza for dinner. My dad is in a bad mood because of the traffic when he walks in. They both seem tired, and hardly talk while we eat.

That night, my dad, Jack, and I watch a movie in the den. My mom goes up to bed with her book. But I can't really focus on the movie. I'm wondering about my mom and dad. They're together here, but they don't seem happy. Or maybe they were both just stressed earlier because of the traffic and the storm. Hannah and I don't seem as close as we used to be. I'm also wondering what's going on with Katherine. Is she the same here? Or different? At least Jack seems fine. But he's always fine, and now that I think about it, maybe that's his way of coping with actually *not* being fine. Other things I'm wondering:

Why am I still here?

When, exactly, is this going to wear off?

What should I do in the meantime?

And, finally, if I'm *here, then where is the Gracie who actually belongs in this life?*

At bedtime, I try to calm down by convincing myself that this will probably be over in the morning. That I'll go to sleep and when I wake up, I'll be back to normal. And then I'm going get rid of that journal. Get it out of my room, and out of my life, for good. Before something happens that I really can't come back from.

Outside, the moon reflects off the snow, casting everything in an eerie light, like a Polaroid that hasn't fully developed yet. It takes forever for me to fall asleep.

When I open my eyes in the morning, I start to fully appreciate my predicament. I stare out the window, taking in the backyard, the swing set, the snow. A chill sweeps through me, as cold as the Norwegian wind from the last universe I dropped into. What if this is permanent?

I don't hear the coffee maker gurgling in the kitchen yet and I realize that's because everyone must be sleeping in. It's a Saturday, which at least means I'm not expected to go to school; I've got some time to work things out.

I pace around my-bedroom-but-not-my-bedroom.

The journal.

I wrote myself into this. Maybe there's a way to write myself out of it.

This is *my* (well, sort of) room, after all. Not a frozen tundra. I get down on my hands and knees and look under the bed. There are several shoeboxes there, two that actually contain shoes and one full of these weird bendy hair curlers I bought but never use. There's an empty suitcase. And several dusty stacks of old books that I used to read when I was a kid. That's it. I scan the room. Maybe in this reality, I keep it somewhere else? The closet? In a drawer? But I sense that it's probably not here. In *this* house. What I need to do is go to the source. I need to do what I wasn't able to do yesterday.

I need to get to Katherine's.

"So can I take the car to go visit Grandma?" I ask my mom as soon as she's had her coffee.

"Well, I was going to go grocery shopping, but I suppose I can take your dad's car," she says. "The roads seem okay today." And then she studies me, like she's trying to figure something out. "Why the sudden urge to go see Grandma? You know we're going over for Sunday dinner next weekend."

I need a plausible reason.

"I thought it would be nice to have some one-on-one time."

Her face softens. "Okay. Let me just give her a ring first to make sure she's not doing her docent thing today at the museum."

This *definitely* doesn't sound like the Katherine I know. Which is the best thing I've heard since I arrived here in this other life of mine.

As I drive west toward Pittsburgh, I formulate a plan. I'll visit with Katherine, and at some point, excuse myself to use the bathroom upstairs and see if the journal is in her vanity drawer. Or under the bed in my room. Which I guess isn't *my* room *here*. But what if I don't find it? Or . . . a little ember of worry begins to smolder in my gut. What if it doesn't even exist here at all? How will I get back? *Can* I get back? I shake my head. I'll just have to cross that bridge when I come to it.

"GRACIE!"

I lose track of all my intentions when Katherine opens the front door. Immediately, it is clear this is not the grandmother I know. She doesn't sound like her, and she doesn't look like her either. Her hair is done and she's wearing a thick cable-knit sweater and slacks. Most notably, there's no purse hanging from her arm.

I'm so bowled over by her saying my name that I'm momentarily speechless. She steps out onto the porch and pulls me into a hug. "Aren't I the luckiest to get you all to myself today?" She smells like cinnamon, something I remember from when I was little and she used to bake. I hug her back tight as a huge lump forms in my throat. She's okay *here*. *This* is what okay looks like. "Hi, Grandma," I say. I haven't said those words in so long.

And then I burst into tears. Big, messy, red-faced, waterfall tears.

She holds on to me and rubs my back as I cry.

"Oh, Gracie-girl, what's wrong, honey?"

Everything, I think. *Everything*. Except . . . right here, right now, in this universe that is not my universe, where everything is familiar but also so very strange, she is okay. *Really* okay. And isn't this what I wanted the most? *A home you can't return to, or that never was.* But I don't know how to tell her any of that.

"Let's go inside," she whispers to me. "It's cold out here."

Gently, she steers me into the entryway and helps me with my coat as I wipe my face and look around.

The house is different too. Less stuck in time. I take in the newer, more comfortable-looking furniture in the sitting room. The crafting table and knitting supplies in the study. Something is indeed baking in the kitchen.

"I'm making your favorite," she says. "Apple pie. It's got about ten more minutes and then we can go out for a walk while it cools."

"Okay," I say, finally managing to speak.

"Let's go sit by the fire."

And sure enough, there's a small fire going in the fireplace, which we've never used since my mom, Jack, and I moved in to this-house-but-not-this-house. My mom was too worried about Katherine not paying attention, getting too close, and getting burned.

I stand in front of the fire and warm my hands while Katherine—or, I guess I can call her Grandma here—sits in an armchair.

"Tell me what's going on with you, Gracie," she says. "Your mom mentioned you've been a little blue lately."

My stomach flip-flops as the utter weirdness of the whole situation washes over me. I hesitate for a minute, unsure of what to say. The Gracie she is asking about is not *me*, right? But also *is* me? Why is she sad lately? And yet again this makes me wonder: Where *is* the Gracie she's asking about? Have I booted her out of her own life? I feel like I might be ripping holes all over the fabric of the universe. And who knows whether they can be repaired?

I try to think of something to say that's vague enough not to raise any eyebrows.

"It's nothing, really . . . School is busy. Mom is overreacting."

She studies me. "Those tears didn't seem like nothing. Everything okay at home?"

Which home?

"Everything is fine," I tell her. "I just . . . wanted to visit to make sure you were okay. With all the snow."

"Oh." She swats the air with her hand. "I paid Dorothy Mortimer's grandson to shovel the walks. And I'm not scheduled at the Carnegie until Tuesday, so I don't need to drive in it. I'm all right."

She does seem all right—more than capable of taking care of herself, in fact—and it makes me smile.

"How's that going?" I ask, changing the subject. "Your docent thing, I mean. I want to hear all about it."

I want to hear about a million things. *Everything.* But I'm not sure what I can talk about without raising suspicion and being found out as an imposter Gracie.

As she tells me about the latest exhibit she's giving volunteer tours for at the Carnegie Museum, I keep glancing at the framed photos on the mantel. There are a number of me and Jack. And my mom at various ages. My grandparents in their wedding photo. My mom and dad's too. There's also the one of Katherine and her brother and sisters in front of the old farmhouse. And there, with the others, are photos of Katherine and the boy that I *think* is the one *my* Katherine talked about that day we walked back from Park Manor: Henry. The photos I found in the hat box. There's the one where she's wrapping her arms around him and the one from the party, where they're both looking at each other and laughing. Right here. Not tucked away under a bunch of junk in a drawer. Which is . . . surprising, to say the least.

It's already out of my mouth before I can stop myself. "Is that Henry?" I ask, pointing to the photos.

She gives me a curious look and then answers. "Yes, of course."

"Where was that one . . . the party one . . . taken?"

All I can think about is the day that I showed my Katherine

that photo and she couldn't remember the name of the place. How sad and frustrated she looked.

She smiles. "That was the Variety Club. We saw Duke Ellington that night! I don't think I've ever danced so much . . . Why do you ask?"

Should I tell her everything right now? What will she think? But I don't want to ruin this moment. This moment that I can't have in my real life. Not yet. Because once I do, I don't know if I'll ever be able to get it back again.

"I've just . . . always been curious about it. You both look so happy."

"We were," she says, her voice wistful. "We were." A *ding* sounds behind the kitchen door.

"Oh, that's my pie," she says. "I'll be right back."

Once the pie is out of the oven, we go for a walk in the park. The sun has come out and snow glitters all around us. I still can't quite bring myself to ask about the journal, so for a little while we talk about mundane, everyday stuff—the book she's reading, upcoming holiday plans, her favorite spot at the museum—which at first seems like a waste of this time we have together. But it's also, in a way, wonderful. I don't ever get to talk to my Katherine about anything rooted in the everyday. Not usually. Sometimes she comments on the weather. But mostly it's all about "where they put the letters."

I remind myself to get my head back on straight as we turn onto Shady Avenue. I've almost forgotten why I've come here today. I need to find that journal. I need to figure out a way to get myself home, even if, at the moment, part of me wants to stay.

When we get back to the house, Katherine and I kick snow off our boots before climbing the stairs to the front porch. I glance over to the Broders' house. Thoughts of Tom have been in the back of mind since we set off on our walk. Does he live across the street . . . *here*? And if so, is he home? Even if he is, would he know me? Not the other Gracie. Me. *Probably not.* Unless . . . A desperate hope takes hold: Could I have somehow pulled *my* Tom—or probably not my Tom anymore, but the Tom I know—into this universe too? It's a long shot, but if he *is* there, maybe he can help me figure out what to do.

"Grandma," I say. "Do you mind if I just pop across the street for a second? I wanted to say hi . . . to a friend."

She looks across the street and then at me. "You have a friend at the Mortimers'?"

My face falls. He's not there. Of course he's not. At least not in that house. Could he be somewhere else nearby? I could look in the phone book, maybe . . . but what if his family never left Chicago in this universe? What if he doesn't even *exist* here?

Katherine studies me for another long minute. "I don't think whoever you're looking for is there."

I lock eyes with her, something in her tone making me uneasy.

She pauses, like she's choosing her words carefully, then she says: "You're not the Gracie who belongs here, are you?"

For a few seconds, I'm so stunned I don't know what to say. Finally I ask, "What do you mean?"

She tilts her head. "You're acting very strange. In a way that makes me think that you must have found my book."

Immediately I get goose bumps. And it's not from the cold.

She *knows.*

Which means there's definitely a journal here, somewhere. And she's used it, or is at least aware of what it can do. Which means I can tell her everything without her thinking that I've lost my mind, and maybe she can help. Maybe she can even explain how it's supposed to work and I can finally get to the bottom of why it exists and what it's for.

"I did," I say, my eyes filling with tears. "I did find . . . your book. And I think I've made a big mess of things."

She nods and then seems to come to a decision. "Let's go inside. Have some lunch and some pie. And then we can sit by the fire and *really* talk."

While we have lunch, I confess to her: "I think I'm *stuck.*"

"So it seems," she says. "It's interesting . . ."

"It is?"

"Well, I'm wondering about *my* Gracie," she says. "Did you boot her out of this reality? Take over her consciousness?"

For a brief second, I feel like she's slapped me. I am not *her* Gracie, and she knows it. Is she angry? And now that it's all out in the open, I have to come to terms with the fact that she is not *my* Katherine, which breaks my heart.

"I don't know!" I admit. "I didn't intentionally try to come here. It was all kind of an accident. That journal doesn't exactly follow any logical rules as far as I can tell."

She nods and sighs. "I can see why you would think that."

I have so many questions—about how it works, where she found it, how long she's had it—and they spill out of me so fast, there's no way I'm even making much sense. I also ask her if my mom knows about the journal, if *my* Katherine does, and if she can help me get unstuck.

Finally, there's the question I don't ask, but it's probably the most important one of all: *Can you help me set things right?*

Katherine blots her lips with her napkin and sets it down next to her plate. "Well, your mother doesn't know about it *here*, but I have no idea what she does or doesn't know wherever you're from. And I don't know if I can get you unstuck, but we can try. All I can tell you is what I've learned."

So she begins to tell me her story. And even though it sounds like fiction, I know that it's all true.

"I found the journal long ago, when I was close to your age, in an old trunk that used to belong to *my* grandmother. And much like what I expect you have experienced, I learned what it could do quite by accident." She smiles. "I was a dreamy girl when I was young. I loved to make up stories. And when I found that journal, I don't know . . . I can't really explain it, but it just felt like the perfect place to write them down. So I did. And then something strange happened. I wrote this silly story about a girl who brought good luck to everyone she met—and it echoed in my real life, but in unexpected ways. My neighbor's chicken started laying a prodigious amount of eggs. My brother found a twenty-dollar bill on the street. Back then, that was quite a lot of money! I didn't make the connection right away, but once I noticed what was going on, I started experimenting. It was thrilling at first, to have the power to bend reality, even if I couldn't quite control it. But after causing a little too much trouble a few times, well . . . I put it away. Back then, you see, my family was very religious. We went to Mass every Sunday and even sometimes during the week too. I came to believe there was something sacrilegious or perhaps even evil about that book. Like it was a test sent by God for me to resist."

She shakes her head and continues, glancing up at the mantel. "Some years passed, the war came, and I lost someone very important to me, as you know. It was a very scary time, for everyone. There were things I thought I could fix, or perhaps even undo. But as I suspect you've learned, the book doesn't always interpret the words you write in the way that you think it will."

"Are you talking about Henry?" I ask. "I actually *don't* know much about him. You've only ever mentioned him once . . . in my world."

She seems surprised. "You don't know? Henry was your biological grandfather," she says. "We got engaged in 1943, right before he went overseas. Three weeks later, he was killed in Tunisia. It wasn't long after that I found out I was pregnant with your mother." She pauses for a few seconds and then she continues: "In those days, this was not the best situation to be in, as you can imagine. We hadn't married yet. And later, when his letters arrived, it almost broke me. The mail was delayed, you see . . ."

A connection clicks in my brain: *his letters.* Are they the letters that my Katherine is always asking about? They must be. A lump forms in my throat.

This Katherine gets this faraway look. "I hardly remember how I got out of bed during that time. But I think, in a roundabout way, that journal may have sent Charles to me, right when I needed him most."

"Grandpa Charles?"

She nods. "He was a friend of my older brother, Frank. And, through Frank, he knew about my situation."

"So you used the journal . . . to do what?"

"I wrote that I wanted my child to have a father, but I had no idea things would happen the way they did. At the time, I just wanted Henry back. I was grief-stricken, devastated. But I don't think resurrection is one of its abilities, which, as I've grown older, I've come to realize is really for the best."

"Yeah, you could have had a *Pet Sematary* situation on your hands."

"What's that?" she asks.

"It's just this creepy book by Stephen King. Probably don't read it . . ."

"Oh . . ." she says. "Charles disliked those kinds of books.

He was such a snob about things sometimes." She laughs. "Charles was *very* different from Henry in so many ways. Serious. Quiet. Thoughtful. Henry was light and carefree. Oh, he made me laugh! But, in the end, Charles was a good father to Maggie. And a good husband to me."

I'm starting to think that in this universe, the grandfather I know must have passed away years ago. Maybe this Katherine waited to put up those pictures of Henry until after he died. Something *my* Katherine never had a chance to do.

"But," I say, "weren't you always worried that it wasn't really Grandpa's choice to marry you?"

She thinks about this for a minute. "Well, I don't know if this is true for you, but it has been true for me. Anything I did with the journal when I was . . . experimenting . . . it eventually wore off. There was no permanence to the effects. Once, I even changed the color of my own eyes! They were blue for two weeks before they turned back to brown, and nobody remembered my eyes had switched colors at all, not even my mother. The only thing that didn't fade was Charles. He remained steadfast our entire marriage. And I didn't have Charles in mind when I wrote that entry—I hadn't even met him yet. So maybe it delivered on something I really needed, but only because it was meant to be? Or maybe it was just a coincidence—I don't know."

"Well," I say, "my Katherine had a Henry and a Charles, so maybe you're right. Maybe it *was* all meant to be. Although, she also had the journal. I found it in *her* vanity drawer. But it was blank when I came across it, so I don't know if she ever used it or figured out what it could do."

"Why didn't you ask her?"

I pause. She doesn't know. But of course she doesn't—how could she? I need to tell her, though.

"I did ask her. She doesn't remember. She—*you*—are not okay . . . in my . . . world. You have Alzheimer's. You don't remember anything. You don't remember me and Jack. You don't remember Mom. You don't even remember much about those photos with Henry, even though I know you want to, so badly. Mom is not okay either. She's overwhelmed. Sad . . ." I stop. I don't know if my heart can handle talking about it more when the person who Katherine could be—resilient, witty, capable, her mind still active and filled with memories—is right here, in front of me. I try to hold in the tears that are threatening to fall. "*That's* how I ended up here, I think. Because I wished it was otherwise and I wrote this word in the journal—hiraeth—that sort of, I don't know, *embodied* that wish? And then I got dropped into this world where you are okay and my life is closer to how it was before we moved in with you. I mean, before we moved in with the *other* you."

"Ah, I see." Her face gets a troubled look. "Alzheimer's is my sister Anna's fate in this world. A terrible, terrible disease. I know all too well what's it's like to want to wish it away. But my being sick is not your fault, or something that you can fix. And your mom . . . well, your mom is not entirely okay here either. I think your parents need to figure some things out. But also, happy or unhappy, sick or well, okay or not okay . . . that's *life*. I know this can be very hard to hear when you are young, but the sailing is not always going to be smooth."

I get up from my chair and start pacing around.

"But then what is the point of that journal? Why does it even exist if it can't save the people you love?"

"I've asked myself that many times," she says. "You and I are very similar, Gracie. We're both restless souls. Maybe we needed to learn that any story—any *life*—no matter how exciting or dazzling it seems, still has bad moments mixed with the good. And that being *more* than just ourselves isn't necessarily better. Just different. I've come to understand that there's a reason we can't control every aspect of our lives, or fix everything that's broken, or undo our mistakes. I mean, even with the power of that journal, the two of us couldn't do it in a way that didn't have unintended consequences and ripple effects. Maybe our real power—the power that matters—lies in our ability to learn and grow and become better people *because* of the challenges we face."

I study the photos on the fireplace mantel again. Katherine's sister Anna. My grandfather. Henry. Her story has not been without sadness.

"Plus," she adds, "if everyone had the ability to rewrite

reality, I think that life as we know it might devolve into pure chaos."

And when she says this, I am reminded of that day in the car when Tom was explaining Benford's law. How he seemed reassured by the idea that there was possibly some kind of mathematical order to the universe. *Like it's not all chaos.*

Katherine stands up. "It looks like *you* may be the reason I've hung on to the journal all these years, however. Let's see if there's a way to get you back to where you came from, and my Gracie back from . . . wherever you've sent her."

I follow her up the stairs, into her bedroom, where she unlocks the bottom vanity drawer. Her journal, I note, is not blank. Together, we open it up and turn to the first empty page. She looks at me. "In my experience, simple and specific is the best approach."

I nod.

She picks up a pen from the vanity. "How about I write, 'In the morning, Gracie Byrne wakes up exactly where she is supposed to be'?"

I nod—hoping that covers both of us, me and me-but-not-me—and she commits the words to ink.

After we put the journal back in the drawer, I phone my-mom-not-my-mom and ask if I can spend the night with Katherine. I briefly consider also telling her that she and my dad should talk and decide what will make them more happy—staying together or splitting up—and that Jack and I will be okay either way, but in thinking about it, I decide not to. This is not really my life to shape.

Katherine and I have a magical night. We go out to dinner at the Italian restaurant on Murray Avenue. We have more pie when we get home. We sit by the fire until it's later than late, and through it all she tells me all about her life when she was young, about my mom as a little girl, about my grandfather Charles, and about Henry. Like the pages of a blank book, being filled in.

I want to stay up all night, as long as possible, but I need to go to sleep eventually, so that I can hopefully wake up back where I'm supposed to be. And when, in a reversal of our usual roles, *she* tucks me in, there is a split second where I think maybe it's *here*. Maybe *here* is where I'm supposed to be. Where Katherine is okay.

But there is another Gracie who really belongs here. And it wouldn't be right to take her place. And also, Tom doesn't even know me here. Nor does Mina, or Daniel, or Leo and Isaac. There's no Hank. Ashley will never be born. There is so much I would miss.

"Remind your Gracie to call Hannah in the morning," I tell her. "They're supposed to get together tomorrow." Maybe, in this universe, this will be the spark that rekindles their friendship. Or maybe not. Maybe they're both just moving on to new things.

Katherine brushes the hair away from my eyes. "I'll be sure to tell her. As for the rest, whatever is supposed to happen is going to happen. That's what I think. Give me a hug."

I hug her so, so tight, trying to commit every detail of her, and this night, to my memory.

"Good night, Gracie."

"Grandma!" I stop her before she turns to leave. "One more thing."

"What is it?"

"Where do you keep Henry's letters?"

Maybe they'll be in the same place at home. And maybe I can show them to *my* Katherine, read them to her, and help her remember.

For a little while, at least.

When Katherine disappears through the bedroom door, my eyes fill with tears.

It's strange to try and sleep in this bed. This my-bed-but-not-my-bed in this hiraeth universe. It's strange to want to both leave and stay, like a string being pulled in two directions at once. But I have to go. This is not my story. This is not my life.

There's still a crack in the ceiling in this reality, however, and I stare up at it, my mind turning over everything that's happened. Unintended consequences. Ripple effects. I hope what we've done to try and fix things actually works, and I hope

I *haven't* done anything to make things harder for the other Gracie. Or for *her* mom or dad or Jack or anyone. But although there was once a moment when I wished I'd never found that journal, that I'd never written a single word inside it, I can't say that anymore. Because even though it has sometimes proved to be an instrument of chaos . . . it's also been a gift.

It takes a long while, but eventually, I drift off to sleep.

DENOUEMENT: THE RESOLUTION OF A NARRATIVE.

Someone is shaking me. Shaking me hard.

I hear sounds, but they seem far away.

Footsteps running up the stairs.

Voices.

Wake up, Gracie, wake up!

What's going on?

She won't wake up! Is she . . . dead?

She's breathing.

But why won't she wake up? Why won't she wake up!

I don't know. I'm going to call 911.

And then it feels as if I'm fighting my way to the surface after being held underwater. I just need to get to the light. The air.

My eyes fly open, and I take a huge, gasping breath.

Jack is standing above me, his face white, tears streaming down his cheeks.

And Tom is there too.

"What's wrong?" I say, my chest tightening, thinking that maybe someone has died.

"You wouldn't wake up!" Jack says. "I thought you were—"

"We came over to get Jack's clothes for school and he found you in here," says Tom. "Like this."

"Like *what*?"

"He was trying to wake you up and you wouldn't wake up. I was about to call 911."

"Are you okay?" Jack asks. "I was so scared, Gracie."

I sit up and put my hand on his arm. "Yeah, I'm okay. I'm okay."

Someone is honking a car horn outside.

"That's my mom," says Tom. "Hang on."

He leaves the room and runs down the stairs. I hear him calling to her to hold on a minute.

"I'm okay," I reassure Jack. I take the edge of my sheet in my hand and wipe his face. "Go on to school. It's okay. I must have just been *really* asleep. It was a long night." I give him a hug. "Love you."

He hugs me back tight and runs out.

I look around the room one more time. *My* room. *My* desk, mirror, posters, pile of clothes by the closet door. And next to the bed, the journal. I pick it up off the floor and turn to the first blank page and see that it's not entirely blank. The words *hiraeth, hiraeth, hiraeth, hiraeth* are indented into the paper—a ghost version of the original copy that I scrawled on so aggressively and then tore out. Maybe that's why . . . I shake my head. It doesn't matter. Because I'm back.

I'm *back*. I'm back, I'm back, I'm back.

As I hear Tom coming up the stairs, I wonder if this is going to be like a *Wizard of Oz* situation, where I wake up and everything that happened since I found Katherine's journal never really happened, just like how Dorothy wakes up back in Kansas and isn't totally sure that she really ever went to Oz. But as soon as Tom walks in the room, he gives me a curious, wary look.

"You went somewhere else again, didn't you?"

I nod. "Somewhat accidentally. I wrote something, and then I ripped it out, but it happened anyway."

He shakes his head. "You are very accident-prone. Where to this time? The Great Wall of China? Machu Picchu?"

I sit up straighter in my bed. He still keeps his distance.

"Home. I mean, my old house. But not just the location. I guess I went to an alternate version of my life? One where I still lived where Jack and I used to live. And then I got stuck. For a couple *days*. Katherine—a different version of Katherine—got me out."

Is the other Gracie back where she is supposed to be too?

Does she know she was gone?

Does time pass differently in different versions of reality?

These are all questions I'm probably never going to get the answers to. And I'll have to live with that. But if I am back where I'm supposed to be, my hope is that she is too.

Tom lets out a long breath. "Good thing you took me to Norway with you, otherwise I'd never believe you right now." His expression softens. "What was it like, this other version of your life?"

My eyes well up. "Tom. She was fine there. Katherine. Not like she is . . . here."

"Oh," he says quietly. "That must have been . . . I don't even know."

I don't even know either. I don't think I can put into words how I feel about it. On the one hand, it makes the card fate has dealt her here seem even more unfair, but on the other, it helps to know that she's at least okay *somewhere.*

I want to tell him more. I want to tell him everything about it, but I don't even know where to start or how to put it all into words.

"I think I still need to make sense of it myself."

"It's okay."

"You didn't live across the street from her there," I say suddenly.

His face shows just a touch of his usual humor. "So you were looking for me . . ."

"Of course I was looking for you," I tell him.

We stare at each other. It's so uncomfortably quiet.

"I wish we could just start over," I say, finally. "Because

now we'll never know if I made everything happen—with us, I mean."

He steps closer and then perches on my bed, next to me. "What was it you wrote again?" he asks.

My face warms. "'Please let Gracie get what she wants.'"

His lips twitch, like he's trying to hold back a small smile. "And you think that your journal interpreted that to mean *me*."

I shrug. "Maybe? I mean, not *just* you, but maybe."

He shifts to face me. "This was the night that Katherine got lost?"

I nod.

He's quiet for a minute. "Okay, but . . . here's the thing: maybe you already had me. You just didn't know it yet."

I raise my eyebrows, waiting.

"Maybe you already had me that first day you picked me up in the Seville." He pauses. "I guess what I'm saying is, even if the journal *did* play a part in this"—he gestures between us—"you getting what you want also means I get what I want. What I've *wanted* for a while now. It's basically a win-win situation."

"I don't believe you," I say. "You looked like you wanted to jump out of the car the day I asked you to homecoming."

"Well, first of all, at that point I thought you had something going on with Luke."

I think back to that day he saw Luke and me in the hallway together. He's not altogether wrong, even if I was already regretting it by then. *Luke.* My gut churns thinking about him.

About what I did. I decide I'm going to apologize, even if he has no idea what I'm talking about.

Tom continues, "And secondly, I'm not *impervious* to awkwardness, you know. You have this tendency to sort of take people by surprise. But that's what I like about you, Gracie Byrne."

"What if you just *think* that," I say.

Tom runs both hands through his hair and sighs. Like I've exasperated him. Like he finds me exasperating. He moves closer. "Ask Mina if you don't believe me. I confessed all one afternoon in math class—because you know I talk too much—and it was definitely before homecoming. Also, and I can't believe I am having this incredibly nonscientific discussion right now, but didn't you say that some of the other stories you wrote, like, wore off or something?"

"I think so . . ." The other Katherine mentioned this as well.

"Well," he says, "maybe we should just . . . keep going and see what happens? If it's meant to be, it's meant to be, you know?"

Meant to be.

I nod yes. "That would be okay with me."

"But how about you stay *here*, in the real world? When I said that Talking Heads song reminded me of you, I think you might have taken it too literally."

He leans toward me, touching his forehead to mine.

"Deal," I whisper.

After Tom leaves for school, I put the journal in the hat

box and then take the hat box up to the attic—putting it in the most hidden corner I can find. I was going to burn it, but I don't know what that might do. I keep the photos, though. I'm pretty sure my mom will want to see the ones of Henry. Her father. My grandfather. I want to ask her what she knows about him. And then I go into Katherine's room and sit at the vanity where I found the journal. I open the bottom drawer on the right side, opposite the one that was locked. And there, underneath another pile of junk, is a stack of old letters, tied with string. Henry's letters. They were right here, all along.

Later in the day, I go to meet my mom at the hospital in the post-surgery lounge. Katherine's hip surgery went well, but she will be in rehab for several weeks. "And then we'll have to figure out what to do next," she says.

"Can I go in and see her?" I ask.

"She was still sleeping when I went in earlier," she says. "But let's try again now."

We walk down the polished floors of the hallway to her room. Katherine is sitting up in bed when we walk in. She looks tired, and so tiny in her hospital gown, but she's awake.

Immediately, her eyes lock on mine as if she recognizes me and my heart leaps. *What if* . . . I don't know, what if me getting sucked into that alternate universe allowed me to somehow bring back some of the pieces that Katherine has been missing? Her memories, her spark, her essence . . .

Her eyes search my face. "Anna?" she asks.

"No," I say, a hard lump forming in my throat. "I'm Gracie."

"Oh," she says. "Oh."

I think back to what the other Katherine said to me: *There's a reason we can't control every aspect of our lives, or fix everything that's broken, or undo our mistakes.*

Maybe the reason is because the things we can't control, and the broken parts, and the mistakes are all part of what makes us who we are. For real.

But next time I come visit, I'm still going to bring my boom box, play some Duke Ellington, and read her Henry's letters.

When I get home later, I call my dad.

"Hey, Gracie," he says. "How is everything?"

And instead of saying "fine," I tell him the truth. "Actually, not so great."

"Tell me what's going on," he says.

And I do.

We talk for a while, and when I finish updating him on Katherine, I ask a question: "You remember when you told me to let you know what you could do to help?"

"Of course I remember," he says.

"Well, I have some ideas."

After I hang up, I wander into the sitting room and look out the window. It's starting to snow. Maybe we'll get enough for Jack to go sledding when he gets home from school. Maybe I'll join him. Maybe I'll call Mina and Daniel later and see if they want to come along too. And I'll for sure call Tom when he gets home from practice. Now that we are going to keep going. I think back to this morning and smile. Tom being there for me. Tom making me laugh. Tom *forgiving* me.

I really like this boy.

All this time, I've been thinking of him—with his easy smile and quirky sense of humor—as the embodiment of sunshine, appearing on the sidewalk in front of Katherine's house one humid, sticky September day to light up my earth. But I realize now that maybe it's the reverse. Maybe he is my earth. He is solid and real. Grounded. And I am the star. Electrically charged, chaotic, and sometimes lost. Hurtling through space. Looking for a home.

KATHERINE AND I SIT ON THE PORCH WATCHING A LIGHT, delicate rain. This last week, the weather has turned definitively spring-like, with new grass coming up and blossoms on the trees. When the rain stops, everything is vibrant, greener.

Tom pulls into the Broders' driveway. I watch him as he gets out of the Beetle, runs across the street, and bounds up the porch stairs. I love that my house is always his first stop.

"How was practice?" I ask.

"We got out early," he says. "The rain."

He greets Katherine with a hug and Hank with an ear scratch.

"Aren't you a sweetie," Katherine says. "Do you know where they put the letters?"

"Gracie has them for you," he says.

She looks confused at his mention of my name until I tell her, "I'll read you a few later."

"Oh, good." My dad and Kirsten helped finance a rehab specialist, and Katherine's hip healed faster than even her doctors had hoped. But she has a walker now, and is losing some of her fine motor skills. She still needs more advanced care than she can get here at home. Next month, she's moving into Park Manor full-time. It's not home, but it's close enough that we can visit her every day, and bring her back here to join us for dinner or hang out on the front porch whenever she likes. But no matter what, I'm for sure going to keep up our Sunday evening tradition: we put on some Duke Ellington, I read her a few of Henry's letters, and we look at old photographs. Not just the ones of Henry. My mom helped me put together an album for Katherine—with photos of Henry, my grandfather Charles, her siblings, and all of us. Sometimes the music and the letters and the photos make her happy, sometimes they make her eyes fill with tears, but every time they help her recall *something*—a moment or a place or someone's name. She often forgets about it all again later, but it's nice to be able to help her fill in a page of her story, even if it's only for a little while.

Tom joins me on the porch swing, sprawling out sideways so that he can rest his head in my lap. I weave my fingers through his hair.

Our mutual attraction hasn't worn off yet. Maybe the journal brought us together, or maybe it didn't. But there's no doubt anymore about why we're *still* together.

The Broders' Volvo pulls in behind the Beetle. Jack, Isaac, and Leo spill out. Trish waves. Jack comes across the street to dump his backpack in the house.

"Grosssss," he says, as he passes us on the porch.

Tom ignores him and closes his eyes. "I love that smell. After it rains. What's the word for it again?"

I'm about to tell him, but then Katherine says, "Petrichor."

Tom opens his eyes. We both look at her. She smiles, and for just a fraction of a second, she looks like the other Katherine. The one from the other place. This happens every so often. And every time it does, it makes me ache.

"Is that right?" Tom looks back at me. "Petrichor?"

"Uh-huh." I nod. "It comes from the Greek word *petra*, meaning stone, and *ichor*, meaning the blood of gods and goddesses." I shrug. "I guess that's what the Greeks thought it smelled like when raindrops hit dry ground."

Tom grins. "I love it when you talk obscure words with me. Give me another one . . ."

"Stop," I tell him.

"I'm completely serious," he says.

I lean down and kiss him.

"*Grooooooosssss.*" Jack's voice, inside this time, comes through the screen window that faces the porch.

Tom and I are 100 percent in the phase of our relationship where we are annoying to everyone but each other.

Jack comes back out with Hank's leash. "When's Mom getting home?" he asks.

"Late," I say. "She has a date."

She and Rob have been seeing each other more. It's nice that my mom has met someone who makes her happy. Jack and I like him too. And the cooking part is a pretty sweet bonus.

Jack takes off in the direction of the park, Hank dragging him toward Leo, Isaac, and Hypatia, who are waiting at the corner. Cherry blossoms dance in the breeze.

"That dog is a real piece of work," Katherine says.

"He really is," I agree.

A few minutes later, Mina and Daniel walk up the sidewalk with a bag from the bakery on Butler.

"How'd you do on that trig exam, Broder?" Mina asks. She's wearing black capris and a Breton striped shirt.

"Ninety-seven percent," says Tom.

"Are you freaking kidding me right now?" she says as they join us on the porch. "That's what I got too!"

Daniel and I give each other a look. Mina and Tom have this annoying math rivalry that neither one of us can relate to.

"I don't see the problem here, do you?" I ask.

Daniel shrugs.

"The problem," Mina says, "is that he doesn't even *study*, and it irritates me."

"Well, in his case, I think that's only a successful strategy in math . . ."

"True," says Tom. "It's not working out so well in Spanish."

Mina opens the bag. "Macaron, anyone?"

Daniel rolls his eyes. "She really commits to her daily theme."

"Oh! I'd love one," says Katherine.

"So are you two in for *Rocky Horror* tomorrow night?" Mina asks, after setting Katherine up with a macaron. She's been begging me to bring Tom to the midnight show for weeks.

"I already have my costume," Tom says.

"You do?" I ask. "What is it?

"It better be Frank," Mina says. "Those legs were made for fishnets."

He laughs. "You'll just have wait and see."

Wait and see.

And that's exactly what I'm going to do, because Tom's story is not mine to tell. Nobody else's story is mine.

I look around at everyone on the porch and think back to that idea: *sonder*. The awareness that out of billions of life stories, we'll only ever get to be the main character in one—our own. And although we may be featured players or have bit roles in other lives, there are so many more that we'll never even be aware of at all. And the main characters in *those* stories? They'll never be aware of us, either. I mean, somewhere out there, I'll bet there are plenty of people who've never even heard of Prince.

I originally thought this was a lonely idea, but maybe it's not. Not if I imagine all of our stories—mine, Katherine's, my mom's, Tom's, Jack's, Mina's, my dad's, Daniel's, everyone's at school, everyone's in the universe, even the ones I'll never know about—intertwining and overlapping and connecting together as part of some bigger narrative, a narrative written by a multitude of authors, but united by all these common threads across time: Birth. Death. Happiness. Heartbreak. Joy. Sorrow. Loss. Love.

As for me, I have no idea what the next chapter of my life is going to bring. I mean, I have some things that I hope for, but I know there are no guarantees.

But I guess the not knowing part is what makes things interesting.

And the right now part is all I can really live in.

This moment. This me. This us. Good or bad, sad or happy, bitter or sweet—maybe a little of all of it, all at once. I wouldn't trade it for anything else.

This is the story of Gracie Byrne.

It's all true.

Even the stuff you probably don't believe.

A WORD ABOUT GRACIE'S WORDS . . .

Like Gracie, I love interesting words. When I come across one that intrigues me—because of how it sounds or what it means—I add it to a list that I keep, in case it might inspire a character, or a scene, or even an idea for a complete story. And, sure enough, my word list turned out to be one of the sparks that brought *The Totally True Story of Gracie Byrne* to life. I asked myself, *What if there's a girl who collects words, and it turns out that the words she collects have special powers?* The final story strayed a bit from that initial idea, but Gracie's habit of collecting words remained as a core part of her character. Throughout the novel, she often uses the words she finds to inspire the scenes she writes in her grandmother's journal or to fuel her internal thoughts and daydreams.

As I was writing the book, I knew that in 1987 Gracie would

not have had the benefit of the internet to search for words, so I had to come up with other sources. Dictionaries, I decided, or from other books in her grandfather's library, or through conversations with people. However, one of the words that Gracie "finds" in the novel didn't exist in 1987, at least not in the way it is used in the book. That word is *sonder*. I came across *sonder* via an internet article on interesting words, and it was coined in 2012 by John Koenig for *The Dictionary of Obscure Sorrows*, which is this really cool online project that creates new words to match specific emotions. (As of 2021, *The Dictionary of Obscure Sorrows* has been officially published in book form.)

I loved the concept of this word so much that I decided to keep it in the book. So . . . in a story that involves a magical journal, alternate realities, and a rare owl showing up in the hallway of a high school in Pittsburgh, I hope you will forgive me (and Gracie) this one small anachronism.

—Shannon Takaoka

ACKNOWLEDGMENTS

Whew, second books are tough. When I was drafting this one, there were times when I couldn't help wondering if my first novel was a fluke—an accomplishment I'd be unable to repeat. Maybe I'd turn out like one of those stressed-out authors depicted in books or movies, all bleary-eyed, staring at a blank screen, ignoring their agent's texts about missed deadlines. Thankfully, I have many people in my life who help me channel my (sometimes) overactive imagination in more positive directions, and I couldn't be more grateful for their kindness, enthusiasm, wisdom, and support.

To my editor, Kaylan Adair, thank you for everything. Thank you for your ideas, your thoughtful feedback, your patience, your encouragement, and your friendship. Thank you for falling in love with Gracie and for helping me shape this story into a final product that I am really proud of. And thank you, also, to Juan Botero. How lucky am I to have not just one but two amazing people on my editorial side? Your great notes and story ideas were so helpful as I worked on revisions.

Thank you to the entire team at Candlewick Press. You all continue to be wonderful to work with. Matt Roeser, you hit it out of the park again with Gracie's cover. It's beautiful and magical and a perfect complement to your earlier work on *Everything I Thought I Knew*. Thank you. Thank you to Maya Tatsukawa for the gorgeous interior art. Thank you to copyeditors Maggie Deslaurier and Maya Myers for your attention to detail, your notes that made me smile, and for making sure that my story time lines (eventually) made sense. To Martha Dwyer and Matt Seccombe for proofreading. And thank you to Stephanie Pando for all your hard work in publicity, and to everyone in marketing and sales.

To my agent, Nicki Richesin, thank you for being my sounding board, my "does this make sense?" gut-check, and the person I can call anytime I find myself at sea while navigating the ins and outs of the book world. I'm so glad to have you in my corner. Here's to many more brainstorming sessions (and celebrations) at California Gold! Thank you also to the team at Dunow, Carlson & Lerner.

Thank you to my amazing and talented YA critique partners: Eva Gibson, Jenn Moffett, Alex Richards, and Shana Youngdahl. I guess the one silver lining about debuting in a pandemic is that we figured out that if we had to launch our first books on Zoom, we could also do a critique group that way too, even if some of us lived thousands of miles apart. I don't think I could have finished this book without our regular meetings, and I'm so thankful for your insights, your suggestions, your moral support, and most of all, your friendship.

And speaking of 2020 debuts, a big thank-you to Nora Shalaway Carpenter for getting such a great group of authors together for a retreat at the wonderful Highlights Foundation in Pennsylvania. Nora, your energy and generosity of spirit are contagious! To Cathleen Barnhart, Rocky Callen, Sarah Kapit, Cameron Lund, Janae Marks, Cindy Otis, Diana Pinguicha, Erin Riha, Jess Rinker, and Josh Roberts: it was so wonderful to get to meet you all in real life, especially after such a long period where none of us was able to meet anybody. (Eva and Alex too!) I'm so glad we got to bond over our "pandemic debut" experiences and share our stories. You are a wildly talented bunch. To the rest of the #Roaring20sDebut group: it's been lovely to swap ARCs, advice, and laughs online, and I hope I get to cross paths with more of you in the years (and books) to come.

Thank you to Jeff Bishop, Chelsea Sedoti, and other authors I've already mentioned for agreeing to read early copies. I'm so appreciative of your time and generosity.

In the San Francisco Bay Area, I'm also lucky to have a wonderful group of author friends right in my backyard. Mae Respicio, Kath Rothschild, and A.J. Sass—I love getting together and talking about writing, publishing, and our favorite books. And to my longtime writing pals Dorothy O'Donnell and Mindy Uhrlaub, you know I wouldn't be where I am at now without you. I'm so grateful for all our lunches, getaways, and years of friendship.

The list of friends and family who continue to cheer me on and celebrate all things book-related with me is so long, I hope I haven't forgotten anyone. Thank you to the Shahs, Hunts, Blauvelts, Landes, Yanaris, Kurths, Mokelkes, and Springers. Thank you to the Hamiltons for loaning me their awesome backyard office whenever I needed a quiet place to work, to my book club gals, and to the rest of my Lucas Valley village. Thank you to Julie Bloomberg and Suse Barnes. Thank you to Dan Reidy, Robyn Fernsworth, Tara Kusumoto, Amanda Orr, Annette Shimada, and all my work colleagues, who not only give me the flexibility to do what I do, but also talk up my books like the PR specialists that they are. There are so many more of you from all the phases of my life—Pittsburgh, Penn State, DC, the Bay Area—who have been so kind and excited for me, and I appreciate you all. I couldn't be happier to have such a great group of people in my life.

While *The Totally True Story of Gracie Byrne* is, of course, fiction, there are some inspirations for the story from my real life: my love of weird words, growing up in Pittsburgh in the 80s, and, most personally, my grandmother Veronica, who lived for a while with my mom, dad, brother, and me when she was suffering from Alzheimer's. There are so many things that stay with me from that time: how Veronica carried her black patent leather purse with her everywhere and, if the TV remote went missing, that *might* be where to look; how much she loved ice cream and donuts; how she'd light up and suddenly seem like a different person when we played music that she liked. I'll never forget her sweet nature, and I'll also never forget the unconditional love my parents showed as her caregivers. I'm so thankful for your kind hearts, Mom and Dad, then and now. Love you both.

My family is my everything. Scotty, thank you for always being my most enthusiastic champion, for giving me the space and support I need to live this wild, creative life, and for keeping me very well fed along the way. Emi and Evan, watching the two of you grow into such creative and independent young adults has been the greatest joy of my life. Thank you for all the nicknames and the hugs, for making me laugh, and for making me so proud. Love you all to the moon and back.

Finally, to all the readers, word nerds, bookworms, and daydreamers out there—thank you for picking up *The Totally True Story of Gracie Byrne*. I hope you've enjoyed reading it as much as I've enjoyed writing it!